A Case of Bloodshed in Benidorm

A Midthorpe Murder Mystery (#2)

David W Robinson

www.darkstroke.com

Copyright © 2019 by David W Robinson
Cover Photography by Adobe Stock © aanbetta
Design by soqoqo
All rights reserved.

No part of this book may be used or reproduced in any manner whatsoever without written permission of the author or Crooked Cat Books except for brief quotations used for promotion or in reviews. This is a work of fiction. Names, characters, and incidents are used fictitiously.

First Dark Edition, darkstroke. 2019

Discover us online:
www.darkstroke.com

Find us on instagram:
www.instagram.com/darkstrokebooks

Include **#darkstroke** in a photo of yourself
holding his book on Instagram and
something nice will happen.

About the Author

David Robinson is a Yorkshireman now living in Manchester. Driven by a huge, cynical sense of humour, he's been a writer for over thirty years having begun with magazine articles before moving on to novels and TV scripts.

He has little to do with his life other than write, as a consequence of which his output is prodigious. Thankfully most of it is never seen by the great reading public of the world.

He has worked closely with Crooked Cat Books and darkstroke since 2012, when The Filey Connection, the very first Sanford 3rd Age Club Mystery, was published.

Describing himself as the Doyen of Domestic Disasters he can be found blogging at **www.dwrob.com** and he appears frequently on video (written, produced and starring himself) dispensing his mocking humour at **www.youtube.com/user/ Dwrob96/videos**

The Midthorpe Murder Mystery series:
A Case of Missing on Midthorpe
A Case of Bloodshed in Benidorm

The STAC Mystery series:
The Filey Connection
The I-Spy Murders
A Halloween Homicide
A Murder for Christmas
Murder at the Murder Mystery Weekend
My Deadly Valentine
The Chocolate Egg Murders
The Summer Wedding Murder
Costa del Murder
Christmas Crackers
Death in Distribution
A Killing in the Family
A Theatrical Murder
Trial by Fire
Peril in Palmanova
The Squire's Lodge Murders
Murder at the Treasure Hunt
A Cornish Killing

A Case of Bloodshed in Benidorm
A Midthorpe Murder Mystery (#2)

Chapter One

Dominique Masters stormed into her husband's office, dug deep into the pockets of her coat, and came out with a flimsy pair of panties which she threw at him.

"That's it. I've had enough. This is the last pair of stray knickers I deal with. I'm on my way to see my lawyer. I want a divorce. I want you out of the house this weekend, and by the time I'm done with you, you'll be out of the company too."

Gil Masters took the threat in his stride. "Yeah, yeah, yeah. I've heard it all before. Now get the hell out of here, Dom. Some of us have work to do."

Her voice was the hiss of an angry viper. "Make the most of it. Just remember whose money built this company. When my lawyers are through with you, you won't be able to afford cheap hookers, never mind loose-legged secretaries. Out of the house by the end of the week."

Dominique turned and dashed from the office with the same hurricane speed she had arrived.

Masters glared at the door as it slammed behind her. It was a situation that had been in the making for at least a year, possibly longer. Fifteen years of marriage to a witch – albeit a disgustingly rich witch – like Dominique was enough for even the most masochistic of men, and Gil Masters was not a masochist.

An innate arrogance coupled to three years at Oxford, another two years at Harvard Business School, then a decade working at one of the largest publishing corporations in America, had created a mindset where he could never accept culpability, no matter what the problem. There was always someone else to blame, and this time it was his stupid secretary. How the hell had she come to leave her pants at his palatial Surrey home? What was she wearing under her skirt on the drive back to London? Fresh air?

If Xavier Vadaro was to blame for his present predicament, there was no way he could allow Dominique to determine his future.

Sure, she could throw him out of the house. It had been in her family for a couple of hundred years. True, she could secure her divorce if that's what she really wanted. The number of women he had enjoyed down the years, many of whom would be willing to talk to Dominique's lawyers for the right price, would make it impossible to defend against such an action. But could Dominique really remove him from his office?

Shortly Publishing was his baby. Dominique's money might have laid the foundations, but it was his enterprise, his business acumen, his persuasive, smooth-tongued skills which had attracted the big names, the bestsellers, the writers who made Shortly the company it was today, the giant it would become in the future. He was not about to let Dominique bring that down on the back of his shortcomings (or her miserliness in matters carnal). Not if he could help it.

Gazing out from his eighth floor window, on a bright, sunny day, he calculated the odds against him.

Dominique had injected a huge amount of capital in the company, and she owned 49% of the shares. He was left with a crummy 16%. The remaining 35% was spread across various friends, family, and one or two carefully selected investors and institutions, all of whom had seen a good return on their investments thanks to him: him, not Dominique.

And yet, she needed only 2% of those shares in order to kick him out. And what could he do about it?

Fight. That's what. Hadn't he been a fighter all his life? Anyone christened Jeremy Pratt would have to fight. Changing that goddamn awful birth name as soon as he was legally old enough to do so had signalled his intention to fight.

And would he fight dirty? Damn right, he would.

He spun his chair and gazed through the windows at the

leafy suburbs of West London. Normally, the sight would relax him, but today he seethed with indignation.

Who signed up Philippa Killairn? One of the bestselling historical romance authors in Europe. Who signed up that snooty Ray Baldock? Without question the single most popular crime novelist in the UK, Europe, possibly the world. He did. Gil Masters. That's who. And in the case of Baldock, he actually discovered the man working as a hack for a crime magazine.

And Dominique thought she could…

His thoughts came to a halt. Killairn and Baldock. They were the rock upon which Shortly's success was built. If he could show the shareholders how tightly they were bound to the company, and how those bonds were due to him, and how he could take them elsewhere at the crooking of his index finger, they wouldn't dare replace him.

But how to achieve it? Both authors were quite happy with Shortly. Neither had expressed any inclination to go elsewhere, and Masters knew for certain that Baldock had been approached by at least one or two of the really big houses.

Naturally, they were contractually bound to Masters and his company, but there were ways and means of getting round contracts. He should know. He had pulled many such stunts in the past to steal authors from other houses, and all without penalty.

What he needed was a means of ensuring that they would never be tempted, *could* never be tempted. How could he arrange that?

The sight of the frilly underwear Dominique had thrown at him gave rise to the obvious idea. Sex. Killairn was in her mid-40s and happily married. Not an insurmountable difficulty, but an obstacle nonetheless. Baldock… he wasn't sure about Baldock. The man was an out and out misery. A wealthy misery, sure, but nonetheless a misery, and Masters had never heard mention of a wife, fiancée, or even a girlfriend. Perhaps he was gay. But if Baldock wasn't open to that level of persuasion, his agent, Bernie Deerman might be.

The scenario began to develop in his head. All he needed was a location, and it would have to be somewhere really seedy. He thought of his PA the other side of the office door. A naturalised Brit, she was Spanish by birth, and that thought prompted his final decision on the location. Where better than the Costa Blanca?

He would also need a lever, something to ensure that they showed up. His computer expertise would soon deal with that.

He needed a third target, too. If he simply went for Killairn and Baldock, it might be too obvious, too suspicious. He needed a solid midlister, and Shortly's stable of authors had plenty of those in the stalls.

He jabbed the intercom on the telephone. "Get your bare ass in here. Now."

A moment later, the door opened and Xavier Vardaro came in. She was wearing a 1950s style pencil skirt (Masters insisted upon skirts amongst his female employees) and a translucent, white blouse which showed the line of her bra beneath. Tall, brown-eyed, dark-haired, she was a fine looking woman. just the right side of 40, unmarried, skilled on her back, a woman who knew how to keep her legs open and her mouth shut even if she didn't always remember to take her knickers home with her.

He held up the offending garment. "Did your ass feel cold when you went home last Tuesday?"

Her ears coloured. "How do you know I didn't leave them there deliberately for Dominique to find?"

That was another thing he liked about her. She wasn't intimidated by him.

"Are you still screwing around with that jerk off, Linkman?"

"If you mean are we still dating, the answer is yes."

"Get onto him. I want him here next Monday, ten o'clock, no argument. The same applies to Bernie Deerman. Pencil her in for eleven o'clock. There'll be at least one more, but I haven't made up my mind who, so leave the twelve o'clock slot free. Got all that?"

"Yes."

"Good. Get out and get on with it." He watched her turned to leave, and as she reached the door he called to her. "Oh, and take these with you." He threw the errant panties to her.

The door closed behind her and Masters turned to look through the window once again. He had work to do. The plan was only half formed in his mind, and it would need development. Beyond that there would be the finer points to tweak.

But he was already anticipating the end product, salivating at the thought of the look of defeat on Dominique's face when she learned she had been outmanoeuvred. He had not changed his name to Masters for nothing.

Chapter Two

Raymond Baldock signalled for a waitress. When she arrived, he handed over a plate of jam, cream, and a scone with a bite out of one side, and in a voice loud enough to be heard all around the busy cafeteria, said, "Take that back and bring me a fresh one."

"It is fresh."

"Then your baker must have mistaken Portland cement for flour."

"I can't answer for that, sir. All I can say is they were delivered today, and as far as we're concerned, they're fresh."

"No. They *were* fresh. About two days ago according to my estimate. I am not paying good money for food which is obviously past its sell-by date. Now kindly exchange it for one which is more palatable."

Her cheeks burning, the waitress carried off the offending food. On the other side of the table, Baldock's agent, Bernadette Deerman shook her head in bemused wonderment.

The Pantry, a city centre café, was full. Baldock could not recall a time when it was not full. Outside the door a queue had formed as it did every day, and Baldock and Bernie had waited almost twenty-five minutes for a table. Its popularity came down to an approach which prided itself on a 1920s/30s ambience. The waitresses (all female) wore black, with white, frilly aprons, and silly little caps, which bore the café logo across the broad front. Tea was served in bone china cups and saucers, poured from matching teapots and tiny, individual milk jugs. Cube sugar stood in decorative EPNS bowls, complete with matching tongs, and everything about the place spoke of a more refined age.

"Everything but the prices," Baldock had grumbled when they ordered.

He was aware that he spoke too loudly and was often blunt to the point of rudeness, but he considered it an asset rather than a liability. "It makes people realise I am not one to be trifled with," he would say when challenged on the matter.

The argument with the waitress and his forcible opinions had made them the centre of attention, but Baldock did not experience a single second of discomfort. If anything, it made him even more defiant. He felt like turning on these customers and ordering them to get on with their afternoon tea.

"How do you manage it, Raymond?" Bernie asked.

"Manage what?"

"Manage to upset so many people."

"I meant what I said, Bernie. I am not paying eight pounds for two cream teas only to be served food that is two or three days old."

Bernie sighed. "How much do you earn?"

"That's not the point. I was born a Yorkshireman, remember, and if there is plenty that I'd like to erase from my early life, thrift, value for money, is not a part of it. When I pay for the fresh article, I expect it to be fresh."

"Scones are always a little, er, stodgy."

Bernie did not appear too embarrassed by the incident either. Probably because she had spent the much of the last decade representing her most successful author, and that representation included all those facets that were not related to producing and placing novels: nurture in the early days, encouragement when he needed it, negotiating with both him and Shortly Publishing, smoothing the way when tantrums disrupted it, and generally doing whatever was needed to ensure he got on with the job he was best at – writing the books. They had met many times, both here in Norwich, where he lived, and in London, and there had been a number of incidents such as that with the waitress. Bernie, he concluded, was used to it.

She had however, commented that his patience had deteriorated since a visit to see his mother in Leeds during the summer. Baldock denied it, but somewhere deep inside he knew it to be true. He was still haunted by the vision of Lisa Yeoman in his rear-view mirror as he drove away, leaving her in the middle of the road, calling after him.

Less than half an hour after he had ended their relationship so rudely and abruptly, he regretted his hastiness, and wished he could turn the clock back. But it was too late.

His mother had brought up the matter in her regular emails and telephone conversations, but he refused to talk about it. She even hinted that she knew what it was all about, but he obdurately refused to be drawn into any discussion, and instead sat in his magnificent riverside house in Wroxham , brooding upon what might have been, and wallowing in his loneliness.

The cringe-inducing memory haunted him and not only when he was alone. At times like this, waiting for the waitress to deal with his complaint, it forced its way to the front of his mind.

Baldock had always known that he had no small talk. Richard Headingley, the hero of his detective novels, was smooth, charming and blessed with the ability to talk about almost anything. His creator was not, and Baldock became acutely conscious of it (and the way in which he had hurt Lisa) in the silence that followed Bernie's last comment on the stodginess of scones. To kill a few seconds while waiting for the waitress to bring them fresher food, he asked, "How are Oliver and the boys?"

"They're fine, thank you, Raymond."

Bernie was a few years older than his thirty-six years, and married with twin sons, who were ready for their first year at some expensive boarding school in Hertfordshire, not far from where Bernie and her husband lived. It was another reason, as if anyone needed one, why she was so determined that Baldock should keep churning out the rampantly successful *Detective Inspector Headingley* novels. The Deermans' large house in Potter's Bar was mortgaged to the hilt, and at the time Bernie first took Baldock on, Oliver's income as a golf professional at a nearby club left their finances strained to the limit. Even with her share of the rapturous income from the Headingley books and the anticipated additional royalties from the forthcoming TV series, Bernie's situation had not improved much. Adding fees for the boys' schooling would not make the arithmetic any the more appealing, and Baldock anticipated a lot of pressure from her in the coming years.

He realised that another long silence had followed his query and Bernie's response. He tried to think of something he could talk about, but his mind had gone completely blank. This was a business meeting, but to open business discussions while waiting for a slow waitress to attend their needs would be almost criminal from the point of view of both confidentiality and etiquette.

And the stalwart, British standby of the weather was inadmissible as a topic of conversation.

Baldock recalled a line from one of his Headingley novels: *three weeks ago November had reared up like an angry cobra.* It encapsulated perfectly his feelings towards the first month of winter. Autumn was nearly through in the northern hemisphere and the biting eleventh month had sufficient snap to warn them of the weather's potential, end of year ferocity.

The month, however, was August, not November, and aside from a week or two in June, the summer had been predictably wet and gloomy, offering little in the way of conversational themes. Baldock did not do sport of any description and he was reasonably certain that neither did Bernie. And if he was politically-minded, she was not.

Small talk, then, was out and uncomfortable silence was the order of the afternoon.

He was saved further discomfort by the arrival of the waitress with fresh scones. She placed them on the table and smiled sarcastically at him. "The manager's compliments and apologies, sir. He says to tell you he'll instruct the bakery to use more water with the cement in future."

"Go away," Baldock ordered, and the girl tromped off to

seek customers new. "Sorry about that, Bernie," he apologised as he cut through the next scone and reached for the jam. "Now, you were telling me that the latest Headingley is selling well."

Bernie bit into her scone and her eyes lit up. Baldock guessed that whatever diet she was on was a sacrificial lamb to her sweet tooth. Chewing delicately, then swallowing, she nodded. "So far, it's outsold the previous eight books by some thousands. A master-stroke releasing it in the run up to Easter."

"It was a spring title," Baldock pointed out as he nibbled on his scone. "There wouldn't be much point releasing *Headingley and the March Murders* in the middle of summer, would there?"

"Even allowing for that, sales have exceeded expectations. Headingley is now officially a phenomenon. The TV series goes into production soon and although he hasn't said how much, Gil would have pulled top dollar for the rights. And eighty percent of those rights are yours."

Minus your fifteen percent of my eighty percent." Baldock gave her a weak smile to how he was only ribbing her. "Good. Very satisfactory. I can safely anticipate a large payment at the end of the next quarter, then?" He drank a mouthful of tea. "I'm sure you didn't trail all the way from London just to tell me this. You could have emailed. You usually do."

"No. Gil is more than happy with the performance of the books, but he has reservations."

"That's a contradiction," Baldock pointed out, and spread a thin layer of jam on the second half of his scone. "How can he be more than happy yet have reservations?"

"His reservations are not about Headingley. They're about you."

His mouth open, ready to bite into the scone, Baldock stopped, and for a moment, gaped. Making up his mind, he bit the scone in half, chewed vigorously, and swallowed. Washing it down with tea, he asked, "Me?"

"Well, to be honest, it's not just you. There are other

authors he feels the same about."

"No. Wait. I'm sorry, Bernie, you're losing me. You haven't said what reservations."

She finished off her scone, and wiped her fingers on a napkin. "Gil may be British, but he's very Americanised in his approach to business."

Baldock already knew that after graduating from Cambridge, Gil Masters, the founder and CEO of Shortly Publishing, had spent time at Harvard and ten years working with one of the big publishers in the USA. Baldock also knew that he did not like Gil Masters. He further knew that because of the way the contracts had been written, he had to put up with Gil Masters, but he preferred to do so at a distance. Why else would he hand fifteen percent of his income to Bernie, if not to deal with the permanently smiling, permanently demanding, permanently painful Gil Masters?

"He's very much in favour of corporate teamwork," Bernie was saying.

"An attitude of which I approve." Baldock finished his scone, picked up the teapot and poured a fresh cup. "Remember, Bernie, I served my writer's apprenticeship with *Sleuth Monthly* magazine and our editor placed great stress on teamwork."

"I'm glad you feel that way, Raymond. Gil called several agents in for individual meetings last week. He feels that Shortly Publishing could become one of the giant brands in the paperback and electronic book market. To do so, he needs us all pulling together."

"Us?"

"All of us. The staff at Shortly, the agents, the authors. Everyone."

"Don't think I'm being picky, but I don't work for Shortly. Neither do you. We're self-employed. We're simply contracted to them."

"And a part of that contract says that the authors and their representatives will work to promote both their own works and the Shortly brand."

Baldock dropped a half teaspoon of sugar into his tea and

stirred milk in. "And I do. I attend books signings, I turn out for TV slots when he – or you – arrange them. And I might add that I don't even get travelling expenses for them."

"You get increased sales," Bernie pointed out as she, too, helped herself to more tea.

"There's no way of establishing that. For all we know the books may have sold in such number without all the fooling around in bookshops and TV studios." Resting his elbows on the table, Baldock lifted his cup and cradled it in both hands as if warming his palms. "I've known you long enough to know when you're hedging, Bernie. Shall we get to the point?"

"Gil wants authors and agents to become part of the team."

"And he's going to pay me some kind of retainer, is he? Say twenty thousand a year?"

"No. It's just that when he was in America, he was quite impressed by the effect that corporate weekends had on company morale and individual performances. It's an idea that's caught on in this country." She smiled sweetly. "As he often points out, there is no 'I' in 'team'."

"There's no 'I' in 'piddle off' either—"

"Yes there is," Bernie interrupted.

"All right, so there's no 'I' in sod off."

Baldock had raised his voice a little and once again, his announcement could be heard by most of the room. It drew sharp glances from staff and patrons alike, and one middle-aged woman, who had clearly been listening in from the adjacent table, almost choked on her toasted teacake.

It dawned on him that putting aside the disagreement with the waitress, he and his agent were even more the centre of attention and that his invective was likely to make the front pages of tomorrow's tabloids, Baldock considered the old adage on bad publicity. There was, according to legend, no such thing. He raised his voice further and chose his words deliberately.

"I am Raymond Baldock, one of the most successful novelists in this country, not some hick executive trying to claw his way up the greasy, corporate pole, and if Gil Masters thinks I'm going to waste a weekend in the woods outside Harrogate, re-enacting the Battle of the Bulge with paintball guns, while he pretends he's Eisenhower, he can bloody well think again."

Bernie shushed him. "It's nothing like that, Raymond."

From the corner of his eye, he noticed the manager, clad in his company uniform of black trousers, white shirt and bow tie, and a narrow waistcoat which did not allow for his portly abdomen, making his way towards them.

"What is it like, then?"

"He's arranged…" Bernie trailed off as the manager arrived.

"Excuse me, sir, but is everything all right?"

Baldock glowered up. "No it is not all right. I'm being dragooned into a World War Two fantasy, and the food in this place calls to mind the rations our troops had to manage with on D-Day, with prices that remind me of the cost of the allied shipping used to facilitate D-Day."

"Could I ask you to keep the noise down, sir?" the manager asked with an icy gleam. "And may I suggest that if you are unhappy with our goods or service that you take your custom elsewhere. Otherwise, I'll have you removed from the premises."

Baldock glowered. "I'd like to see you try…"

Chapter Three

Janet Baldock checked her list. "So, for the hen party, it's Winners on Thursday, Blackbeard's on Friday, Crown & Anchor on Saturday, and for the stags, it's Blackbeard's on Thursday, Crown & Anchor on Friday and Winners on Saturday." She looked up, peering over the rim of her reading glasses. "Agreed?"

Across the kitchen table, Tim Yeoman nodded. "Fine with me. Are you all right carrying the bill for the shirts?"

To his right was a large carrier bag in which were thirteen T-shirts, in day-glow lemon, each with its own logo on the rear. To Janet's left was another, similar carrier, containing fifteen T-shirts, this time in black, with lurid pink lettering.

"I put it on my credit card. Raymond sends me money every month, so when that comes, I'll pay the bill off, and I'll be all right as long as everyone pays me."

Tim reached into his hip pocket for his wallet. "Here. I can pay you for mine right now."

"Oh, don't be so silly. There's no rush. Besides, you don't ask me for half the bill when you take me out for a meal, and I won't ask you for your shirt money."

"Hey. I'm an old-fashioned man. I don't ask any woman to pay her way." He toyed with the handle of his carrier. "Trouble is, Janet, when the bars are shut, there's nothing to stop Wayne and Chloe meeting on the beach for a bit of how's your father."

Janet pretend-shuddered. "It's unheard of for the bride and groom to meet on their hen and stag parties, and it's up to us to do what we can to stop them. But if they're determined, I don't see how we can. They're not children. Maybe the local police can, though. They take a dim view of shenanigans in the sand."

Tim obviously agreed and took his copy of the agenda. "That's it, then. The Midthorpe Maidens and the South Leeds Stags, all in Benidorm over the same three days, and never the two shall meet in the middle."

Taking off her glasses, Janet smiled coyly. "Once the stag and hens are shipped off back to Leeds, we have an extra three days to ourselves, and I'll expect us to meet a little closer then."

Tim came around the table, leant over her and kissed her, his hands automatically circling her trim waist. She broke away from his lips and removed his hands.

"Save it for later," she ordered. "Right now, after all this organising, I need a cup of tea."

"You put the kettle on, I'll get the cups ready."

They crossed Janet's spacious kitchen together, Tim diverting right to the overhead cupboards, Janet moving left to the worktop where the kettle stood. Although they did not live together, they had been 'an item' long enough for Tim to know Janet did not use the best china except on special occasions. He took down two beakers, and set them up on the table. The sugar basin joined them, and finally, he retrieved a carton of milk from the fridge.

"Don't need the milk jug, do you?" he asked.

"Carton will be fine, Tim." Preparing a novelty teapot which was in the shape of a London double-decker bus, Janet considered their relationship. They were the same age (sixty-five) and had grown up on Midthorpe estate. They had known each other since schooldays, but while she met and married Nicholas Baldock, Tim had spent six years in the army, during which time he had met his wife, Margaret. Now, in later life, both single again, they had come together thanks to the local tenants' association. They had been seeing each other for over a year, and for the present, it was an arrangement that suited them both.

The kettle snapped off. Janet filled the pot and carried it to the table.

"Talking of children," Tim said, "is Ray happier about us

these days?"

"I think so. You know Raymond. He tends not to get involved other than to look out for my welfare. Keith's not interested. Now that he's found yet another woman in Manchester who's willing to put up with him, I hardly hear from him, and I know he and Raymond haven't discussed us."

"You sound certain of that."

"Absolutely. They don't talk to each other."

Tim chuckled, lifted the teapot lid and stirred the brew. His smile faded. "Lisa was very hurt, you know, when Ray drove off the way he did."

Janet shuddered and closed her eyes and mind to the memory of her youngest son driving away and leaving Tim's daughter, the woman with whom Raymond had spent the weekend, calling after him in distraught disbelief.

"I've tried to talk to Raymond about it, but it's so difficult on the phone. He just cuts me off. And he refuses to talk about it in his emails. I'll smack the back of his legs when I see him at Christmas."

Tim laughed. "He'll be here, will he? For God's sake, don't tell Lisa. She'll go for him with a carving knife."

"And I don't blame her. Her old boyfriends are none of his business."

"Lisa had it out with Gary Lipton, you know. It was a lie. She had one date with Gary, just after your Raymond left for Cambridge, and it never went further than a bit of heavy petting. Apparently, Gary told your lad that they'd gone all the way. Well, you know Lisa. It's a wonder she didn't kick Lipton all over the estate. Even so, like you said, it all happened years ago, and it's really none of Ray's business."

"But he disapproved." Janet sighed. "He disapproves of everything these days."

"Didn't he say that if he had his way, he'd demolish Midthorpe and spread the tenants over the rest of the country so they couldn't cause any more trouble?"

Janet allowed her despondency to show through. "He was never a true Midthorper. Keith won't have anything to do with him, and you know how Nick reacted when Raymond won his place at Cambridge." She put on a deep, mock-male voice. "He should gerrout to bloody work, never mind lolling about at some fancy bloody college." She reverted to her normal tones as Tim poured tea. "That ex-husband of mine could never understand the advantages of a university education, and I'm sure his time at Cambridge helped Raymond when it came to making his large salary."

"Royalties." Tim poured a little milk into his tea, and a half spoon of sugar.

Janet frowned as she watched him. "Diabetes, Tim. It means no sugar at all."

"Type-2. I can cope with half a teaspoon."

"What were you saying?"

"Raymond's mega-earnings. They're royalties, not a salary." Tim stirred his tea vigorously. "Does it bother you, Janet? Raymond's money? Are you worried he won't send you money if we get together permanently? Cos I reckon if we put ourselves on a proper footing—"

"It's not his money," she interrupted as she stirred her own tea and clicked one saccharin tablet into it. "He doesn't send me that much anyway, because for all his money, he has a lot of outgoings, and anyway, I have asked him not to send me anything at all. It's just… Oh, I don't know. I just don't feel like listening to one of his tedious lectures on the scourge of Midthorpe and proper behaviour." She sipped her tea with approval. "Anyway, after what happened with Lisa, how does she react to you and me?"

"You know how. It's over three years since Margaret died, and Lisa is more than happy that I'm seeing someone, and more than happy that it's you."

"Good."

Tim shook his head. "She never asked me, you know. She only found out after that Fiagara business. And she doesn't poke her nose in. She appreciates I need my own space as much as she does." He grinned. "University never changed her. She's still a Midthorper. You wait and see in Benidorm. She knows how to let her hair down, that girl of mine."

"I wish Raymond did. I don't think he's happy, Tim."

"Well, I always said money doesn't buy happiness. It just makes you more comfortable in your misery."

Janet rested her elbows on the table and cradled the beaker in her small hands. "So true. I'm like any other mother. I just want to see my boys happy. Keith's been married and divorced twice and Raymond... well he has this friend. Bernard. I say friend, but Bernard is actually his agent, and to listen to Raymond, Bernard has been responsible for everything. 'I sold a hundred thousand books last year, mother. That was Bernie's doing.' 'We've negotiated a brilliant TV contract. Naturally, Bernie did most of the work.' 'Bernie was saying just the other day that we can expect a huge reception in America. I'm very popular over there.' Do you see where I'm going with this?"

A gleam in Tim's eyes told her he did. "Raymond is gay."

Janet nodded sadly. "I think so... well, after the weekend with Lisa, I don't know. Perhaps he's er..."

"Both sides of the fence?" Tim cleared his throat as a preamble to his next announcement. "In this day and age, I don't think it's quite the... oh, what's the word... stigma that it used to be. And he can't be the only Midthorper who turns the other cheek."

"I said, didn't I, that Raymond was never a Midthorper. But you're right. I'm not disappointed and obviously, whatever he is or isn't, he's still my son. If he's happy with his lifestyle, then who am I to argue? But it looks like I'll never see those grandchildren I wanted so much. Keith's ex-wives took his and *he* never sees them, never mind me, and Raymond will never have any."

Tim reached across the table, took her hand and squeezed it. "We have each other, Janet."

She smiled. "And a thumping good weekend to come in Benidorm."

Chapter Four

Seated on a bench outside British Home Stores, watching the sparse Tuesday afternoon shoppers and traders going about their business, Bernie buttoned up her coat against the unseasonably chilly weather.

"I don't think I've ever been thrown out of a café before."

"I'm sorry," Baldock apologised.

"Pubs, yes. Clubs, discos, and one time, I got thrown out of a cinema, but never tea rooms."

"Why did you get thrown out of a cinema? Were you making too much noise?"

"The film was coming to a climax." She giggled. "And so was I."

Baldock's ears coloured. "I… oh…"

"Well I was young, so was my boyfriend, the film was a little bit saucy, and we were both quite excited. Not that the manager saw it that way."

Now his cheeks began to burn. "Surely you weren't…?"

Bernie stared into his shocked eyes and laughed. "Hell, no. He just had his hand in my shirt, and mine were busy where they shouldn't have been."

Baldock hastily changed the subject. "You were saying that Masters doesn't intend to start World War Three in Yorkshire."

"Raymond, do you imagine, for one moment, that I would take part in such a farce? No thank you. Like you, I wouldn't be seen dead chasing through woodland in North Yorkshire while we shoot paintballs at one another. No, it's nothing of the kind. He's arranged a weekend away. Three nights in Spain, where we can, er, what was the phrase he used? *Bond*. Make everyone feel that we are part of a team."

"I don't want to feel part of a team. Where are the team

when Headingley is knee deep in scroats and murderous psychopaths and I don't know how to get him out of it? And the only bonds I'm interested in are tax-free, high yield... oh and 007." Having made his point, he demanded, "Dare I ask who's going to pay for this?"

"Shortly Publishing. It won't cost you a penny."

About to protest further, Baldock hesitated. A good few years had passed since he was last in Spain, yet he still recalled his overawed impressions at the sheer size and splendour of *La Sagrada Familia* church in Barcelona.

His enthusiasm rising, he asked, "Where in Spain? Madrid? Granada? Not Bilbao, is it? I went there once. Arrived on a Sunday morning and it was shut."

"Not Bilbao. The Aranjuez."

For the first time since he met with Bernie in the railway station at eleven o'clock, Baldock felt a flush of excitement. "*Palacio Real de Aranjuez*," he said in almost perfect Spanish. "The Royal Palace of Aranjuez? Rodrigo's concerto is one of my favourite pieces of inspirational music. I know every note, every phrase, every nuance of all three movements. I don't even need to have it playing. I can hear it in my head and never skip a beat. I've never actually visited the palace, but I've seen pictures of it. One of the most magnificent—"

Bernie cut him off. "It's not the Aranjuez Palace."

Baldock chuckled. "Well, of course it isn't. That place is a World Heritage site, not a bed and breakfast joint. I presume we'll be staying in a nearby hotel."

"Not quite. It is the *Hotel Aranjuez*... in Benidorm."

At that precise moment, the sun chose to shine through a gap in the leaden cloud, and lit up Bernie's face so that she appeared almost hallowed one of God's smiling angels. Baldock looked anything but. His colour drained, and for a moment, he slobbered, and his features became less beatific, more satanic.

"Benidorm?" He took hold of himself. "No. Never. Not in a thousand years. I don't care if Shortly sinks to the level of putting out books on a dot matrix printer and binding them in plain cardboard, I am not going to Benidorm."

"But Raymond—"

"Have you ever heard the term Midthorper?"

Cut off, Bernie stared vacantly into the windows of BHS, and it seemed to Baldock as if she were seeking some kind of answer from the dummies clad in their summer outfits. A window dresser, busy fitting a pair of brightly-coloured swimming shorts to a dummy, turned and stared her in the eye, compelling her to look away and back towards Baldock.

"Yes. I've heard you say it. Is it membership of some society you joined at Cambridge?"

"No. Midthorpe is a council estate in South Leeds. I must have told you before."

"No. You just told me you were born on a council estate you never told me what it was called."

"Midthorpe. And because I was born and raised there, I am, by definition, a Midthorper. It is the most appalling place in Christendom. It outstrips Las Vegas, Bangkok and every other hellhole in the civilised world. It is Hades incarnate. It has rightly been described as the anus of Leeds. To give you an idea of what it's like, there's a large pub on that estate named the Midthorpe Hotel. It's known locally as The Midden because you can get anything you want in there, and that includes buying back your own property from people who stole it from the people who stole it from you in the first place." He paused to let the layered complexity of his argument sink in. "I come from Midthorpe, ergo I am a Midthorper. Not by choice. By accident of birth and upbringing. I spent most of my youth working and working and learning and learning and learning, and when I got tired of learning, I forced myself to learn some more. All of it in a desperate effort to get away from Midthorpe. I did it. I made it all the way to Cambridge and since coming out of there with a moderate degree, I have spent the last fifteen years of my life shaking off and burying my past on that damned estate, to such an extent that I have completely dissociated myself from it. I refuse to even acknowledge its existence other than under exceptional circumstances such as now...

oh, and occasional visits to see my mother."

Bernie countered his unbridled vitriol with calm logic. "Raymond, no one is asking you to go to Midthorpe."

"I was coming to that. If you recall, I was back home during the summer for a weekend, and while the place may have changed a little, the people have not. The man who runs the local shop is also a fence for stolen car wheels. One of the teachers at the local comprehensive passed his spare time manufacturing fake Viagra and murdering the odd drug dealer or two. Benidorm, Bernie, is full of Midthorpers. Even those who are not from Midthorpe are still Midthorpers in spirit, as if they're striving to join that select band of scum. Benidorm is the kind of resort where the thieves, rogues, dole fodder, scroats and underclass of Midthorpe go for their holidays."

"If they're all unemployed, how do they afford it?" Bernie wanted to know.

"Usually on the back of ill-gotten gains or working while claiming from the state for imaginary disabilities and numerous children, most of whom were deliberately conceived to ensure the parents did not have to work for a living. Benidorm is full of working class wasters. Benidorm is the same kind of low-life dump as Midthorpe, and inhabited by the same kind of low life as you find on Midthorpe. It is the kind of holiday resort I swore I will never, *never* visit. It is a cesspit of the worst kind. It fits with Sodom, Gomorrah and the other sewers I mentioned. The best thing that could happen to Benidorm and all the other resorts of the same ilk, would be the arrival of the demolition crew... preferably carrying a lot of dynamite."

Bernie took a deep breath and let it out slowly, while silently counting. "Your ideas are steeped in 1970s and 80s stereotypes. Benidorm may appeal to the young or young at heart in the same way that Blackpool does, and it probably has more high-rise blocks than it should, but the hotels are smart, comfortable and very modern."

"So are the accommodation blocks at Yarl's Wood Immigration Centre, but I wouldn't want to spend four days there. I am not going, and that's an end of it."

"Oh dear. That's a bit awkward."

Baldock was about to rant further, but Bernie's words stopped him as he was drawing breath. "Awkward? What do you mean, 'awkward'?"

"Well, I gave Gil the impression that you would be all for it."

The anger began to rise again. "Wouldn't it have been better to consult me first?"

"He didn't really give me time. He demanded assurances there and then. And he made it clear that for those who won't play ball, there will be sanctions."

Baldock chuckled nervously, arrogantly. "Other writers, yes, but not me. My god, am I his best-selling author or not? My books are what made Shortly the company it is."

"That's not true, and you know it. The company was well-established before they signed you up. You're simply the cream on the jam and scone."

Baldock jerked his head backwards in the direction of The Pantry. "After what happened in there, you could have chosen a better metaphor."

Bernie drew breath again and spoke in terms of enforced patience. "You're contracted to one Headingley novel per year, and the contract stipulates that it must, I quote, meet the standards defined by the company. Since those standards are not actually defined anywhere, they can shift the goalposts as often as they wish; kick your manuscripts back and back and back until you reach breaking point. That is the kind of sanction Gil is talking about. Making life difficult for you."

Baldock could not have cared less. "If he even tries it, I'll take my work elsewhere. The success of the Headingley series means every publisher in Europe will jump at the chance to sign me up."

"Ah, now you can't do that, Raymond. You gave Shortly exclusive rights to your work."

"The Headingley novels, yes. But I have other projects in development. I can go where I like with those, and with a track record as a best-selling earner, any house will…"

Bernie looked uncomfortable. Baldock trailed off and waited to hear the bad news.

"You gave Shortly exclusive rights to *all* your work for ten years," she said at length. "That contract still has about five years to run."

It was obvious that she was waiting for the explosion. He felt it building up deep inside, then hurtling upwards until it burst into his brain and came out through his open, twisted mouth. "WHAT?" The single word roared so loudly that it attracted the attention of a nearby Police Community Support Officer, did not convey enough of the volcanic fury he felt, so he went on. "When the hell were you planning on telling me about this?"

"Raymond, you're making a fool of yourself. Everyone is looking at us. Even the police."

He threw a sour glance at the PCSO. "She's not police, and anyway, I don't give a damn if they can hear me in Great Yarmouth. Answer me."

"Well, I don't really remember, but Gil assures me you were told about it on the day you signed the general contract, and he showed me that contract to prove it."

"I don't remember that."

"Neither do I specifically. It was after the runaway success of the first and second Headingley novels," Bernie replied. "We were looking for a larger advance on the third, and Gil was playing hard to get. Those were some of the toughest negotiations I've ever been involved in. Eventually, Gil agreed to pay you a hundred and eighty thousand up front, but it appears he did so only on condition that you grant Shortly Publishing exclusive rights to all your work, even that as yet unwritten. I think you may have been blinded by the size of the advance. In fact, I'm sure of it. You were looking for a house in Wroxham and so eager to get your hands on the cheque that you would have signed away your first-born child for it."

Baldock stood. His entire body stiffened. His fists clenched and unclenched. "I do not believe this. It must be some kind of nightmare."

"Raymond, please calm down."

He barely heard her. "Here I am one of the most successful authors in the country, and you, you stupid bloody woman, have sold me into penury, beholden to a company run by an Anglo-American halfwit."

"Hardly penury, Raymond," Bernie protested weakly. "You made over two hundred thousand last year."

"Less than a hundred thousand by the time you and the taxman had taken your cuts. Let's call it slavery then. I'm a bloody eunuch. Tied to this sodding company whether I like it or not."

His stentorian ranting drew further attention from the PCSO, who now made her way towards them.

"I'm getting my lawyers onto this," he went on. "I'll have them tear that contract apart word by word, clause by clause and find a way out of it. It's punitive. It's restrictive practice. It's criminal. I'm sure of it."

"It's not so bad, Raymond. Only another five years."

"It shouldn't be another five minutes. I am a free agent. Or I should be." He rounded angrily and towered over her, his eyes ablaze. "What is to stop Masters from cutting my royalty rates?"

"He definitely can't do that. Royalties are at a fixed rate. If he tried to juggle them, it would be a breach of contract, and at that point we would have the right to either renegotiate or cut out."

"But even so, everything I write, from the next short story to a Christmas card for my mother has to go to him, and even if he rejects, I cannot take it elsewhere."

"I don't think it's quite that tight, but…" Bernie trailed off, looking into the concerned face of the PCSO.

"Is everything all right, madam, sir?"

Bernie, accustomed to dealing with recalcitrant authors, editors, journalists and publishers, put on a benign smile. "Yes, thank you. He's just had some bad news."

The officer turned to Baldock. "Oh dear. I'm sorry to hear that, sir. You know, sometimes, when we hear things that are distressing, it's good to let it all out, but we don't want to attract too much attention."

Baldock's eyes blazed into her. "And who are you? Norwich's answer to Dr Phil?"

"I'm a Community Support Officer, sir, and we are trained to help those in distress."

"I'm not in distress. I'm bloody annoyed."

"It's the same thing in my book. Wouldn't a nice cup of tea help?"

Her unction got to Baldock. "Why don't you just go away, you gormless gargoyle?"

"Now, sir—"

"If you look hard enough and long enough, I'm sure you'll catch a child dropping a toffee wrapper, and you can get your jollies giving him a ticket…"

Chapter Five

As her last client of the afternoon left, Lisa Yeoman watched the door close, and sighed. "It's been one of those days, girl," she muttered to empty room.

Spinning her chair so she could stare through the window at the thin August sunshine struggling to compete with a chilly, northerly wind, the view of Midthorpe Primary School across the road, prompted her memory.

She had spent much of her working life in counselling; ever since leaving university. The stresses and strains which were part and parcel of the job were something she had long ago become accustomed to. When the vacancy for a full time counsellor at the Midthorpe Health Centre came up, it was too good an opportunity to be missed. She was a Midthorper. She was born in the council-owned town house on Nimmons Crescent where her widowed father still lived. She had gone to the school across the road, and if she had moved on to Matthew Murray Comprehensive, it was only because there was no equivalent on Midthorpe Estate in those days. The only time she had been away from Midthorpe for any significant length of time, was her four years at Manchester University, and after that, a few more years in the Midlands where she pined for Yorkshire. Even then, she had made a point of getting home whenever she could. Midthorpe was in her blood. She was a Midthorper.

But that very fact had its downside. She knew many of the people who were referred to her, and although her work was supposedly directed towards those with medical problems – serious illnesses, potential surgery, coping with the stresses and strains of troubles such as bereavement – the appointments always overran thanks to men and women who wanted to gossip, those with debt problems and young men hitting on her.

University graduates from Midthorpe were thin on the ground. Indeed, the only two which readily sprung to mind were herself, and Raymond (after the way he treated her in June, she hated herself for even thinking of his name) Baldock. While she could not claim anything like the fame and fortune he enjoyed, she was nevertheless well-known on the estate as a resident who had 'bettered herself'.

Midthorpe and its rough and ready population held this inexplicable, magnetic attraction for her. People were not queuing to live on Midthorpe. If anything, they were queuing to get out, and the moment a home address was identified as Midthorpe, the person concerned became the subject of discrimination on a level that would have the European Commission bleating 'foul' so loudly that it would be heard on the International Space Station. Crime levels on the estate, from simple pub brawls to drug-dealing, were at an all-time high, policing at an all-time low. There was a rumour that the Leeds police had declared Midthorpe a no-go area, preferring to leave everything to the local community constable, a man who, in Lisa's humble opinion, would be hard pressed to maintain order in a children's class.

Her last client was a case in point. A woman of twenty-three swallowing anti-depressants as if they were liquorice allsorts, seeking advice on how to deal with an adulterous and abusive partner. Since she also worked as a casual prostitute, what she really needed was relationship counselling. Either that or a carving knife to her partner's reproductive organs, a suggestion Lisa had been careful not to make for fear that the girl would take it literally. She also needed to move away from Midthorpe, but the chances of that happening were so low that no sensible bookie would offer a price.

And yet, the estate was locked into Lisa's mindset. The streets, the schools, the parks, the people (especially the people) were part of a rich tapestry of memories dating back to her childhood, and if she no longer lived on Midthorpe, her upmarket flat on the edge of Leeds city centre symbolising her increased earnings and social status, she was still tied, historically and emotionally to the area.

The telephone buzzed, bringing her out of her mental meanderings. She snatched it up.

"Janet Baldock to see you, Lisa."

"Send her through."

Putting down the receiver, she turned her chair to watch for the door opening.

Janet was not a client, and Lisa had a shrewd idea what the visit was about. Chloe Taplin's hen party, a wild weekend in Benidorm, was a month away, and Janet had been appointed the organiser.

Lisa had always considered herself good-looking. Not beautiful, but attractive. Five and a half feet tall, she kept herself fit and watched her weight, ate sensibly and did not drink to excess. The result was a thirty-six year old, curvy figure, accentuated by the kind of attire designed to enhance. 'Nice arse, nice tits, come-and-give-me-one eyes' as the men of Midthorpe would put it when they thought she was out of earshot.

Janet Baldock was the kind of woman Lisa wanted to become. At the age of sixty-five, she had about her that kind of serene beauty often denied middle-aged women. A slim and trim body, a wicked sense of humour, signalled by a twinkle in her baby-blue eyes, and an air of implacable calm. Lisa was content in the knowledge that her father and Janet were in a relationship, and although both were children of the swinging sixties, that era of tune in, turn on, drop out and all that it suggested in the way of free love, neither had ever displayed any temptation to entertaining multiple partners. They were happy with each other.

Wrapped in a large, brown corduroy coat with a fur-lined hood, and wearing a pair of black trousers and sensible shoes, Janet was carrying a small, plastic bag, which she dropped on Lisa's desk.

"One hen party T-shirt," Janet announced. "And you owe me twelve pounds."

Lisa reached for her purse.

"There's no rush, luv," Janet insisted. "I didn't mean you had to pay me now."

Lisa nevertheless opened her purse, took out a ten-pound note and a two-pound coin and handed them over. "Let's keep the books straight, Janet."

She took the shirt from the bag. Still wrapped in its own cellophane bag, it was jet black; on the front, in the left breast area, written in lurid pink and bright blue was the legend, *Chloe Taplin, hen weekend, Benidorm*. On the rear, in a position where Lisa guessed it would appear right across her back, written in large, bright pink, cursive script, it read, *Lusty Lisa*.

She guffawed. "Lusty? Me?"

By comparison, Janet merely chuckled. "I had a real struggle to come up with naughty nicknames for everyone. I'm Juicy Janet, Chloe is the Battleaxe Bride and her mother is Leggy Linda. The easiest one was Mandy Cowling."

"Randy Mandy?" Lisa suggested and Janet laughed.

"How did you guess?"

Lisa put the shirt back in its bag, and dropped it on the floor next to her handbag. "Dad's organising Wayne's stag party, and I think he's had trouble dreaming up the nicknames for them. I know he's Timid Tim." Her smile faded. "It's odd, don't you think, having the hen party and stag party both in Benidorm, both on the same weekend."

"It was how Chloe and Wayne wanted it. Your father was at my place over lunch so we could work out the schedule; make sure we kept the two parties away from each other over the weekend."

"Done deal?"

"We're organised."

"Good. You and Dad are staying on for a few days afterwards, aren't you?"

Janet nodded. "We are, and we're looking forward to it."

Recalling the near miss when her father had been poisoned by a fake Viagra substitute Lisa's eyes narrowed on Janet. "Tell me to mind my own business, but make sure you're carrying Cialis."

Janet smiled and the twinkle appeared in her eye again. "It's in my bag, packed with the KY Jelly."

***

"Well, it's been an interesting afternoon," Bernie said as she checked the railway station clock. "We've been thrown out of the local tea rooms and you've had an £80 fixed penalty notice for abusive behaviour. They say these things come in threes, so I hope my train gets to London in one piece."

"I've had my three," Baldock sulked. "Four if I stop to think about it. I was the one who got the ticket, remember, and I was with you when we got thrown out of The Pantry. In addition, I've learned that I'm a slave to Shortly Publishing and I have to go on a god-awful weekend to Beni-bloody-dorm of all places."

"It won't be so bad, Raymond. There'll be plenty of sunshine, and you can laze around the pool or on the beach most of the time."

"I don't want to laze around a pool littered with a mob of plebs sleeping off the previous night's alcohol, and I don't like the beach. Remember, Bernie, my lawyers will be looking over that contract."

"I doubt that there's much they can do."

The station announcer's voice echoed incomprehensibly around the station. Neither of them heard what was said, but Baldock caught the word London Liverpool Street.

"That sounds like your train. You'd better hurry."

"Fine. Remember: September third, Stansted to Alicante. Masters will need your passport details."

"He needs to see it before immigration, does he? Decide whether it's up to the Shortly Publishing standards?"

"Advanced passenger information, and you know it." Bernie stretched up and kissed him on the cheek, then made for the platform. "I'll email you all the details."

Chapter Six

With the time approaching one o'clock, Baldock stepped out of his room on the eighteenth floor of the *Hotel Aranjuez*, and caught the lift to the ground floor.

Matters so far had lived down to his worst expectations, beginning at four thirty a.m. when he checked-in at Stansted Airport. Met by Bernie and Gil Masters, he was already in a bad mood.

"I had to leave home just after half past two to get here," he complained, "and now I find we're travelling with Flythere. Do British Airways not go to Alicante?"

"From Heathrow and, I think, Gatwick," Masters replied. "And the price is way too high, Ray. Besides, it's only a coupla hours, so what's the problem?"

Aged about fifty, slim and fit, his head of tidy, dark hair lacking any trace of grey, Masters spoke with a loose, American drawl, intermingled with occasional words delivered in a classless, British accent. The effect came across as insincere, and it had always grated on Baldock.

"Playing Sardines on an overcrowded Boeing 737 is the problem," Baldock retorted. "Even when I'm press-ganged into going to a public lavatory like Benidorm, I would prefer wide-bodied jets, and I like to travel first class, not compulsory economy."

As usual, Masters managed to ignore most of Baldock's complaint. "Hardly press-ganged. Bernie assures me you were all for it."

Baldock glowered at his agent. "Bernie was obviously practising for the day when she turns to writing fiction instead of selling it."

The Shortly team consisted of eleven people. Three writers

and their agents, and three staff editors from the company's London offices, along with Masters and his personal assistant, Xavier Vardaro, a Spanish national who had made her home in the UK. Baldock knew most of them, but he had never met Xavier. A dark-haired vamp in her late thirties, when she made an effort to introduce herself, he remained true to himself and responded with monosyllabic grunts that were barely polite.

Everyone, he noticed, was casually dressed, in direct contrast to him. He had put on a business suit, collar and tie. The rest were in jeans, T-shirts and trainers. The only other exception was Ian Linkman, the agent of romantic novelist, Phillipa Killairn, who had put on a pair of baggy trousers, the cuffs of which were frayed and settled generously over a pair of tatty, leather loafers.

"He has financial worries, according to scuttlebutt," Bernie told Baldock when he commented.

"But I thought Phillipa was a big seller."

"She is. Not in your league, but she is his only client, and I don't think I could live on his earnings."

The flight was about as bad as he had anticipated. After some shuffling around to ensure that Linkman could sit with Masters and Xavier, Baldock was crammed into the centre seat in a row of three, and his tall frame left him little room to manoeuvre. Eventually, Bernie, who was on the aisle seat, agreed to swap places so he could at least stretch out his legs. They departed just after six, and by the time the sun rose they were northwest of London and above 20,000 feet. The trolley began to make its way along the single aisle, and Baldock had little choice but to bring his extended leg back in. Since they were seated just a few rows from the front, and its single toilet, he remained that way for much of the journey, while so many people jostled and nudged him as they queued for the lavatory, that work on his laptop became impossible, and he settled for reading and making the occasional comments on the manuscript for his next Headingley novel.

Masters, he had noticed at Stansted, was determined to make as big a nuisance of himself as he could. He had borrowed Harry Ingels' laptop at the airport, so he could check something out on the Web, and as the aircraft made its way over the Pyrenees, he asked Phillipa if he could borrow hers while he roughed out a couple of memos. Since Phillipa was sat in the window seat alongside both Baldock and Bernie, it meant a major shuffle to get the machine to him, and back again.

"Wouldn't it have been simpler to borrow mine?" Baldock asked.

"You looked as if you were busy on it, Ray, and I don't like to disturb my authors when they're working."

The uncomfortable journey reached its absolute nadir, along with Baldock's temper, as they were approaching Alicante and the cabin manager came over the tannoy. "Ladies and gentlemen, we will be landing in about fifteen minutes. We have only half an hour to turn the aircraft round, so may I ask you to collect any rubbish and drop it in the bags as you leave. Thank you."

"Shove a brush up my backside and I'll sweep the gangway," Baldock fulminated.

He ensured his voice was loud enough to be heard by the cabin manager, who twisted her face into the mean scowl she had reserved for him throughout the flight.

Bernie, too, was embarrassed. "Honestly, Raymond, you've been so snappy since you visited your mother in June."

"That weekend reminded me of many things. Mainly that I'm still a Midthorper at heart, and I still have this Midthorpe habit of telling it like it is."

He did not tell her of the hurt he had caused and the vitriolic self-recrimination he had suffered at his appalling treatment of Lisa Yeoman during the summer. Confronted, for the first time in his life, with the prospect of a true relationship, he had blown it on the strength of information which came from a dubious source and which, if it were true, was none of his business anyway. He had driven away from his mother's house in a furious temper, having summarily ignored Lisa's pleas to hear her side of the story. The manner in which it had haunted him ever since exacerbated his tendency to blunt and downright rude treatment of others.

The aircraft touched down in Alicante five minutes ahead of schedule, and twenty minutes later, having avoided the luggage carousels thanks to travelling light, they were fighting their way through a crowded arrivals area where huge queues of holidaymakers badgered their resort reps for their transfer coach details.

An argument between a rep and a short, chubby man took Baldock's attention.

Dressed in an ill-fitting shirt and jogging pants, his flat cap pushed back on his head, sweat pouring from his brow, his glasses slipping to the end of his nose, he was clearly at the end of his tether. "You told me the bus was only waiting for me and the wife. You're wrong, it isn't waiting. It's bleeding well gone."

The rep did not appear to be remotely put out. "Well, I'm sorry about that, sir."

"Not half as sorry as you will be if you don't get me and Her Indoors to Benidorm."

Viewing the scene with a thin smile, Baldock felt some sympathy and a sense of comradeship for the harassed holidaymaker. "Excuse me," he said, tapping the man on the shoulder, "But you're not from Midthorpe, are you?"

"Oldham," the man replied. In need of something to polish his glasses, he lifted his shirt hem and revealed an overhanging, hairy belly. "It was perishing cold and hammering down when we left at four this morning, but at least there were no cock-ups with the frigging taxi."

"Quite," Baldock said and re-joined his companions.

Ten minutes later, they were climbing aboard a 20-seater minibus for the forty-five minute journey to Benidorm. "But I noticed Gil Masters and his secretary have taken a private limousine," Baldock grumbled as he got on the bus.

It was at that point he realised his laptop was missing, and a further delay followed when he harassed both the airport and the airline over its disappearance.

"You were carrying it when we got off the plane," Bernie

pointed out.

"Then where the hell is it?" he demanded.

"Perhaps our driver has already stowed it on the bus. It'll turn up when we get to the hotel."

No one had any alternative answer for him, but the airport did promise to investigate.

Once the driver had stowed their luggage, they were away from the airport, and soon travelling along the motorway past the city of Alicante, heading northeast towards their destination. A little under three-quarters of an hour later, the bus was passing through the outskirts of Benidorm, making its way to the north end of Levante Beach and the *Hotel Aranjuez*, and Baldock had to grudgingly admit that Bernie had been right. The hotels, many of them tall and narrow towers blocks, were modern and well kept, the streets were spotlessly clean and devoid of the drunks he had imagined populating them.

When they finally pulled into the grounds of the Aranjuez, instead of ramshackle, broken doors, scrub or concrete approaches littered with empty beer cans and pools of vomit, he found neatly trimmed and tended bushes, small lawns and a tiled, palazzo-style entrance, leading to a smart lobby which could have come from a five-star hike anywhere in the world. White settees and glass-topped tables were dotted around the spacious area, pot plants added to the ambience, and the walls were decorated with reproduction oils and watercolours depicting various views of the *Palacio Real de Aranjuez* after which the hotel was named.

He was further relieved to learn from Masters, who had been there for almost half an hour, that the hotel did not cater for same-sex parties larger than three people.

"Which means we won't be plagued by stag and hen parties."

But if Baldock was slightly mollified by the standard of the hotel and its policies, it did not last long. As their driver unloaded their luggage, it became obvious his laptop was still missing. It had not, after all, been placed on the bus.

A long conversation between Baldock, the hotel manager

and the bus driver was to follow. Acting as interpreter, the manager challenged the bus driver who insisted he had loaded everything from the kerbside at the airport, while Baldock threatened legal retaliation on a nuclear scale against the airline, the airport, the bus company and the whole of Spain. Eventually, the driver left them with a flood of vitriolic Spanish and drove away while the manager apologised profusely and said he would be in contact with all the relevant parties on Baldock's behalf.

"Was there much on it that was important?" Bernie asked as the bus drove off.

"Not really. One or two private documents and the outline for the next Headingley. Anyone who has hold of it could steal the script, rewrite it and pass it off as theirs."

"We'll have to keep an eye on new releases then, won't we," his agent said, and led the way into the hotel.

Still furious, Baldock followed her, to join Masters and Xavier, where he learned he was expected to share a room with Harry Ingels, a fellow novelist from Preston.

It pushed Baldock to breaking pointed. "I am sharing with no one. I demand a room of my own."

"The budget wouldn't run to it, Ray," Masters explained.

"And who are you sharing with?"

"I have a room of my own, but that's because—"

"You're not constrained by the budget. And neither am I."

With that, he marched back to reception and a few minutes of negotiation with Señor Jimenez, the manager, who, after the laptop business was only too pleased to cater for him. With the flash of his credit card, he was moved from the fourteenth floor to the eighteenth and a double room of his own.

"It's nothing personal, Harry," he said to his fellow scribe, a rotund Lancastrian in his late fifties. "I just prefer to be alone."

"No problem, Ray. After all, we're in Benidorm, and even you should be able to get your legover here."

Making a mental note to ensure he never included Ingels on a dinner invitation list, Baldock re-joined the rest of the party, to be told that they would be taking lunch in a private meeting room at one o'clock.

"This weekend is about teamwork, not meetings and stuff," Masters explained, "but I need a half hour of your time to spell out what's happening. So: one o'clock in the Sports Bar. Be there."

Baldock's room was worth the extra eighty pounds he had paid for it. A comfortable, king-sized bed afforded him the opportunity to catch up on a little sleep and the tea/coffee making facilities allowed him to savour a good cup of coffee, unlike the washing-up liquid they had served on the aeroplane, and what's more he could enjoy it in relative peace and quiet out on the balcony.

While waiting for the kettle to boil (the appliance was a sop to British tourists, and Baldock would have preferred room service) he threw off the suit, shirt and tie he had travelled in, dragged on a pair of Ted Baker Shorts and a body-hugging, plain white, Hilfiger Denim T-shirt.

If Benidorm was not as bad as he had anticipated, the glorious sunshine bathing the town from a cloudless sky, brought with it the first hint of his low expectations. From his high vantage point, he had a view of Levante beach interrupted only by the tower of the *Hotel Praia* next door. The sands were crowded. From here he could not see a single space amongst the loungers and parasols. Children and younger men and woman frolicked in the shallows where surf frothed invitingly. Many people were either asleep or simply passing the time horizontally, and on the inshore waters, various small craft, from fancy pedalloes up to fishing boats, could be seen bobbing on the slight swell. Further out, near the sloping clump of rock known as *Isla de Benidorm*, a larger boat, some kind of pleasure cruiser (a booze cruise, if Baldock guessed correctly) chugged over the placid sea.

To the working classes from which he had come, and which he so despised, the view was a classic, holiday idyll. To Baldock, it spelled out his worst nightmare. These people, be they English, Irish, German, Scandinavian, knew nothing of Spanish culture or history, and they were driven by a determination not to learn anything. They were here for the cheap tobacco, cheap drink and cheap or preferably free fornication, using the sun-soaked days to sleep off their nightly excesses.

Baldock recognised the hypercriticism of his notions, and in an effort to vindicate them, he reminded himself that his degree in Modern History meant he, too, knew very little about Spain, its history or culture, but it did not mean he was not prepared to make an effort. The loungers and scroungers on the beach were as dedicated to doing nothing here as they were back in England.

Satisfied with his biased diagnosis that a good proportion of those on the beach were signing for unemployment benefit and working in the black economy, he finished his coffee and made his way down to the lobby, where an attendant directed him to the *Bar Deportivo*, and he stepped in to find his fellow authors, agents and the Shortly employees already eating lunch

Chapter Seven

"Ray," Masters greeted him from the head of the table. "Glad you felt able to join us."

"Well, it was a toss-up between here and the fast food joint down by the beach. On the whole, the company at the fast food place might be preferable, but the food's better here."

Having delivered what he fondly hoped was an acerbic *coup de grace*, he moved to the carvery, picked up a plate and shuffled along, choosing items from various cold cuts and salad vegetables, before taking the seat allocated him next to Bernie.

"We don't have long," Masters informed the table. "I managed to secure the room for a maximum of forty-five minutes, so you'll forgive me if I carry on speaking while we eat."

He reached down to a box alongside his seat and began to take out shirts, each wrapped in cellophane, each bag carrying a participant's name scrawled in marker pen.

"If you could pass these along," he asked of Xavier to his right, and Ingels who was on his left.

Baldock could see that others were as puzzled as he. Sat furthest from Masters, his parcel was the first to arrive. He opened it, and held the shirt up so he could examine it properly.

It was, as far as he could judge, the correct size. A short-sleeved T-shirt in bright orange, the front sported the Shortly Publishing logo beneath which was the wording, *Shortly Cooperation Get-together Benidorm*. On the back, was inscribed the legend *Rampant Ray*. Cramming it back into the bag from whence it had come, he dropped it on the floor and returned to his meal.

While he ate, he watched others examining their shirts. Ingels was the first to slip it on over his Adidas T-shirt, after which he muttered a few words to Masters. Greasing, if Baldock had it right; sheer, naked crawling.

Prompted by Ingels, others began to put their shirts on, including his agent, and as she half turned to do so, Baldock noticed that she was billed as *Battling Bernie*. His lip curled and he helped himself to a dash of balsamic vinegar to take away the smirk of disgust.

"Not trying yours on, Ray? I expect to see all of you wearing them."

"I expect an advance of at least a million for my next book. I think the chances of that happening are about the same as me turning out like a refugee from the Dutch World Cup football team."

Alongside him, Bernie physically cringed. Masters did not. He merely smiled, causing Baldock to wonder what he had to do to really get up the man's nose.

Casting his eye over Masters' pristine white, short-sleeved shirt, Baldock asked, "If you expect everyone to wear these abominations, where's yours?"

Masters stood, unbuttoned his shirt and removed it, revealing his orange tee beneath. He turned his back so they could all read the words, *Glorious Gil*.

"I'm a team player, Ray. I don't ask the team to do anything I won't do myself."

"I'll remember that when you tell me to bugger off and never darken your door again."

If Baldock's candour caused ripples of shock round the table, Masters did not bat an eyelid.

"Okay, folks. Good to see us all getting it together. Now, please carry on with your meals and if you could lend an ear as you do so, I'd be grateful." He paused a moment to allow everyone to get back to their food. "Ray's attitude, regarding both the shirt and his comment when he first joined us is entirely symptomatic of the gulf that exists between authors, agents and the staff at Shortly. We don't cooperate as we should. We are separate entities orbiting around each other, exerting some influence, but not enough. I want to see us work as a *team* and I had to figure out a way of encouraging you to do so."

"If I may just interrupt," Baldock said, and swallowed a mouthful of ham and lettuce. "I don't call blackmail cooperation."

"No one blackmailed you, Ray."

"Threats were uttered."

"Not threats," Masters disagreed. "Tools, levers, if you will, designed to get you to come along and enter into the spirit of the thing. These are legitimate negotiating tools."

"Richard Headingley, my fictitious detective, would describe it as duress; coercion. I'm practically certain any competent lawyer would use the same term. Mine are looking into it as we speak."

"I wish them well, but I don't think they'll get very far." Masters ignored the spearing glower from Baldock, and spoke again to the whole table. "I was saying I had to think of a means of achieving this goal of cooperation. I came up with this."

Masters reached down to his box again and came up with a large sheet of white card which read $E=MC^2$. Beneath it was written: *Earnings = Marketing x Cooperation^2*.

Having finished with his food, drinking from a glass of iced water, Baldock almost choked. "E equals MC squared is a mass-energy equivalence formula, you ignoramus."

"I know what it is, Ray. But like you, I'm a creative, so I adapted it." His next words were once more directed at everyone. "So what does it mean? Our marketing department work hard on your behalf. The more you cooperate, the more books you will sell and the higher your earnings will rise. And that, ladies and gentlemen is what this weekend is about." His gaze narrowed on Baldock. "Ray, you are one of the company's biggest sellers and without giving away precise information, you earned six figures last year. You reckon you could have done that on your own?"

"A pointless question, and one we can't answer because it didn't happen," Baldock replied. "When it comes to cooperating, I do. As I pointed out to Bernie when this farce was first mentioned, I attend every interview, every book signing, every reading in every poky little library or old people's home in the country. I even turned up here. What more do you expect of me?"

"I expect you to drop the attitude and be pleasant about it."

It was the first direct challenge, and Baldock felt a spark of anger, but before he could rise to it, Bernie got there.

"Raymond doesn't have any attitude when he's reading, signing or speaking to the media, Gil. His demeanour in other circumstances is entirely his own affair."

"Not when he's telling a professional editor to get back to school and learn English."

"I told her to learn British English." Baldock snapped. His glare settled on twenty-something Katie Enderby, one of Shortly's editors, seated across the table. "I told her to go back to school and learn the difference between the way we Brits and the way our American cousins speak. When I write the word 'arse' I expect to see 'arse', not 'ass'. In Great Britain, an ass is a donkey."

"You're thinking of a mule," Katie replied in an effort to stand up to him and ease her embarrassment.

"No. A mule is the offspring of a male donkey and female horse. A jack and a mare."

"Well, I didn't—"

Masters cut Katie off. "The details don't matter. Insulting the crew when they make mistakes is not in the spirit of cooperation. You were the same when Dean changed 'tosser' to 'jerk-off'." Masters indicated Dean Quarmby, sat two places down from Baldock on the same side of the table. "You have a great many American readers, and they don't understand the term 'tosser'."

"It's British vernacular. I am British, the novels are set in Great Britain, I write as I hear British people speak, and I will not have my work changed by a pair of idiots who pay more attention to the son of an onanist than they do their mother tongue."

Masters smiled thinly. "Son of an onanist? I take it you

mean me? Wrong, Ray. My father was Church of England."

"What a pity." Having scored a major point, Baldock silently congratulated himself.

"To be charitable, Ray, I'll assume you're still upset about your stolen laptop, and I sympathise with you. However, putting theft, religion and personal disagreements to one side, this weekend is designed to help you all cooperate with each other. And to that end, I have some challenges for you, which I will detail at dinner this evening. They're not for today, but tomorrow onward, and they won't take up much of your time. There are eleven of us. I'll be dividing you into three teams of three. One Shortly employee, one writer, one agent. And you will all be comparative strangers. Writers, you will not be teamed with your own agent or editor. Each team will be given a challenge for tomorrow and a second challenge for Saturday. In order to complete these challenges, you're going to need to cooperate."

"Three doesn't go into eleven," Baldock pointed out.

"Xavier and I will be observing," Masters said, indicating his personal assistant. "However, as I said, other than spelling out your tasks at dinner this evening, this is all for tomorrow onwards. For today, we're going to get to know each other in a social setting, here at the hotel, and we'll be taking in the town and its bars this evening." Masters put on his most serious face and ran his eye round the table to take in each individual. "I do not expect anyone, anyone at all, to embarrass Shortly Publishing."

Baldock laughed. It was forced and there was no genuine humour in it.

"I said something amusing, Ray?"

"You want to trawl the bars of the largest, cheapest urban whorehouse in Europe while wearing bright orange T-shirts, and you expect no embarrassment for you or Shortly Publishing? Tell me, Gil, have you ever thought of becoming a novelist? Because you certainly come up with some great fantasies."

***

A hundred yards down the street, as blissfully unaware of her son's presence as he was of hers, Janet took her post-lunch ease by the pool of the *Hotel Praia*, and watched a few of the younger women from their party fooling around in the water.

So far everything was going smoothly, although Chloe, the bride-to-be, had complained that she was missing her intended. Given that both hen and stag parties had travelled on the same flight and they had only parted company when the shuttle bus dropped the men off at the *Hotel Dolce*, it was a sign, so Janet thought, of true love.

"Either that or the sunshine is making her feel frisky," she had confided in Linda Taplin, Chloe's mother.

"Judging by the noises coming from their bedroom at home, our Chloe don't need sunshine to turn her on."

"Distracting, is it?"

"It is when you're on your own. Well, you don't need me to tell you that, do you? Not after the time you were alone when Nick left." Linda left the idea hanging in the air.

"You're right, Linda, but I have Tim now, and John is still around, isn't he?"

"Aye. Living the other end of Midthorpe with his fancy piece."

Janet leaned in conspiratorially. "Well, he's here with the boys on the stag party. There's nothing to stop you trying to win him back."

"And nothing to say I want the little snot back."

Lisa appeared from the hotel exit, looked around the busy pool area, spotted Janet and made her way across. She looked good. Dressed in a pair of short shorts and a thin top through which her nipples poked. Janet felt a twinge of envy. She wished she had the kind of bustline that would let her nipples poke through sun tops.

"Now here's a girl I would have loved as a daughter-in-law."

"Lisa?" Linda asked. "She wouldn't have looked twice at your Keith."

Janet tittered. "Not Keith. Raymond."

Linda's face fell. "Oh. Him."

Janet would have taken Linda to task, but Lisa arrived and took the next sun lounger. But she did not lie down. Instead, she sat on the edge, facing Janet, and kicked off her sandals.

"I thought you were having a rest," Janet said.

"I was going to," Lisa replied, "but Mandy decided to start the weekend in classic style. I went back to the room after lunch, and I heard the bed creaking as I walked in. Didn't make the connection until I saw his backside thrusting away."

The two older women laughed.

"Blimey," Linda said. "She's started early. Who is the poor sod?"

"One of the porters. According to his shirt, which was on the floor by the way, his name is Gaspar."

"Fatal, that," Janet commented. "His name begins with G."

"He was certainly living up to his name. All that gasping." Lisa shuddered. "Honestly, I've never been so embarrassed. I didn't know where to look."

"Good job it wasn't the other way round." Linda laughed loudly. "Mandy would have asked you to hold on while she got her camera out."

"She has a smartphone Linda," Janet said. "She'd have videoed it." She beamed on Lisa. "You'd have been on YouTube before dinner, luv."

Lisa, obviously did not find it funny. "Any chance I could move rooms?"

Janet gave it some thought. "Well, I suppose we could ask Sandra Scranton if she'll ship in with Mandy. They're of the same bent, aren't they? But you'd have to crash with Angie Gallacher."

"I don't mind. At least Angie won't be trying to screw her way through the staff."

"Fine. We'll talk to Angie in a bit."

Satisfied, Lisa threw her legs up onto the lounger, and from her bag, pulled out a pair of Ray Bans. She lay back, arms behind her head, and yawned. As quickly as her mouth opened, it closed again, and she stared intently at the tower block of the *Hotel Aranjuez*.

Puzzled by this behaviour, Janet asked, "Something wrong?"

"No. Yes. I mean no. For a moment there, I could have sworn I saw Raymond on a balcony up there." She pointed to the top of the Aranjuez block.

"Raymond? You mean my Raymond?"

"Yes. Up there. Top floor… oh. He's gone now."

Janet found it deliriously funny. "Our Raymond in Benidorm? I think it was a trick of the light, Lisa. Our Raymond would never be seen dead in Benidorm."

"Hmm. You're right. Trick of the light and a tired mind. It must be." Lisa yawned again. "And it's a good job. If I caught him here, they'd hear his screams in Valencia."

Chapter Eight

Lisa's eyes opened. A clutch of four Midthorpe Maidens were larking about near the edge of the pool, and one of them (Becky Wainman if Lisa was not mistaken) had just fallen in, giving rise to a bout of screeching, hysterical laughter from her friends.

The rest of the group, particularly the older women, were sleeping off lunch in the shadier part of the pool area, and having moved her light luggage from the apartment she shared with Mandy Cowling, Lisa had taken her cue from them, grabbed a sun lounger, dragged it into the shade alongside Janet's, spread her towels on it, and flopped down. She had been on the point of drifting into sleep when the gambolling of the younger Midthorpers disturbed her.

Automatically her eyes travelled to the tall tower of the Aranjuez which in turn called to mind the man on the very top floor who had so reminded her of Raymond Baldock.

Janet had dismissed the notion in a fit of giggles similar to those given out by the cavorting hens in the pool, but at the time Lisa had been so convinced that she would be willing to bet a week's salary on it.

Janet, of course, was right. Her youngest son would not be seen dead in this town. He would be unlikely to visit the Costa Blanca under any circumstances, but if he did, he would stay either in Alicante, or if he chose to visit the coast, it would be in a more upmarket, sedate resort like Albir. In his eyes, Benidorm was hedonism personified, far too free and easy, and much too far outside his comfort zones.

His attitude, best described as haughty, was the foundation upon which most Midthorpers based their dislike of him. To be truly accurate, it was not his stringent standards, but his insistence upon maintaining them and letting everyone know that he disapproved of any behaviour which failed to meet them. Sensitivity was vital, even on a rough-and-tumble council estate like Midthorpe, and Raymond had none. He was blunt, to the point, and it was asking for trouble. With a few exceptions, the Midthorpe women sniggered at him behind his back, and the Midthorpe men considered goading him to be a first-class sport. It had always been the way.

And yet, for all his foibles, Lisa loved him. She had been distraught when he left for Cambridge almost 20 years ago. She had been delighted to see him in June, but four days later he had left, unwilling to listen to her denunciation of Gary Lipton's outrageous lie. She was as furious with Baldock as she had been with Lipton, but beneath her rage, she still could not suppress her love.

When she saw him on the balcony... correction, when she saw someone who looked like him, she wanted him in front of her. She wanted to rage at him, beat him into submission, and then tend his wounds.

Looking up at the Aranjuez, shielding her eyes against the glare of the sun reflecting from rows of windows, she scanned the top floor again, looking for him, hoping against hope that it was him, almost willing him to be there in Benidorm right next door to her.

A few floors lower down, a dark haired woman staggered against her balcony, and leaned over as if she were going to be sick. Lisa could not help a chuckle at the thought of anyone immediately below her. It would give a new meaning to the phrase projectile vomiting.

Her humour died. To her horror the woman's feet were raised, presumably by someone behind her, someone Lisa could not see, and she toppled over, free-falling through the air, her arms flailing feebly.

Lisa was not the only one who had seen. Cries of alarm went up all around the Praia, and from next door, they could hear the screams of guests at the Aranjuez.

***

On the sun terrace of the Aranjuez, Bernie had chosen to pass the afternoon exchanging text messages with her husband.

Her thoughts, too, were of Baldock, but she was not in love with him. True, she considered him a close friend, but that was as far as it went. In common with many people, his approach to life both irritated and worried her. He was outspoken to the point of rudeness, and it never occurred to him that there was anything amiss in such candour. It never seemed to dawn on him that he might be hurting other people's feelings. And other than on those occasions when he set out to deliberately irritate someone, such as he had with Gil at lunchtime, he could not understand why people got angry with him.

He was possessed of a high IQ, he was a supremely talented writer, took pride in the meticulous planning and construction of his works. But he was a social Neanderthal.

Bernie had a small list of clients on her books, but Baldock was the most important. Her income was heavily reliant upon his success, and it was no exaggeration to say that she would cancel a meeting with the senior executives of any and all publishers if Baldock or Shortly called.

She had no more idea than anyone else what game Gil Masters was playing with this apparently pointless weekend in Benidorm, but she was seriously concerned about the way in which Baldock constantly threw down challenges. She had an awful feeling that matters were going to come to an unpleasant head.

Although Masters was a few years older than her, she had known him very briefly at Oxford, and even then she had found him a singularly unpleasant and manipulative man. The intervening years, especially the time he had spent in the cutthroat business world of North America, had done nothing to diminish his ability to swing any and every situation to his benefit. She did not trust him. Conversely, it was their brief entanglement at Oxford which had opened the Shortly door to Baldock, and it was the bedrock upon which the company rode the crest of commercial success.

The antipathy between the two men concerned her, but

more importantly, Baldock's social naiveté could possibly blind him to whatever hidden agenda Masters had in mind.

It was while she was tossing ideas back and forth with her husband on this very subject that a rising tide of screams filled her ears, and distracted her attention.

She glanced over to the sunlit corner of the terrace just in time to see a familiar body smash down onto the marble-effect tiles.

Xavier Vardaro landed on her back with a sickening crunch of bone, and as her head struck the ground blood began to seep from her shattered skull.

Chapter Nine

Finding the raw heat of a Spanish day overwhelming, Baldock spent most of the long, sweltering afternoon in the comfort of his air-conditioned room, dozing on the king-sized bed or working on his iPad.

Occasionally, wearing nothing but his trunk underpants, which could legitimately pass for shorts from a distance, he stepped out onto the balcony, to take in the view, and once he could have sworn he'd seen Lisa Yeoman's shapely figure, strolling round the pool of the Praia next door.

Wishful thinking, he diagnosed. A guilt-induced hallucination after the appalling way he had treated her three months previously. And with that conclusion, he went back to work.

Many people thought him strange for carrying both a laptop and iPad, but he had always been a belt and braces man. Without a folio case/keyboard for the iPad, he had to work with the on-screen keyboard, and for that reason, he preferred the laptop, but the files on both portable machines were the same.

Thoughts of his missing laptop threatened to irritate him once again, but before he could get properly wound up, he was disturbed by an insistent pounding on the door. Pulling on his Ted Baker shorts, he padded barefoot across the room, opened the door and found Bernie in a state of high anxiety.

"What on earth is the matter?"

"Xavier," Bernie gasped barging past him into the room. "She's dead."

Baldock closed the door. "Just calm down, Bernie. What do you mean Xavier is dead?"

"I mean dead. As in no longer alive. D-E-A-bloody-D. She

is the late Xavier Vardaro."

Forcing the thrill of shock that ran through him, Baldock dug into the minibar, brought out a miniature brandy, cracked the cap, poured the contents into a glass and handed it to her. Bernie gulped half of it down.

"What happened? Do we know?"

"She came over the balcony. Landed in the pool area."

"Long drop?"

"She was on the fourteenth floor, Raymond. And the pool area is... the pool area. It's tiled, not a bouncy castle. It's chaos down there. Half the guests are in shock, the other half are drunk as skunks, the hotel staff are flapping around like headless chickens, and the police want to speak to everyone in the Shortly group, including you."

It was as if he had not heard her. "She must have made a hell of a mess when she landed."

"And that's another thing. The hotel cleaners are demanding extra pay for cleaning up the blood and brains."

"I really must make some notes on this."

Bernie's eyes almost popped. "Raymond, Xavier is dead. Never mind your next Headingley novel. The woman is dead."

Her insistence seemed to wake him up. He gestured at her glass, indicating that she should finish it off. When she had done so, he led the way out of the room, ensuring that the door was locked behind him, and they took the lift down to the ground floor.

As Bernie had said, the place was in chaos. The management had closed the pool, and sealed off the outer area, and many of the guests were protesting on two fronts. Some were complaining that a body had actually arrived on the ground at high speed, while others, especially those on all-inclusive packages, were complaining that closing the pool interfered with their right to soak up the ultraviolet and free beer.

Flanked by police officers, the members of the Shortly group were silent and white-faced and sat in a huddle, off to one side of the general melee. Baldock and Bernie battled through the crowds and joined them.

Linkman and Ursula Franklyn were in tears and comforting each other, Philippa Killairn and Harry Ingels were talking grimly between themselves, while the rest of the party remained locked in their own thoughts, Masters was busy talking into his mobile phone.

When Baldock and Bernie arrived, Masters broke off his call, and spoke to a police officer standing nearby. "This is Raymond Baldock, one of our authors. He's the last of our party."

Baldock was kept busy over the next few minutes giving a brief statement to the police, but when asked if he could throw any light on Xavier's death, he simply said, "I've been alone in my room all afternoon. The first I knew of it was when my agent, Mrs Deerman, came for me a few minutes ago."

"If you would wait here, senor, Inspector Suarez will maybe need to speak to you."

Baldock cast a glance through the panoramic doors and windows which led to the swimming pool. Across the far side were several police officers and medics standing over Xavier's covered body. The sight sent a shudder through him, but with his customary air of detachment, he made mental notes of the scene.

"Tragic," he muttered, "but excellent research material for any crime novelist."

Bernie's eyes widened. "For God's sake, Raymond. How many times do I have to say it? The woman is dead."

"What? Oh. Yes. Of course. I said, didn't I, it's tragic." He turned his attention on the disapproving Masters. "Do we know what happened?"

Of them all, the chief executive appeared least distressed. "No. After lunch, she did like you and went back to her room. Some of the guys were taking their ease around the pool, and the next thing I knew was young Linkman screaming his head off like some chick who been groped for the first time. Five minutes later, Philippa rang me and told me what happened. Where the hell were you, Ray?"

"In my room. Resting."

"Yeah, well, that's about your mark, isn't it?"

"And what do you mean by that?"

"When it comes to socialising, you don't."

Masters shuffled to a more comfortable position and yawned. Baldock got the impression that it was a deliberate act designed to show his lack of interest in anything his most successful author might have to say.

Time passed and eventually a senior police officer wearing a black insignia and two laurel leaves on the epaulettes of his pristine white shirt entered. Tall, muscular, with the slightest trace of a paunch about his midriff, he addressed them as a group.

"Good afternoon, ladies and gentlemen, I will not detain you any longer than is necessary. I am Inspector Suarez of the *Policia Nacional* and I am looking into the death of Señorita Vardaro. My officers will need to speak to you all again one at a time."

Masters took immediate umbrage. "Why? You've already had our statements."

"Yes, señor. However, that was before the doctor reported to me. I suspect that Señorita Vardaro did not fall from the balcony. She was assaulted before she fell, and it could be that we are looking at a case of murder."

The announcement sent a ripple of shock through the party. Once again it was Masters who pressed for an explanation. "What are you talking about?"

"She has extensive bruising to her face."

"Forgive me for stating the obvious, Inspector," Baldock said, "but she has just fallen fourteen floors."

"This we already know, señor. But she landed on her back. Her injuries are consistent with that, but how do you explain the bruises about her face and eyes? No, señor, she was assaulted before she came over the balcony, and as her closest friends and colleagues, it is from you we must take the statements. This is not to say that any of you were involved, but you may have information which can help us."

The process began immediately, and Masters pulled rank,

insisting that the police speak to him first. Baldock was at the back of the queue, and an hour passed before he finally gave a statement to one of Suarez's officers, and it was no different to the statement he had given when first asked.

Relieved to be away from the lobby, as he made his way to the lifts, he found himself accosted by a half drunken young man who spoke with a thick Geordie accent.

"Buggered the day up, that has. Bloody attention seekers. Allus gotta spoil it for everyone else."

Baldock rounded on him. "She's dead, you moron."

"Proves my point then, dunnit. She wanted attention, and her name'll be all over the papers tomorrow. Can't get more attention than that, can she?"

***

At six thirty, Baldock took a shower before putting on his shorts and the ridiculous, bright orange, Shortly T-shirt. Notwithstanding Xavier's death, Masters insisted they attended for dinner, and Bernie had impressed upon him the need to appear as if he were toeing the line, even if he did kick now and then.

Sliding his feet into comfortable Dune Flounder espadrilles, and carrying a shoulder bag for his wallet, smartphone and keys, he joined the others for a self-service dinner in the hotel restaurant (the lack of waiters caused him to mark down the place one star) and settled for roast chicken with potatoes and a selection of other vegetables, supplemented with a glass of house red, and followed by a fresh fruit salad.

The police had finished their investigations of the pool area and he was pleased to note that Masters had commandeered three outdoor tables, and had the staff push them together so they could literally have dinner as 'one family' (Masters' description, not Baldock's).

During the meal, conversation was muted, strictly non-controversial and non-business. Masters told one or two tales from his days at Harvard Business School, Baldock delivered a couple of anecdotes from his early career as a staff writer on *Sleuth Monthly*, while Phillipa Killairn reminisced on her early days as a romantic novelist. The subject of Xavier was never mentioned, but it was impossible to raise the general air of gloom, and Baldock noticed that Ian Linkman was not eating, and he was constantly comforted by Ursula Franklyn.

"He had a thing with Xavier," Bernie whispered when Baldock queried it.

With dinner over and the sun dipping towards the horizon, Masters finally brought them round to business.

"Ladies and gentlemen, we have lost a good friend today, but I knew Xavier well. She worked or me for the last four years, and she was thoroughly committed to the Shortly vision. For the time being Ursula has been appointed my PA." He smiled benignly on the young woman. "And I'm sorry, Ursula, but that doesn't get you out of the team game." He addressed the whole table again. "I know Xavier would have wanted us to carry on in spite of her passing, so without further ado…" He dipped into his pocket, came out with several small envelopes, stood up and began to move along the table, handing them out to individuals.

"Remember, people," Masters went on, "This weekend is quite informal. However, here are your orders for tomorrow. You can take your time about them. The card will detail your team and your task. I expect you to report back at dinner tomorrow evening."

Baldock opened his envelope and removed the finely printed card inside, Harry Ingels, sitting close to Masters, spluttered.

"Bloody hell, Gil. This is a tall order."

"And this is Benidorm, Harry. You should find it easy."

"You expect me to get some stranger to pull my shorts down while my teammates take pictures?"

Masters gestured along the table. "I'm assured it's easy to arrange in any of the bars here. Isn't that right, Ray?"

"How would I know?" Baldock responded. "I hate Benidorm."

"Which means you must have been here before."

"No. Never. I simply loathed it on sight of the brochure."

Masters ignored him, and faced the clutch of tables. "The name of the game, people, is cooperation. It doesn't much matter whether you succeed or not, it's learning to cooperate with your teammates that counts."

While their self-appointed leader spoke, Baldock read his card.

The Team:
Ray Baldock
Ian Linkman
Ursula Franklyn
The task:
Remove a woman's panties in public or in private while your two teammates look on and gather the photographic evidence.

He felt the colour rushing to his cheeks, and the smouldering anger building up from deep in his gut. "Forget it."

"Ray—"

Baldock interrupted Masters again. "If you think I am propositioning some woman in the middle of the street, you are mistaken. I won't do it."

He returned to his coffee. At the head of the table, Masters drained off his and took out a pack of cigarettes. "Ray, let's take a little walk, huh? Just me and you. A short constitutional around the pool so we can clear the air."

Baldock finished his coffee, pushed his plate away and stood, kicking his chair back with a loud scraping noise on the terracotta tiles. Bernie grabbed his wrist and he looked down into her worried eyes.

"Be careful, Raymond."

Baldock raised his eyebrows. When Bernie did not answer, he fixed her gaze with his. "What is it?"

She looked away and shook her head.

"Bernie—"

Her head spun back and she cut him off. "Just be careful."

His anger rising further, Baldock turned on his heels and marched off in pursuit of Masters.

He caught up with Shortly Publishing's CEO ambling along by the pool, his tanned features given a blue cast in the ghostly illumination of the subsurface lights.

"I'm beginning to get annoyed with you, Masters."

"And I appreciate you're teed off with losing your laptop, and what happened to Xavier has upset everyone, but even allowing for that, I'm beginning to get a little ragged with your attitude." Masters drew deeply on his cigarette and blew a cloud of smoke into the clear, evening air. "There are only two kinds of people in this world, my friend; winners and losers. I'm a winner. So are you, which means it all comes down to which of us has the bigger balls. I figure it's me."

"Don't be too sure of yourself."

"Oh but I am sure of myself, Ray. I have whip hand." Masters stopped, turned, and looked up at Baldock. "I believe Bernie told you of the sanctions I'll impose… well, she must have done or you wouldn't even be here."

"She did. She also told me of those absurd and restrictive clauses in the contract. My guess is they're illegal and my lawyers are looking into it." He did not add that his lawyers had already reported back and found nothing out of place.

Masters smiled, turned and began to walk again, turning left around the far end of the pool and admiring a couple of young women in their scant evening wear. "They're wasting their time, and your money. I've been in this business a long time, Ray, and I've screwed up now and then. Bought some real turkeys that I thought would be successful, but which bombed. But I've never screwed up a contract. That deal is tighter than your Yorkshire-born ass."

"We'll see."

"But I don't have time to wait or to waste. You will toe the line, boy. You will turn out the stuff I want, you will turn it out to my satisfaction, and you will get out there tomorrow and bring me back a pair of ladies' panties and proof that you removed them. What's more, you'll do it by dinner tomorrow evening, because if you don't, those sanctions will kick in from midnight." Masters stopped again, turned, took a drag on his cigarette and blew the smoke in Baldock's face. "I will freeze you out. I will bankrupt you."

Trembling, his fists clenching involuntarily, Baldock forced control over himself. "I'm known for my stand against violence, Masters. I don't believe in it, I don't approve of it. I will walk away before I'll get into a fight. Despite that, right now, I'm sorely tempted to punch your face in."

In a gesture, which to Baldock smacked of total contempt, Masters dropped his cigarette on the tiles, and crushed it underfoot. "An Oxford Blue for boxing, a student of karate for over thirty years, and you want to punch me? To paraphrase a certain movie, go ahead, chump, make my day."

Baldock took a deep breath and let it out in a long, slow hiss. "Have you ever heard of Midthorpers?"

"Nope. What is it? A bar in Norwich?"

"No. They're people born and raised on Midthorpe, which is the slag heap of a council estate in Leeds where I was raised. I have fought for the last two decades to rid myself of that label. I hate it. I hate the place, the people, I loathe the very thought of Midthorpe and Midthorpers. But there is one thing I took from it which I value. Midthorpers are afraid of no one, and we are sore losers."

"That's two things."

"So it is. There you are then. I've just doubled my Midthorpe assets. Are you a sore loser, Masters?"

"I don't know. I've never lost." Masters walked back towards the hotel.

"Then be prepared for the experience."

Baldock turned smartly and marched back to join Bernie, now left alone at the clutch of tables the Shortly team had commandeered. His agent was staring glumly over the rim of a cup of cold coffee.

"How long have we worked together?" he demanded.

She shrugged. "Ten years. Give or take."

"And how long have we been friends?"

"Even you can do the arithmetic, Raymond." She stared him out. "Is this about your laptop? Or Xavier?"

He shook his head. "Neither. Friends for a decade, yet you never call me Ray."

She could not have looked more surprised if he'd asked her to marry him. "I thought you preferred Raymond. At least that's what you told me."

"No. I told you my mother insists on calling me Raymond because that was the name I was given. When she hears others call me Ray, she has this embarrassing habit of scolding them."

"Raymond… Ray, is this going somewhere or are we just taking a stroll through hell?"

"Well, the point is, after all this time, do you think I can't tell when there's something wrong? So what is it?"

"Nothing. Well, nothing you can do anything about."

"Don't give me that, Bernie. He's just threatened me and he's obviously said something to you. I want to know what."

"I've told you, Raymond, it's nothing you can do anything about. Trust me on this. I was at Oxford a few years behind him, and I heard of his reputation. He's a total scroat."

"I recall you mentioned it when you first took me on. You figured your years at Oxford might open a door. And it helped, didn't it?"

"It did. What I didn't tell you was that he was scum then, he's bigger scum now. Now let's leave it at that. We're expected to follow them into town."

Chapter Ten

At just after nine thirty, they left the hotel to amble through the streets, away from the beach towards the lively heart of Benidorm.

With the setting of the sun, dark clouds had massed over the barren hills in the middle distance. Baldock did not believe they were harbingers of bad weather such as they would be in England, but their very presence seemed to intensify the already overwhelming heat. Most of the party – Baldock included – were comfortable in shorts and casual shoes or trainers, but again, Linkman wore his baggy trousers and shabby loafers, his only sop to the heat being the ridiculous orange T-shirt Masters had insisted upon.

Live music came from the outside bar of a busy hotel; when Baldock checked it was a youngish couple, the man playing keyboards, the woman singing as they ran through a repertoire of old Carpenters' hits, with an audience of young to middle-aged drinkers singing along and applauding them.

Tagging along with Bernie, slowly falling behind the rest of their party, they came off the main road and mingled with droves of people moving into what was known as the Brit quarter, and the further they moved along the narrow *Calle Gerona*, the more the subdued cocktail party air of dinner faded, and the more dispirited and depressed Baldock became.

Young people crowded the narrow streets, some women barely dressed in the skimpiest, and to his way of thinking, most provocative, clothing, the men clad in shabby tees and shorts, or in fancy dress ranging from bearded brides to adaptations of The Blues Brothers, and one group of men dressed in red tops and miniskirts of cheerleaders. Many groups were branded with sashes or shirts identifying the particular stag or hen party to which they belonged, and the ridiculous orange, Shortly Publishing T-shirt made him feel as if he were part of one such group.

A young woman staggered along the pavement and dropped a large, plastic penis she was carrying. A middle-aged man wearing a white T-shirt which read, *Between the diuretics and the Viagra, I don't know whether I'm coming or going*, tapped her arm and said, "Hey up, luv, you've dropped your dick."

The man's wife guffawed loudly, and the young woman picked up her toy.

"Thanks," she slurred. "I'm a bit tanked up."

Bernie giggled, but Baldock found himself equally disgusted by the man's obvious pleasure and the girl's insobriety.

Huge and muscular security men, easily identified in their black shorts and T-shirts, roamed the streets in twos and threes, or stood on corners smoking, ever alert for signs of trouble. From the different, crowded bars came loud music, some of it obviously karaoke, but mostly via DJs utilising overloud disco systems, the lyrics drowned by off-key singing from one party or another, the whole ensemble melding into a tuneless cacophony which insulted Baldock's sensitive, classical ears.

This was Benidorm at its worst; the Benidorm he had imagined and dreaded. Blackpool with sun, someone had said. They were wrong. He did not like Blackpool, but at least there, the noise would be enhanced by the chinking and chiming of games arcades and the sound of children enjoying themselves. Here, there were few children in evidence, their parents rightly keeping them out of the degeneracy and potential danger.

Bernie laughed when he put his thoughts into words. "Degeneracy and danger, my eye. These people are enjoying themselves."

As if to contradict her and reinforce Baldock's concerns, an argument broke out between rival stag parties outside one large and popular pub. Baldock could not work out how the security men learned of it, but they came hurrying from all directions. Rather than calm the situation, their arrival seemed to exacerbate it. Someone threw a punch, a security man reacted and in seconds the street was awash with running, kicking, brawling men... and a few women. As the fight spread across the junction of two streets, an innocent bystander, pausing to watch the action, found himself caught up in it. He raised an arm to fend off a security man who had been pushed towards him. The security man, in the mistaken belief that the bystander was trying to join battle, lashed out, and a single punch floored the onlooker. His head hit the pavement, blood appeared from a wound, and he lay on the ground not moving. Baldock was about to rush to his aid, but Bernie stayed him as others came to help.

"These people are scrapping, Raymond. They have tunnel vision, and they'll hit out at anyone, as that poor man has just found out."

Baldock shook his head angrily. "It makes me ashamed to be British."

To his relief, someone, obviously less inebriated than everyone else, rolled the hapless man into the recovery position, and another got on the phone to call for an ambulance.

They turned to move on and a drunken youth stood in Bernie's face. Dressed in a black and red T-shirt and sagging shorts, he stank of stale booze and his voice was slurred as he told her, "I need a woman," while his friends, with a wary eye on Baldock, tried to drag him away.

"The state you're in you won't be much use to any woman," Bernie told him, and stepped round him, towing Baldock behind her.

They had lost sight of their group by now, but as they turned into The Square, that pedestrian-only interruption to the *Avenida Mallorca* frequented by many of the Brits, Bernie caught sight of Gil going into *Cafe Benidorm*.

"Let them go," Bernie said. "The less I see of Masters, the better I like it." She led Baldock across the street to *Winners*

Bar.

"But you haven't told me what he's done," Baldock complained, following her.

She did not answer.

Forgetting her problems with Masters he clucked as they passed a young man and woman locked in a kiss so passionate that they were oblivious to the rest of the world.

"Sodom and Gomorrah," he grumbled.

Bernie disagreed. "Don't be so sulky, Raymond. They're having fun."

"They're trying to eat each other, and cannibalism is not my idea of fun." He waved a hand at the bawdy carnage all around them. "I'm not particularly religious, but if there was ever any justification for the arrival of the Four Horsemen, then this is it."

Things were no better in Winners.

The interior of the bar was packed to the rafters with bodies. The dress – or alternatively, the lack of it – indicated more hen and stag parties in residence. Many tables on the outside of the bar stood empty, while the inside was heaving. In the very top corner, neither inside nor out, was a mechanical bull, twirling, pitching and yawing, ridden by a young woman dressed in an outrageously short skirt, and a black top, which, when her back was turned, declared her to be *Randy Mandy*.

Baldock had just tutted at this, when a tramp, who was obviously part of the bar's entertainment staff, hopped onto the bull and shuffled up behind her, slipped his arms around her waist to cup both, ample breasts, and then began to thrust at her from behind.

"That is disgust…"

Baldock trailed off. The bull had turned his way, and the woman's eyes caught his, and in a second he was transported to a fairground on Midthorpe estate twenty years back, and that same lusty gaze and 'come and get it' smile.

Bernie noticed his shocked stare. "Whatever is the matter, Raymond? You look like you've seen a ghost."

"I think I have." He half turned and using his eyes,

directed Bernie's gaze towards the mechanical bull.

"The tramp looks like he's giving her one," she observed with a throaty laugh.

"That depends on how you define tramp. I've never seen him in my life, but I know her. I'm sure I do. She's a Midthorper."

Bernie shrugged. "You said Benidorm is the kind of place they come to, so maybe it's not so strange. Who is she?"

"I'm not certain, but I think it's Amanda Cowling. Known on Midthorpe as Mandy the Midthorpe bike."

"Oh. That sort of tramp."

"She's a few years older than me, and when I was a teenager, she was the local biology tutor."

Bernie laughed. "Expensive?"

"Free." He hastened on before Bernie could get the wrong idea. "Not that I took any lessons from her, but I know many of my, er, year did." He glanced into the bar. "I'm not sure that it is Amanda, but if so, I don't want to speak to her. I'll see if I can get us some drinks."

"Bacardi and coke for me, thanks." Bernie nodded at the bull. "I'll see how long she lasts."

"It's not her you should worry about," Baldock insisted. "It's the tramp. That poor sod doesn't know what he's getting into."

"Literally? In public?"

"I wouldn't put it past her. Especially if his name begins with the letter G."

Baldock moved away and into the bar.

The place was crowded beyond belief. There were at least two hundred people crammed into a space designed for no more than a hundred according to Baldock's estimate. And some of their activities did little to endear them to him. In a space cleaved from the crowds, half a dozen young women were playing a game of pass the parcel. While waiting for service at the packed bar, he watched one girl remove a layer of tissue, and pass the parcel on. The woman governing the game waited until it reached a tiny brunette and called a halt. The brunette took off the final wrapper revealing a large, battery operated vibrator. They all laughed as the woman in charge said, "you'll need that on your wedding night, luv. He'll be too full of ale to be any use to you."

His lips curling, Baldock looked further round.

Off to one side, in another clear space, a middle-aged woman stood with a young man. His left arm was draped around and over her shoulder, his hand resting dangerously close to her breast while she blatantly groped him, egged on by her female friends who were busy taking photographs.

More disgusted than ever, he made to turn away. Then his blood ran cold, his colour drained and his eyes widened. He detached himself from the bar and moved closer to make sure of his facts, and the full horror hit him.

"Mother!"

Chapter Eleven

It took a moment for Janet to recognise her youngest son, but when she did, her smile, already wide, broadened further and her eyes lit with joy.

"Raymond. Oh my lord, it is you, isn't it?"

Logic displaced his shock. "I called you 'mother'. Who else could it be, other than Keith or me?"

"Well smack my bottom with a cold fish. Lisa said she saw you earlier on the balcony of the hotel behind ours, but I said it couldn't possibly be you. Not in Benidorm. What are you doing here?"

"I'm… never mind what I'm doing. What the hell are you doing?" He pointed a shaking finger at her left hand, firmly gripped on her young attendant's crotch.

"I'm having my picture taken," she said, and the flash of cameras picked up again.

With the photographs done, she reached up and kissed the youngster on the cheek. "Thanks, Chris. I'll make sure you get a drink."

He nodded and grinned. "My pleasure, Janet."

Janet addressed the clutch of female photographers who had been eyeing and capturing her performance. "Look who it is, everyone. It's our Raymond."

Baldock found himself smothered in a welter of greetings from the Midthorpe Maidens, some of whom he recognised, others he was uncertain of.

"I think we need to talk, Mother," he said urgently, but before Janet could answer, his eye caught Lisa and her grim stare.

Everything around him melded into a background blur of noise and colour. Lisa had been an attractive teenager, and the years had enhanced her beauty into that of a desirable, thirty-something woman. And during the summer, she had been his for that one weekend, and he had let her go, cast her off in a fit of furious chagrin after revelations from her former boyfriends... well, one former boyfriend.

He tried a weak and diffident smile. "Hello, Lisa."

The response was stiff, formal. "Hello, Raymond. You're staying at the Aranjuez, aren't you? I saw you on your balcony earlier today. I saw someone fall off one of the balconies and I thought it might have been you." There was no warmth in her greeting, and memories of that awful day in the summer, came back to haunt him. If she had added, 'In fact, I was *hoping* it might have been you,' he would not have been surprised, and he would not have blamed her.

"I, er, yes." The memory of seeing a woman he was almost convinced was her ambling round the pool of the adjacent hotel, hit him. "So you're staying where? The Praia?"

Lisa gestured around her. "We all are. About fifteen of us."

"I, er, oh. Yes. Forgive me, Lisa, but I need a word with my mother."

"Be my guest. I wouldn't want to hold you up."

It was difficult to ignore the ice in her voice, but he had more pressing matters to deal with. Taking Janet gently by the elbow, he led her outside where they found an empty table. "I'll get us both a drink," he said and signalled a waiter. "What is it you drink? A snowball, isn't it?"

"A snowball in hell, you mean. I'll have a vodka and orange."

He frowned. "It was always a snowball. Perhaps the odd sherry or brandy at Christmas."

"Yes, well that was before your father..." she trailed off and swallowed a lump in her throat. "A vodka and orange, Raymond."

The waiter arrived. "*Vodka y naranja, y una cerveza, por favor.*"

"We only speak English in this bar, mate," said the waiter in a thick Liverpool accent. "Usual is it, Janet?"

"Usual, Roger, and Raymond wants a beer."

"I got that bit, luv."

Baldock poured scorn on their acquaintanceship. "Then perhaps you'll understand plain English when I invite you to move it. We're thirsty."

"Beer and a voddie and orange coming up, pal."

With the waiter gone, Baldock rounded on his mother. "What was that all about?"

"You were ordering drinks, dear, and Roger pretended he didn't understand your pidgin Spanish."

"I'm not talking about his lack of brain cells. He knows you by name. So did the idiot inside. The one you were groping."

"Of course they know me, Raymond. I come to Benidorm two or three times a year and when I'm in town, I always drink here, and I'll take lunch in Friar's at least once, maybe twice."

"But... but..." Baldock took a deep breath and tried to sort the muddle in his brain. "When we were younger, holidays were always Scarborough or Bridlington or Filey."

"They were your father's choices, not mine. These days it's Benidorm or Magaluf, or San Antonio, but I must admit, Benidorm is my favourite."

"And would you care to explain what the photograph was all about?"

"Fun."

"Depravity from where I stood."

Roger, the waiter, returned and before them. "*Vodka y naranja, y una cerveza. Cuatro euros y cincuenta centavos, señor.*"

Determined not to be beaten by him, Baldock laid a five-euro note on the table. "You can keep the fifty cents. Use it to ring a few publicans. I'm sure there must be openings for a man of your obvious talents."

With a grunt, Roger took the money, and left them.

Janet picked up her glass and sipped. "You do talk some rubbish. I'm having fun, luv. Something I haven't known for years. Even when your father was with us, I didn't know the meaning of the word. His idea of fun was a night in the

Midden with him playing darts in the tap room and me in the lounge listening to young people squawking on the karaoke. Now that he's gone..."

Baldock suspected a tear in the corner of her eye and his irritation rose. "You're doing it again. Talking as if Dad is dead instead of living with his tart in York."

"As far as I'm concerned, he might as well be dead. I don't weep for him. Only the way he hurt me."

Somewhere deep inside, Baldock could not argue with his mother's sentiments. He felt the same way about his errant father.

In an effort to gain some purchase on the discussion, he asked. "Mother, what on earth has happened to you?"

"Life has happened, Raymond. I've realised what it's all about, and it's not about taking second place to your father's wishes. These days, I'm living it up."

"With half of Midthorpe by the looks of things."

"It's a hen party." She plucked her T-shirt from her left breast, brought it forward and thrust it at Baldock. "I came up with the name, Midthorpe Maidens. I thought it was better than Chloe Taplin's hen weekend." Releasing the shirt so that it fell back into place, she picked up her theme. "Young Chloe is getting married in a month. Like Lisa said, there's about fifteen of us." Janet waved back into the bar. "Most of them are whooping it up in there."

"Well, your behaviour was disgraceful."

Janet tittered. "It's not the first time I've had a handful of Chris."

"And I suppose Tim took the pictures last time, did he?"

"Well, as matter of fact, he did. How did you guess?"

"I haven't forgotten the Fiagara fiasco and the wax impression you took of his reproductive organs." Baldock tutted his disgust. "At least I understand how come I saw Amanda Cowling on that bull thing, with some tramp who looked like he was... er..."

"Shagging her from behind?"

"Mother!"

"What's wrong now?"

"Your language."

"There's nothing wrong with 'shagging'? It describes what Mandy does perfectly well." Janet tutted. "You're so stuffy, Raymond. Honestly, you've been like that ever since you went to Cambridge."

"I am not being stuffy. One simply doesn't expect to hear one's mother coming out with that kind of vernacular." Baldock took a sip of his beer. His face screwed in distaste. "Tart."

"She still is."

"What?"

"Mandy Cowling. She's still a tart. Lisa caught her with one of the hotel staff within half an hour of us arriving."

"I was talking about the beer. It's a bit tart."

"Oh." Janet sipped her vodka. "So, what happened at your hotel this afternoon? Lisa saw it, you know, and we all saw the police arriving."

"A woman fell off a balcony."

"Do you know you're hopeless when it comes to gossip. I already knew that. Who was she? Was she drunk or sober."

"Her name is… was Xavier Vardaro, and she was member of our party. Beyond that, I can't tell you anything because I don't know anymore, but the police think she was murdered."

Janet's mouth fell open. "Murdered? Oh, the poor girl."

"Girl? She was forty if she was a day."

"You know what I mean." Janet took a gulp of her vodka. "And what party is this that you're with? Not a stag party, obviously. Not if there are women with you. It must be something special because Benidorm's not really your type of place. You never liked Blackpool or Scarborough or Bridlington."

"Or even Filey." Baldock took another drink of beer. "I'm on a corporate weekend with my publisher. Bernie dragooned me into it."

Janet's eyes lit. "Bernie's here?"

Baldock nodded glumly. "Watching Mandy on that bull."

"So at last I'm going to get to meet the famous Bernie?" Janet turned in her seat and eagerly scanned the crowds around the mechanical bull. "Which one is he?"

Baldock was so immersed in himself, wondering how many more shocks to his system he would have to suffer before the weekend was out, that he almost missed the remark.

"He? Bernie isn't a he. She's a she."

"A woman?" Janet was as surprised as Baldock had been by her remark.

"Of course she's a woman."

"Well you never said, and I didn't know. I assumed Bernie was short for Bernard."

As if on cue, Bernie appeared from the crowded bar and looked around. Baldock attracted her attention and she strolled over, carrying a multi-coloured cocktail.

"There you are, Raymond. I was busy watching your friend, and when I turned round, you'd disappeared. I managed to get myself a drink, but I couldn't see you anywhere."

"Amanda Cowling, is not my friend," he reminded his agent. "Bernie, may I introduce my mother, Janet Baldock. Mother, this is *Bernadette* Deerman, my agent and a close friend. She prefers to be known as Bernie."

The two women shook hands.

"Raymond has told me so much about you," Janet said.

"All of it good, I hope."

"Oh yes. Well, most of it. I have to confess he led me to believe you were a man."

"I did nothing of the kind," Baldock squealed. "You just assumed it."

Bernie's eyes widened. "A man?"

"Hmm, yes. Raymond never really explained properly, and I thought Bernie was short for Bernard."

Bernie nodded judiciously. "An easy mistake to make, Mrs Baldock."

"Please call me Janet. I'm so relieved. Naturally, I wouldn't disown my youngest son simply because he's gay, but—"

"GAY!" Baldock almost exploded. "I'm not gay."

"There's no shame in it, Raymond," Bernie insisted.

"I didn't say there was. I simply said it doesn't apply to me."

"Well, I thought it did until you hooked up with Lisa in the summer, and then I thought you were both sides of the fence." Janet's announcement sent further seismic waves of calamity through her youngest son. "I'm so pleased to hear you have a proper girlfriend hidden away, luv, but don't you think it would have been better to mention it to Lisa… or at least mention Lisa to Bernie?"

"Mother," Baldock said with enforced patience, "Bernie is not my girlfriend. She is my agent and a close friend, but she's also married with twin sons."

Janet tittered and said to Bernie, "So Raymond is your bit on the side? Good for you."

"I wish." Bernie laughed and sat alongside her. "I'm sorry to disappoint you, Janet, but our relationship is a working one. True, we are good friends, but it's purely platonic." Bernie took a swallow of her cocktail. "God that's awful."

"What is it?" Janet asked.

"Sex on the beach."

"Too many ingredients for my liking. Try an Orgasm. Cointreau, Tia Maria, and Bailey's Irish Cream. Almost enough to give you an involuntary orgasm, but quite tasty."

Baldock clucked. "What would you know about involuntary orgasm, Mother?"

"Nothing, dear. Not until your father left. Not until I got together with Tim."

Bernie stepped in to avoid an argument. "So what are you doing in Benidorm, Janet? Letting your hair down?"

"I am. And I'm trying to persuade my youngest son of it, but he disapproves."

Her defiant stare put Baldock on the defensive. "I do not disapprove of fun, but putting aside having my laptop stolen —"

"Your laptop was stolen?" Janet interrupted.

"Yes, Mother, stolen. If I were in Leeds, I'd swear blind it was a Midthorper. But I'm not in Leeds, I'm in bloody

Benidorm, and considering half of Midthorpe appears to be with you, I still swear blind it was a Midthorper. However," he pressed on before Janet could interrupt again, "putting that aside, along with the asinine demands of a gormless, transatlantic idiot, I am enjoying myself. Or at least I was until Xavier was murdered."

Janet's face fell. "That poor woman." She addressed Bernie. "He's not telling me much. Do you know more?"

Bernie shook her head. "The police are investigating, and they insist she was thrown from the balcony."

"That tallies with what Lisa saw," Janet said, and when Baldock raised questioning eyebrows at her, she went on to explain, "Lisa saw her leaning over the balcony, and it looked as if someone just lifted her up and tossed her over."

"She should speak to the police," Bernie suggested.

"She's a Midthorper. They don't like talking to the police." Before her son could disagree, Janet went on," I expect it's put a bit of a damper on your weekend."

"It doesn't appear to have bothered Masters too much," Baldock grumbled. "He still insisted on dragging us into this godforsaken area where I found my mother in a compromising situation with a man one third her age."

Bernie chuckled again and nudged Janet familiarly. "Have you been getting up to naughties?"

"I'm having a ball, Bernie. Two balls when Raymond found me. I must say, that young fella, Chris, has plenty of balls, too. Now, you tell me the truth, Bernie. Apart from losing his laptop and one of your friends meeting an untimely death, is my son having fun?"

"Definitely. He's managed to upset Masters, the big boss, and wrecked one meeting with a dissertation on abstract mathematics. He also said Gil Masters' father was an onanist."

"A what?"

"One who withdraws before he ejaculates," Baldock explained.

Janet was no wiser. "What?"

"A man who pulls out before he shoots his load," Bernie

translated.

Janet laughed. "Oh, how awful. Raymond you shouldn't belittle your boss like that."

"Belittle him, nothing," Baldock retorted. "The bloody idiot all but thanked me for it. He thinks onanism is some branch of Christianity. And he's not my boss. I'm my own boss."

Janet let out another throaty laugh. "Well, Bernie, that's Midthorpers for you. We're all very outspoken."

"I've been hearing about these Midthorpers. Are you here with a group of them?"

Janet nodded. "Hmm, yes. Hen weekend. In fact, here comes the mother of the blushing bride now."

Linda Taplin hurried towards them, and stopped at their table, catching her breath. "Hi, Janet, hi, Raymond, and hello... er, sorry, I don't know your name."

"Bernie."

"Hello, Bernie."

"You remember Linda Taplin, don't you, Raymond?"

"Yes of course. Hello, Mrs Taplin."

"Great to see you again. I'm in a bit of a hurry. Quick, Raymond, give me your shorts."

Baldock's eyes almost popped. "I beg your pardon."

"The DJ's leading the hen parties in a game. There's about twenty women from different parties involved. We have to get back to him with a pair of men's shorts. Come on, Ray. If I don't get a move on, I'll be last."

"Yes, but—"

"Hurry up, Raymond," Janet urged.

"I'm not taking my shorts off."

"You're wearing underpants, aren't you?"

"That's not the point. These are genuine Ted Baker—"

"This is Benidorm, Raymond," his mother reminded him. "No one will notice, let alone care. Get your duds off."

Grumbling to himself, and under the amused stares of Bernie and his mother, Baldock struggled to let down his shorts without standing up. As he strove to pull them off over his espadrilles, Linda reached down, grabbed them by the leg and yanked them off, and then, waving the shorts above her head, dashed back into the bar like an Olympic sprinter going for gold.

Janet and Bernie laughed as Linda's bulky frame disappeared into the crowds.

"You people certainly know how to enjoy yourselves," Bernie commented.

"Life's too short not to," Janet assured her. "I'd invite you to join us, Bernie, but there are no men allowed and Raymond would look a bit odd in a leotard and blonde wig."

"You two go ahead," he said tartly. "Don't worry about me."

"All right, we won't." Janet got to her feet and picked up her drink. "Come on, Bernie. Let me introduce you to the Midthorpe Maidens."

The two women walked off into the bar, leaving Baldock to stare glumly into his beer

"All on your lonesome, pal?"

The voice belonged to Roger, the waiter who was busy clearing the tables.

"They've gone inside for some fun," Baldock described speech marks in the air with his fingers.

"Not your thing, this place, then?"

"Not really."

"Well, listen, mate, if you're looking for some real action, away from your Ma, I know this bar in the Old Town, and if you can't get your end away there—"

"Yes. Thank you. I'll wait for my mother and friend, if you don't mind."

Roger shrugged. "Whatever turns you on."

Baldock sank into his miserable thoughts, asking himself, not for the first time, how come he had ended up in this awful place.

Right now, he would have handed over most of his money and his house to be somewhere else. Somewhere where his laptop was not stolen. Somewhere where a young woman had not tumbled to her death. Somewhere where he would not have learned that his mother was no different to other

Midthorpe Maidens. Somewhere, where he would not have had to hand over a pair of expensive shorts so those same women could play their childish games. Defining fun, he decided, was entirely at the behest of the individual, and getting roaring drunk and half-stripped did not fit with his definition.

"Hello, Raymond."

The chill in the greeting froze his thought processes. He looked slowly up into Lisa's severe eyes and felt like a schoolboy facing a nightmare interview with the headmistress.

"You bastard."

Chapter Twelve

Baldock was unable to maintain eye contact and lowered his gaze to the ground.

On delivering her final two words, which to his mind constituted a succinct and accurate assessment of him, Lisa did not look around to check whether anyone was listening. With all the noise around them, it was difficult to imagine anyone could hear, but even so, he knew she did not care. If she had had a microphone, she would have happily used it and let the whole of Benidorm know what she thought of him.

And he could not blame her.

His mind shot back to the June afternoon when he stood in Gary Lipton's workshop and his most despised enemy grinned as he told Baldock of his fling with Lisa. *"Didn't she tell you about me and her? Like dynamite we were."*

The fury that had gripped Baldock in that moment had seen whatever possibilities there may have been between Lisa and him, disappear. Her life before him was none of his concern, and if it had been anyone other than Gary Lipton, he could probably have dealt with it. But it was Lipton, and he, Baldock, had shown Lisa no mercy. He had simply driven off leaving her calling after his car. Letters and emails from her and his mother had expressed their concerns and Lisa's distress, but he had ignored them.

In truth, he regretted his reaction, and ever since, he had wished he could turn back the clock and just sulked for an hour or two. He was good at sulking.

Now he had to face her wrath, and whatever came from her in the next few minutes, he deserved.

She sat down, her eyes spearing him. "I never asked about

the women you'd had before me, did I? I meant to, but it slipped my mind."

The change from raw anger to dripping sarcasm hit him hard, and he once again found himself shrinking in shame.

In an effort to recover some ground, he resorted to confession. "I'm sorry, Lisa. Of course, everyone is entitled to their private lives and their past, but it was Lipton. That's what I couldn't handle."

She loosed off her rage in an unstoppable tirade. "And it didn't occur to you for one moment that he was lying? It didn't dawn on you that he was doing what he enjoys doing the most: winding you up? I was a seventeen-year-old girl and the man I loved had just gone off to Cambridge and would only ever come back on flying visits. I had one date with him. I got drunk, Gary tried to get my knickers off in Virgin's Valley, and he got a smack in the face for his trouble. He was lying. I'm old enough to have known one or two men, yes, but never Gary Lipton."

He calculated that her reference to other men was a deliberate attempt to goad him, evoke the envy within.

On the other hand, his knowledge of her sexual appetite, gleaned over that summer weekend in Leeds, suggested that it might not be without foundation. She had known a few lovers; she told him that from the start. But was it likely that she had really been head over heels in love with him back then? He would be the first to admit he was quite naive on the matter of female sexuality, but if she were telling the truth, then it meant he was just as ignorant of his own effect on women... this woman at least.

"Lisa, you have every right to be annoyed. I am sorry I treated you so badly. No, it didn't occur to me that he was lying and it should have done. I lost it over a false revelation which, with hindsight, was designed to do exactly what Lipton intended."

"And that makes everything all right, does it? That makes up for torture I went through? The nights I spent crying over what might have been?"

Every shaft drove into him, tweaking, aggravating the

guilt he already felt.

"You are a class one scumbag, Raymond. Cambridge may have turned you into a cut above every other Midthorper, all the money you're worth may reinforce that image, but it does not give you the right to treat people the way you do. Especially those who loved you."

He had no answer for her.

"If I'd slept my way through the Yorkshire Regiment, I don't see what business it would be of yours as long as I was not sleeping with them when we were together. Or is it that you secretly hate independent women? You know; women who might enjoy a bit of the other with someone you don't approve of?"

Another line designed to sting him. It hurt all the more because it was untrue, but he did not rise to it.

"But do you know what was worse than your childish jealousy?"

He knew all right, but he was not about to interrupt her flow.

"Driving off without giving me the chance to say anything. All you could think of was your precious, bruised, bloody ego." A stern pause. "Well?"

He did not answer. He did not know how to answer.

Lisa permitted his silence for a few seconds, and then took in a deep, frustrated breath before letting it out with a sigh. She was a shade calmer when she next spoke. "Raymond, communication is a two-way process. Unless you speak, I don't know where I'm up to."

He cleared his throat: an unnecessary preamble. "I have no answer, Lisa, because everything you say is absolutely true. I treated you appallingly. Yes, I should have given you the opportunity to explain, and even if it were true, it was still none of my business. And yes, the only thing going through my mind was my bruised ego. All I can say is, I am so, so, sorry, and you should just get it off your chest so we can go our separate ways and get on with our lives."

His words seemed to stoke her anger again. "And that's what you want, is it? Go our separate ways? Live our separate lives?"

"Well, given your annoyance… I, er… The thing is—"

"The woman with your mother? She's your current girlfriend?"

At last, something he could get a purchase on. "No. She's my agent. She's also happily married. Let me get us something to drink." He raised his hand to signal the waiter. "What will you have?"

"Just a small beer. I've had enough cocktails. And don't blame me if I get mad and pour it all over your head."

Baldock gave Roger the order and was glad of the brief hiatus. It allowed him time to formulate was he was going to say so that it did not provoke another round of bitterness.

While they waited for the drinks to arrive, they sat in sulking silence, watching the antics of people around them. A stag party passed, one of the men carrying an inflatable doll. They met with a hen party coming the other way, one of the women carrying a large, flexible penis and testicles around her neck. The man stopped her and suggested her 'wedding tackle' might like to get it on with his 'tunnel'. The girl laughed, the man laughed and the two parties went their separate ways.

It was the kind of scene which would bring out the worst of Baldock's neo-Victorian conservatism, but he was busy rehearsing what he had to say and for once he ignored it. He risked a glance at Lisa, and she too gave the couple no more than a passing, disinterested stare.

Roger delivered the drinks, he paid for them, and finally concentrated on her.

"The weekend I spent in Leeds during the summer, was one of the best I've ever had in my entire life. That was down to you. I'm not just talking about the nights we spent together, but the whole time. We spoke about my visiting Leeds once a month or so, and you possibly visiting me in Norfolk, to see if we had any future, and that appealed to me. I was coming round to the idea that I loved you, Lisa. Then I messed it up. Badly. I hurt you terribly. Whatever punishment I have coming, I deserve. You don't. I naturally assumed you would never want anything to do with me again. I still don't think you should want to know me, because that's what I deserve. What's worse, I don't know how to make it all up so we can at least be friends." He took a self-pitying sip of beer. "I am a hugely successful writer and businessman, but as a man I am a complete loss. I don't understand people, I don't understand women, and if you still want to know me, I don't understand you either."

Lisa, too, drank the head from her beer. "Like you said, you're a novelist. You're good at writing speeches, and if I didn't know you better, I'd swear you were trying to wheedle your way into my good books with some cleverly crafted tales."

"I'm not."

"I know you're not. Unlike you, I do understand people… well, most of the time. I can see it's the truth." She sighed again at the night. "How do you make it up? I don't know either. I'd expect a wealthy man like you to shower me with expensive gifts. Don't bother. That, more than anything, would persuade me you're lying. What you do, Raymond, is apologise, which you have already done, and if you wish, if I wish, we wipe the slate clean, go back to the beginning and start again. But only if you're prepared to make an effort."

His hopes rose faintly. "You're ready to give me another chance?"

"As long as you're willing to make the effort, and I mean make an effort, Raymond. Not pay lip service to it."

His hopes rose briefly, but then crashed again. "I'm sorry, Lisa, but it simply won't work. No. Please. Hear me out." He took another sip of beer. "I'm no good with relationships, but I do know it will not work if we're treating each other with kid gloves. We have to be able to speak and act frankly."

"I quite agree," she replied, much to his surprise. "And we have been speaking frankly for the last five or ten minutes."

"Actually, I think you'll find you've been speaking and I've been listening. Not," he hurried on hastily, "that there's much wrong with that, given the nature of events under debate."

"I said, Raymond, that communication is a two-way thing. It involves listening as well as speaking. If I do or say something to upset you, then I'm obliged to listen while you get it off your chest, and vice-versa. This isn't about kid gloves, but treating each other with respect. Your actions in the summer were appalling, but more importantly, they were disrespectful of me and a part of my past, which wasn't true but had nothing to do with you just the same. If I got any of it wrong, then it would be disrespectful of me not to listen to you and, if necessary, apologise." She toyed with her glass, turning it round and round on the table. "Now, do we try again or not?"

It was more than he could ever have hoped for. Memories of that summer weekend flooded his mind again, and he smiled broadly.

He was about to say 'yes' when a loud cheer came up from within the bar, and Linda Taplin came hurrying out again, followed at a more leisurely pace by Janet and Bernie.

"Raymond," she said breathlessly. "You're needed for the next part of the game."

"I'm taking no part in any game," he retorted. "Where are my shorts?"

"The DJ has them. They're waiting for you."

"Then tell him to send them back."

"No you see, there's a second part of this game and they're waiting—"

"You're not listening, Mrs Taplin. I want my shorts back."

"But—"

"Forget him, Linda," Janet interrupted. "He's not like his father. He doesn't have the bottle for such games."

Baldock took instant umbrage. "Are you saying I'm a coward, Mother?"

"No. Only that you won't put yourself in a position where it might get embarrassing."

"Oh, won't I? Excuse me, Lisa." He passed his shoulder bag to his mother and stood up. "Lead on, Mrs Taplin."

"Raymond…"

Both Janet and Bernie called after him, his mother

sounding as if she suddenly wished she had not thrown down the gauntlet, but he was already striding into the bar, vaguely aware of the two women, accompanied by Lisa, leaving the table to follow. By the time he reached the central area, which had been cleared of dancers and revellers, Mandy Cowling and several more of the Midthorpe Maidens had joined the throng, but he had more concerns.

While the crowd chanted, whistled and applauded their intoxicated encouragement, half a dozen men, most of them apparently younger than Baldock, had lined up facing the wall, their backs to the crowd, and all of them wore nothing but underwear. When asked, after some minor debate, an angry Baldock stripped off his shirt and joined them. But if he appeared outwardly calm, he was shaking inside and beginning to regret his hastiness in agreeing.

Chapter Thirteen

"All right, kids," the DJ announced, "Here we are with a special version of Mr and Mrs. We have our missus blindfolded and she hasn't seen any of the men line up. She can't see, the men aren't allowed to speak, and she has to work out which of them is her partner… using only her hands. So let's have a round of applause for our Mrs, who is Andrea from Northampton."

A rousing cheer went up as the young woman was led into the room. Baldock risked a glance from the corner of his eye. Dressed in a dangerously short, flower-patterned dark skirt, and plain white top, Andrea's fair hair was tied back in a ponytail and she had a black sleep mask covering her eyes. Two attendants, one male the other female, both wearing the black T-shirt of the bar, guided her towards the men to loud cheers from the crowd.

For all their emphasis on sex, Baldock thought, the provision of two escorts, of different genders, indicated that the management were careful to ensure the male staff could not take liberties.

The DJ joined the young woman. "You know what it's about, Andrea. You have to tell us which man is your husband."

"Partner," she corrected.

"Whatever you wanna call him."

Baldock switched off from the DJ's inane nonsense, and concentrated on his irritation. Notwithstanding her denial, it appeared that his mother was determined to embarrass him. The elliptical suggestion that his father, a man Baldock actively disliked, would have gone through this farce and laughed about it, while he, the second Baldock son, would not, had angered him, and his mother had known it would.

When this childish game was over…

"There's only one rule," the DJ was saying. "Backs only. You can't reach round his waist to feel the size of his crown jewels. That'd make it too easy." He laughed at his own witticism, and many of those in the audience joined in. "But you can touch anywhere you want on his back, and I do mean anywhere." He laughed again. "And gentlemen – I use the word in its loosest possible sense – please keep your feet and thighs together."

Sixth in line from the end where she began, Baldock instantly found himself in the grip of a rising panic that bade him run for it. His mind, already overwhelmed with multiple shocks from the events of the day, both at Masters', his mother's and Lisa's instigation, suddenly filled with tabloid headlines designed to pillory him. *"Sexy Secrets of the Super Scribe." "Headingley creator lets it all hang out in Benidorm." "I groped famous novelist." "Game girl gropes Baldock's b**ls and c**k."*

While Andrea from Northampton denounced the first man as too 'saggy' to be her partner, and allowed herself to be guided to the next body, the journalist in Baldock's literary mind automatically censored the final, imaginary headline with asterisks.

Andrea claimed that the next man could not be her partner because he was too wobbly, and amidst howls of laughter from the crowd, she moved up one more.

Baldock racked his brain to think of famous men who had survived such sex scandals, and he could not. But he could think of many men who had been ruined by this kind of Sunday tabloid sleaze.

Lots of people in the audience were taking photographs and flashes were going off with an almost stroboscopic regularity.

'A strong contender' was Andrea's verdict of the third in line, and while she moved along the line, the crowd egged her on.

Women could withstand these onslaughts to their reputation, Baldock decided, but not men.

He became aware that some of the flashes were coming from his right. A quick look in that direction, past the bulky body of the seventh and final man in line, revealed his mother, Linda Taplin and Mandy Cowling, who was in urgent whispered conversation with her friend and fellow tart, Sandra Scranton, all with smartphones aimed in his direction. As he looked, his mother took two quick pictures.

The fourth in line was dismissed and the man's friends, all male, naturally, cheered.

There was one more body between Andrea and him, and Baldock wondered for one brief second whether he could make a run for it; get the hell out of this lunatic asylum while his mind, body, soul and reputation were still intact.

But even as he thought of it, he dismissed the idea. It would confirm his mother's poor impression of him, and knowing that cow, Mandy Cowling, busy snapping away with her smartphone, she would video the entire event. He would be a branded a coward, left a bigger laughing stock than he was now, and the newspaper headlines would take an entirely different slant on it. *"Baldock Not A Cock But A Chicken", "Headingley Runs For It," "Courageous Cop's Cowardly Creator".*

Baldock was not sure which set of headlines he preferred.

Andrea said she was unsure of the fifth contender, and her helper moved her up to stand behind Baldock.

Sweat broke on his forehead. He pulled in a deep breath in an effort to force calm upon himself.

Her hands began to roam his back, testing the fine muscles of his arms, then his legs, and finally worked her way up to his buttocks. To his horror, as her nimble fingers pinched, probed and test the muscles, tried to find a way into the gap between his locked thighs, he felt the first stirrings of an erection.

"Well, Andrea?"

"I wish. Too well-built."

His erection began to grow rapidly.

Her comment drew a loud laugh from the audience, and she moved on.

Baldock sent out mental commands to his member to calm down, but it had no effect. The little strumpet's deft manipulation of his behind had sent the blood rushing to his groin, and the erection continued to grow. While she tested out the seventh and final contender, he tried to think of ways and means of escaping the inevitable embarrassment. He was standing before a crowd of at least a hundred people, and he was wearing nothing but a pair of body hugging, Calvin Klein trunks with a codpiece designed to enhance his masculinity, not hide it, and his growing rod was now forcing out the front of those trunks.

He wondered idly if the young man his mother had been groping had gone through the same awful experience. If he had, he didn't show it. How did men maintain that kind of control?

Off to one side, there were flashes from cameras once more. A quick glance told him that Bernie had now joined the Midthorpe Maidens, and she, too, was taking pictures. But while she and most of them concentrated on his upper body, Mandy Cowling's lens appeared to be aimed lower. His ire rose, and he felt his member beginning to shrink again.

Andrea declared number three to be her partner, the blindfold was removed, and she was proven correct, for which she won a bottle of local champagne.

"Well done, Andrea," declared the DJ. "And let's have a round of applause for the men for being such good sports."

There were cheers and whistles and clapping, soon drowned when the music started again.

Trying to look nonchalant while crossing his hands in front of his errant manhood, Baldock marched briskly through the crowds invading the dance floor, and back out into the open air.

His mother, Linda Taplin, Bernie and Lisa were already at the table, and Mandy Cowling had made her way to stand at Lisa's shoulders. He was vaguely aware of other Midthorpe Maidens following him, but he did not register the presence of Sandra Scranton close behind him. He had seen them head to head whispering when he took part in that ridiculous game, and it should have warned him.

As he neared the table, Mandy raised her smartphone, its camera lens aimed at him. "Come on, Ray, one for the album."

He stopped, let his strong arms hang loose at his sides and tried to smile. As he did so, Sandra grabbed his underpants, and yanked them down.

"What the f…"

He bent to pull them up again, but Mandy was too quick, and the camera flashed before he could cover himself.

A loud cheer went up from many men and women looking on. His mother covered her mouth, but he knew she was laughing. Bernie too, was smiling, but Linda Taplin appeared more worried, and Lisa looked as if she disapproved.

"Have you taken leave of your senses, woman?" he shouted at Mandy.

"No, but I've got a smashing picture of you taking leave of your shreddies." Mandy smiled mock-coyly. "And aren't you a big boy…*Gareth*?"

Ignoring his puzzlement at her use of a non-existent name, he made a grab for the phone, but she backed off. "Ah-ah. Naughty. Be nice to me, *Gareth*, or this goes up on my website."

"Bitch. And my name is Raymond."

He was about to move on Mandy again, but a voice stopped him.

"There you go, pal. On the house."

Taking the wind from the sails of the argument was Roger, the waiter, who placed a fresh beer on the table.

"Gaffer reckons you deserve it for being a good sport. Personally, I reckon any bloke who's as well-hung as you shouldn't have any trouble enjoying himself in Benidorm."

Baldock dismissed him with a glower and then turned his vitriol on Linda Taplin. "Where the hell are my shorts?"

Linda looked uncomfortable.

"Well?"

Linda held them up. "I'm afraid they got spoiled, Raymond." She held up the garment and demonstrated where a large stain of vomit had covered them. "Some poor lass puked on them."

Fury gripped him. "Those are genuine Ted Baker."

"Well Ted needs his flies washing," Mandy commented with a drunken laugh.

"Those, Mrs Cowling cost more than your entire month's dole money."

His remark wiped the smile from Mandy's face. "I beg your pardon. I'm not on the dole. I'm a supermarket manager, as you bloody well know. You called in during the summer."

Baldock turned away from her and directed his anger at Linda. "What are you going to do about cleaning them up?"

"Oh, Raymond, stop making such a fuss over a pair of shorts," Janet said. "Give them to me, Linda. I'll wash them through for you when I get back to my room, and you can collect them tomorrow."

"They're the only pair I brought with me," Baldock ranted. "What am I supposed to wear while I'm waiting for them? A business suit? How the hell am I supposed to walk back to my hotel? Even the police in Benidorm will take exception to men wandering round in their underpants."

"I may be able to help," Lisa said, and hurried off down the street.

"Where's she going?"

"I don't bloody care," Baldock snapped.

"The rest of the Shortly people are across the road, Raymond," Bernie said. "I'll see if any of them can help." She left her seat and hurried across the street to *Café Benidorm*.

As Bernie disappeared into the crowds, Baldock glowered at Janet. "We need to talk, Mother. But not now. I may say too much that I'd regret. Can I pick you up at the Praia tomorrow? For lunch?"

Janet nodded. "I don't think we've any plans."

"Good. I'll collect you … if that's all right with the Midthorpe whores."

"Raymond!"

He dismissed his mother's scolding, but he was still fulminating when Lisa returned and placed a small carrier bag on the table.

"Cows." She nodded at Mandy and Sandra, still giggling as they looked over their photographs. "I'm sorry, Raymond, but at this time of night, these were the best I could do. Good job it's Benidorm and not Scarborough. Most of the shops there would be shut this late."

Puzzled, he opened the bag and took out a pair of bright purple shorts. He looked from them to Lisa and back and back again, his eyebrows rose.

Lisa waved at her co-hens. "They're all rat-legged. To them it's just one big laugh. I don't think it's funny. I think it's humiliating." Now she gestured at his stained Ted Bakers. "The least I could do as the only one who's reasonably sober is buy you a pair of shorts so that you can walk back to your hotel rather than forking out for a taxi."

"Yes... oh... Right. Thank you. Taxi fare wouldn't have been an issue. How much do I owe you?"

"No, no. That's all right."

"Nonsense. I can afford it better than you." Baldock reached into his shoulder bag for his wallet.

"Raymond, please put your money away and get dressed. I think you've been made to look a fool long enough."

"Well, it's what it's all about isn't it?" Baldock grumbled as he snapped off the labels and dragged the shorts on over his espadrilles. "I'm the only one from Midthorpe who has a claim to fame and—"

Janet, who along with other Midthorpe Maidens, had clearly been listening, interrupted him. "There was Freddie Colby."

Baldock looked down his nose. "He was an armed robber. He got twenty years for his part in that bullion robbery in Birmingham."

"He still made the front pages," Janet argued.

"That kind of publicity I can live without," Baldock insisted as he stood and fastened the shorts at his waist. "And now if you will all excuse me, I'm going back to my hotel."

He nodded brusquely to them. "I'll pick you up tomorrow, Mother." He turned and walked off.

Lisa stared at his back, then at the table, then hurried off to catch him up. "Raymond. Wait. Please."

He turned on her. "Lisa, I'm grateful for what you've just done, but don't you have a set of idiots to look after?"

"Not particularly. They're all grownups. They can cope without me. Please, Raymond. Didn't we talk about this earlier?"

"We did and I said, I'm grateful to you, but I don't think you'd find me particularly good company right now."

"You'll be a different man in ten minutes. When you've got over it." She smiled. "You're staying right next door to us."

"I know."

"In that case, you can walk me to my hotel can't you?"

He softened perceptibly. "If you insist."

He turned and began to walk away again, Lisa hurried to catch up.

Chapter Fourteen

Baldock slowed his pace in deference to her. She had forgiven him his unforgivable behaviour in the summer, but he appreciated the fragility of that pardon, and as angry as he felt, he did not want to jeopardise it.

They strolled down through The Square, Baldock largely oblivious to the drunken people cavorting around them until a young woman, wearing the skimpiest of bikinis appeared in front of him, turned her back and began to twerk. He stepped around her, delivered a snarling opinion of both her and her act, and walked on.

Lisa gave him her approval. "One thing I love about you is the way you haven't lost the Midthorpe habit of speaking your mind."

"It's the only thing I brought from that estate which I've kept," he replied. "Everything else I dropped years ago, and that fiasco back there should tell you why."

"It's a hen weekend, Raymond. They're drunk. It's what you do on a hen weekend, and you know them better than that. Sober, they wouldn't have dared think of it, let alone do it… with the possible exception of Mandy."

"Precisely my point. Drunk. A euphemism for Midthorpers."

"I'm a Midthorper, but I'm not drunk."

"You're the exception that proves the rule."

They walked on, crossed the wide dual carriageway of *Avenida del Mediterráneo* and reached the seafront. Looking north and south, the broad sweep of Levante Beach lay in a swathe of bright, white light coming from the powerful lamps running the length of the promenade. Augmented by the multi-coloured lights of hotels, bars and shops, the illuminations conspired to dispel the night and bring back the glory of day. They crossed the narrow road and turned left, walking along the edge of the beach towards the cable ski end. Coming upon a small, stone bench, they stopped and sat to gaze out on the calm waters, letting the sound of waves froth on the sands instil them with something approaching serenity.

"Is it me, Lisa?"

"I'm sorry?"

"Do I have a 'kick me' sign pinned to the back of my shirt?"

"Sorry. I'm still not with you."

"To my certain knowledge you and I were the only two of our year to make anything of ourselves. All right, I made Cambridge, but let's not belittle your achievements. Manchester is good. Only you and me. At school everyone took the mickey out of me, but not you, and as a result, all I ever wanted was to get away from Midthorpe. Now, here I am, twenty years on, a roaring success in the field of popular fiction, and you're equally successful in your chosen field. Shouldn't they be proud of us? Shouldn't they point us out and say, 'there they are. Two of Midthorpe's finest'? Yet, when I was there in the summer, all I met with was cynicism and criticism. I'm treated with complete contempt. A figure of fun. We're over a thousand miles from home, and they do it here. Am I really so bad that the whole of Midthorpe wants to shoot me down? Have I really offended them so much?"

Lisa was obviously struggling with the question. "Well, I have to say, you don't make it easy for people to get on with you."

"My mother joined in tonight."

Lisa chewed her lip. "You'll have to speak to Janet about that. I know some of it, but it wouldn't be right coming from me. I know she was annoyed with the way you treated me in the summer, but there's more to it than that, and she should tell you herself."

Baldock spirits sank lower. "It is me then. I'm so bad that even my mother feels the need to demean me."

"That's not the case at all, Raymond. And that business in the bar... well that's Benidorm. It's fun. Benidorm's idea of fun... wrong, one bar's idea of fun, and that bar happens to be in Benidorm."

"Well, it's not my idea of fun, even if it is sufficient excuse for the Midthorpe Mares – present company excepted, of course – to have a go at me." He turned a disappointed face on her. "You didn't appear to mind. Is that the difference between us? You're happy to fall into their decadence?"

She laughed. "I'd hardly call it decadent. It's not like they were actually screwing on the dance floor."

"I've seen photographs which suggest that kind of thing happens. And the bar's clown looked too close for comfort on that bull with Mandy."

"Part of his act. And you know Mandy. From a Benidorm point of view, the night's young yet. If anyone is going to drop her pants in that bar, it'll be Mandy."

He was about to speak but Lisa carried on before he could utter a word.

"As for any photographs you might have seen, well, you can see the same images from Majorca, Ibiza, the Algarve, even Blackpool. It's over the top. A release from the daily grind of housework, bringing up the brats, husbands getting under your feet, and working at crappy jobs which pay minimum wage. I don't have a problem with it, as long as it doesn't go too far. Goading a man like you, who obviously doesn't care for that kind of thing, into taking part is perhaps going overboard, but it's par for the course. And as for pulling down your underpants and taking pictures, and vomiting on your shorts, I suspect that's a step too far for most of them, your mother and me included." The stern set of her face verified her disapproval. "Were they genuine Ted Baker?"

"So the label says and the price I paid for them, I expect them to be authentic."

To the southeast, a waxing Moon rose above the horizon, its deep copper creating a rippled reflection on the sea. They stood and strolled along, and for the first time since their reconciliation, Lisa linked her arm in his. A thought occurred to him, and he reached into his shoulder bag. "I almost forgot. Tell me again how much do I owe you for the shorts?"

"Just forget it."

"Lisa, please—"

"It's only a few euros, Raymond." Her eyes lit up. "Tell you what, why don't you buy me lunch tomorrow."

"I'm sorry, I can't. I'm having lunch with my mother and I have a lot to say to her, so I'd prefer it to be just the two of us. How about dinner?"

Her eyes continued to sparkle, enhancing her smile. "Dinner would be great. We're technically all-inclusive at this hotel, but the food is garbage."

"Dinner it is then. I'll check on the better restaurants in this town."

"I'm already looking forward to it."

Another silence fell between them, but it was more contented this time. Lisa leaned into him, and to Baldock it seemed as if their shocking parting of the summer had never happened.

And yet still the events of this evening, even if they had brought them back together, niggled him. "Why do they do it, Lisa? Why?"

"I told you. You don't make it easy for people to get on with you. Let's be honest, you do try to lord it over people."

"Not intentionally."

"Of course not. But it's your sense of superiority that goads them." She stopped and faced him. "At your age, you should know that while you may be intellectually above many people, that does not make you superior. Your wealth doesn't count, either."

"I never said it did, and to be frank, I didn't realise I do think of myself as superior." Without thinking more deeply on the matter, he suspected it was a lie. He had always thought of himself as better than others.

"Then stop taking yourself and life so seriously." She stretched up on her toes, and they kissed.

For Baldock, it set the seal on their rapid and welcome, if

unexpected reunion, and reawakened the fires he had experienced during the summer. For the second time that evening, he felt an erection coming on, but it was more acceptable (and better hidden) this time.

"Stay with me, tonight, Lisa," he urged.

"I thought you'd never ask."

They kissed again when they broke for breath a second time, Lisa was more practical. "The Aranjuez is a posh place. Will they mind me shipping in with you?"

"Probably, but if you have your passport with you, I can ensure you're registered and then they won't say a word."

Lisa tutted a combination of expectation and frustration. "Always by the book, Raymond."

"You'd rather they assumed you're a hooker I picked up in the town?"

"I'll call at the Praia and pick my passport up."

They walked on.

"So did I hear right? That poor woman was murdered?"

Her question reminded Baldock of how bad the day had been. "Yes. Well, the police say it was murder, and apparently she had been in a fight. It's another cloud over the weekend."

"And Detective Inspector Headingley wouldn't jump at such a conclusion, would he?"

"You're taking the mickey again, Lisa. And no, Headingley wouldn't assume anything. He would rely on evidence, and as far as I can ascertain, Inspector Suarez had none when he spoke to us today." He stopped, turned, faced her and said, "Forget about that. Let's concentrate on us."

Their pace quickened perceptibly without rushing, and Baldock, spurred by memories of the summer, wondered whether she was experiencing the same sense of excitement and anticipation as he.

Reaching the end of Levante Beach, they crossed the road and walked up the side street between two fast food places and past a British pub, turned sharp right and while Lisa disappeared into the Praia, he waited by the entrance, his impatience manifesting in a brisk pacing back and forth across the automatic, double glass doors causing them to open and shut repeatedly.

She was back in less than five minutes, and they began the short climb up the steep hill to the Aranjuez.

In the lobby, the very autocracy Lisa had criticised came to their rescue as Baldock checked her in. The clerk, Francisco, glancing from Baldock to Lisa, looked doubtful, but a good dose of defiant, British arrogance soon persuaded him and with Lisa duly registered as a guest, they took the lift to the top floor and room 1807.

Once inside, he allowed Lisa to take in the comparative opulence, and as he kicked off his espadrilles, he asked, "Would you like a cup of… compf."

He never finished what he was about to say. Lisa practically threw him to the vast bed, and hurled herself on top of him, clamping her lips to his, her hands ferreting through his shorts. Not slow to react, Baldock began his tactile search of her taut, fit body, and before many minutes had passed, they were naked, lost, buried in the overwhelming desire for each other.

Immersed though he was in the all-consuming need for her, the heat of the night and the trials of the long day, took its toll on Baldock, and as she reached her climax and he spent within her, sleep approached in giant waves, threatening to overtake him.

Bathed in sweat, he lay alongside her, heartbeat settling, his eyelids drooping, while Lisa's lips played around his neck and jawline. He returned her soft ministrations as best he could, but even his hand and arms suddenly felt too heavy to move.

He glanced around the room with half closed eyes, and his gaze settled on the escritoire by the balcony window. What he did not see there sent a spear of disappointment through him.

"Laptop."

Lisa, as obviously drained as him by their exertions, also came to life. "What?"

"My laptop."

"Really, Raymond. I like a cuddle after, and even though I disapprove of smoking, I can handle a post-coital cigarette, but a post-nookie laptop?"

He released her and sat up. "No, no. You don't understand. My laptop. It was stolen from me this morning."

Flopped onto the mattress by his sudden dumping of her, Lisa was clearly aggrieved. "Yes, I remember you saying. I just don't understand why it's suddenly so important. Maybe you'll get lucky. Maybe, when news of tonight's fiasco spreads, the thief took will take pity on you. He'll think poor old Ray hasn't had much luck lately so I'd better give him it back? Course, he won't be aware that you were up for the ride of your life tonight, will he?"

"Yes, but I was talking to the police earlier about Xavier. I could have mentioned it then. I really must get my act together."

"Raymond."

"Yes, Lisa?"

"I'm already sick of hearing about your rotten laptop. Would you like to hear about my problem for a moment?"

"Yes. Of course. I'm sorry, Lisa. It's so annoying, that's all. Of course I'll listen to you."

She threw back the duvet. "I'm on fire, Raymond. Burning for more action and the only thing you need to deal with is me."

The sight made him burn too. "Sorry. I'm distracted. You come first."

"I'd better."

Chapter Fifteen

The sun had only recently risen when Baldock, clad in a plain white, cotton T-shirt and the cheap shorts Lisa had bought for him, sat out on his balcony.

In front of him was his iPad, upon which he had detailed the previous day's events, including the theft of his laptop and Xavier's murder. Suddenly tired of it, he stared out across the uneven and inelegant skyscrapers of Benidorm and the vast spread of Levante Beach.

It had rained briefly during the night. A thunderstorm had deluged the area for fifteen minutes from about two o'clock, and the cream tiles of the balcony floor still retained a trace of the damp. The downpour had eased the searing temperatures, and to the south, the clouds which had brought it had not yet had time to disappear beyond the horizon, but they were distant enough to be less brooding, less threatening than they had been. The sea, which had boiled and frothed in the flood tide the night before, now lapped sheepishly at the sand, and he could see one or two people walking along the beach.

It would be another hour or two before Benidorm came to life, but there were other early risers to be seen in various rooms of the Praia tower next door.

A middle-aged man (Baldock was sure it was the short, dumpy man he had seen arguing with the holiday reps at the airport) sat a few floors below Baldock's level, enjoying a cup of tea and an early morning cigarette.

Several floors above him, a young woman marched about her room, the lights on, blinds wide open, wearing only a pair of dark panties, apparently oblivious to the watching eyes of Raymond Baldock and anyone else looking in her direction. The sight, which at one time would have had his lip curling in anger and disgust, now reminded him of Lisa's magnificent body, still sleeping in the bed just a few feet away, and the way he had greedily enjoyed it twice the previous night… the major reason why the thunderstorm had not troubled either of them.

Three months had passed since that weekend in Midthorpe when she, more than anyone, had instigated small but significant changes in his life, changes which saw a shift in attitude towards that dreadful estate. Not a seismic shift, true, but a softening for all that. Now, after forgiving him his appalling treatment of her back then, she had achieved a similar, inexplicable shift in his mindset. Yesterday, Benidorm was an anathema; an opinion reinforced by the previous night's disgraceful brawling in the vicinity of The Square and the farce outside Winners. This morning, it was merely somewhere he would prefer not to be, but was happy to tolerate as long as Lisa were there and content to be with him.

While iPad waited patiently for him to add to his journal, it amused him to think of the places he would be willing to visit with Lisa; places he would normally, deliberately avoid. Birmingham was one. He loathed the second city with a passion superseded only by his hatred of Midthorpe. Berlin was another. Cosmopolitan it may be, but it was always far too crowded for Baldock's liking. He had found Moscow impersonal and brittle from the moment he stepped off the plane at Sheremetyevo Airport.

And yet, if he could have Lisa at his side, rather than Bernie, he would be happy to be in any of those places tomorrow.

Love? It was an absurd notion. He had spent a total of four nights with her – three during the summer, and last night – and although her company was excellent, it was not much more than raw, exciting and gratifying sex.

A regular clicking noise reached his ears. Leaning over the balcony rail, trying to ignore the dizzying view, he looked down at the pool area where both here and at the Praia next door, teams of attendants were setting out sunbeds, while in both hotels, others operated some kind of robot cleaning machine in the pools.

There was no conversation between them. They would, he imagined, be under orders to keep the noise down and allow their guests to sleep off the previous night's excesses. Each man or woman knew their job and got on with it. When the low drone of the road sweeper, a small machine similar to those used in pedestrian precincts in England, came along, operatives got out of the way and busied themselves with other nearby areas. No instructions were given and none were needed.

The scene called to mind Masters and his demands for teamwork. These simple people had it down to a fine art. They needed no wasted weekends in fancy hotels to tell them how to function as a team. They knew what needed to be done, each man or woman contributed a share of the effort, and the team got the job done.

There was little to compare cleaning the public areas of a holiday hotel and producing a book, but the underlying principles remained the same. If everyone, he, Bernie, the editors, the design and marketing people, simply got on with it instead of idling away days on the pointless and, in his opinion, disgusting exercises Masters had set them, the job would be done cheaper and more efficiently.

Allowing his mind to meander further around the subject, the more he thought about it, the less sense Masters' demands made. Baldock had been to America. He had seen the effect corporate team building had on employees and it paid huge dividends, but hauling in people who were not employees of the company, and from such diverse and disparate areas as writing and author representation, was calculated to do more harm than good.

A midlist author like Ingels, whose annual sales probably accounted for the same as one month of Baldock's, would be happy to jump aboard for the free weekend in Spain, but why drag himself or Phillipa, a talented and prolific, romantic novelist who sold many thousands, along? And why the constant threat of sanctions which if imposed would damage the company as much as they did the author?

Notwithstanding his threats and warnings, his lawyers had already looked at the contract, and found nothing wrong with it.

"It seems to us to be a standard publishing contract, Mr Baldock," they had assured him, "and available for renegotiation only if one or other party should renege on it."

Thinking about it as the sun blazed onto the distant hills, it became obvious that Masters had a hidden agenda. But what? Baldock was uncertain of Shortly's history, but he knew that Masters had founded the company on his return from America, and in less than fifteen years had taken it from producing early electronic books to a major player in the world of international fiction. He retained his position as CEO, earned a seven figure salary, and to Baldock's knowledge, had the support of his board and shareholders. What possible, hidden motive could he have for this level of coercion, and what, if anything did it have to do with the murder of Xavier Vardaro?

"I can't comment on the woman's death., obviously, and I've never met him but I'm guessing the Masters is a control freak," Lisa said when Baldock put the point to her twenty minutes later as she appeared on the balcony dishevelled, tired but still so attractive to him.

She was wearing one his shirts which reached comfortably to the level of mid-thigh, and she had stepped out onto the balcony demanding coffee.

"I have a mouth like a gorilla's armpit," she complained with that raw, Midthorpe simplicity he so detested in everyone else, but adored in her.

Greeting her with a kiss, making fresh coffee for the two of them, he told her of his suspicions while they sat, and she reiterated her opinion.

When she made her pronouncement, he considered it and found it wanting. "You're telling me he does this for no other reason than to establish control over others? Even those who don't work for him?"

Lisa gulped down coffee and nodded. "People like that

have a need to be in control of everything and everyone. You're hugely successful in a highly competitive field. What danger some other house might come along and offer you better terms?"

"Not much," he admitted. "Any competitor would need to offer me seriously large advances to even tempt me. And if they did, it would still come down to the fine print. I'm okay with Shortly, so I don't need to look elsewhere."

"And he's trying to ensure you *can't* look elsewhere. Is it illegal? What he's doing, I mean."

"According to my lawyers, no. They say there's nothing wrong with it. It may be a little stringent, but that's no surprise. Large corporations can be, er, slightly unethical in these matters."

"Ethics tend to be decided by the individual and they're malleable. They can be made to fit his requirements. What you see as restrictive, he sees as legitimate protection, helping him maintain the control he's so desperate for. Tell me, have you looked into the company at all?"

"A routine check when I first signed up, but nothing since. Why would I?"

"You're sure they're not struggling to fight off a hostile takeover?" Lisa leaned forward, warming to her task, and as she did so, she treated Baldock to a fine view of her firm breasts down the open neck of his shirt. "Y'see, Raymond, Shortly has two big name authors on its books; you and Phillipa Killairn. I don't know the ins and outs of the publishing game, but as you've just said, if one of the really big companies wants you or Phillipa, it would cost them a fortune just to buy out your contracts. They can probably go for the shareholders and pick up the company instead. That way they get, not only two bestsellers, but a range of midlist authors too."

"I don't know," Baldock admitted. "But even so, there would surely be room for Masters in the new company."

"You tell me. If, as I've suggested, he's a genuine control freak, he may be trying to ward off the competition by putting a stranglehold on you. He may even be trying to establish his credentials to maintain his position after the takeover by demonstrating that he has you people completely under his thumb." She slurped her coffee and cocked her head to check the time on Baldock's Breitling. "I'd better be thinking about getting over to the Praia for breakfast."

"And I'm due to meet the team here."

"Thinking about this Masters character, what's the possibility that he killed his secretary? Maybe stole your laptop too?"

Baldock was at a loss to answer. "Ask me another. There was a rumour that he was having an affair with her, but then again, there's also a rumour that Ian Linkman is involved with her. As for stealing my laptop, why would he? Any story outlines or ideas I have stored on there will be very rough, and he'll get to see them when they're finished."

Lisa stood up. "In that case, I haven't a clue. Tell you what, though, why did you sign such a restrictive contract?"

He shrugged. "I didn't realise I had. Bernie did the talking and the negotiations were tough. I don't think we went through every clause point by point, and we should have done." He finished his coffee, collected both cups and got to his feet. "I'm sure it will all sort itself out, and whatever game he's playing it will become apparent as we go along. Are we still on for dinner this evening?"

She grinned. "I'm looking forward to it."

Chapter Sixteen

He was in a much better frame of mind when he joined the Shortly team for breakfast at the side of the pool, and his mood was improved further when he learned that Masters was not present. After picking up a plate of bacon and eggs and a cup of coffee from the servery, he came outside to join them, and asked after the CEO.

"He must be out somewhere," Ursula Franklyn replied. "I've knocked on his door and had reception call him, but he isn't answering."

"Let's be grateful for small mercies," Baldock said and took his seat next to Bernie.

"You're very chipper," his agent commented. He noticed that she was anything but.

The same went for most of them. With the exception of Linkman, who still wore the same shabby trousers and black loafers, now tinted with a white salt line, all were suitably dressed for a Spanish seaside resort, wearing shorts and T-shirts or thin tops. Their faces, however, reflected anything but a holiday mood. The death of Xavier Vardaro preying on their minds, he believed.

"Last night turned out really well, in spite of the Midthorpe Mares' efforts to wreck it," Baldock told Bernie. "Lisa has forgiven me my sins of the summer."

"And you spent the night together?"

He beamed. "We did. And now, if you'd like to tell me what it is that's wrong between you and our lord and master so I can tackle him on your behalf, the weekend won't be a total write-off."

"And I told you last night, it's nothing you can do anything about, so let's just drop it, Raymond."

"But, Bernie…"

He trailed off as Inspector Suarez appeared and stood at his shoulder. "Señor Ballcock."

"For God's sake, it's Baldock B-A-L-D-O-C-K. With a D for dipstick, not a C for… never mind."

Suarez's smile reminded Baldock of a lion stumbling across an injured zebra at lunchtime. "You will come with me, please. I need to question you on the death of Señorita Vadaro."

Baldock waved at his half-finished meal. "I'm in the middle of breakfast."

"The hotel will serve breakfast until ten o'clock. I will not take much of your time."

"But I told you yesterday, I don't know anything."

"Señor Baldock, there are matters which have come to light overnight, and I seriously need to speak to you. If you do not come with me now, I will have my people arrest you."

With no option, and acutely conscious of all eyes upon him, Baldock followed the policeman back into the hotel, behind the reception counter and into the manager's office.

Suarez took the chair behind the desk, and gestured for Baldock to take the seat opposite.

"Now, señor, I am informed by other members of your party that you are an author. This is correct?"

"Yes. I write crime novels."

"Like Agatha Christie?"

Baldock considered the question absurd and irrelevant. "No, not like Agatha Christie. Mine are much more down-to-earth and realistic. They're police procedurals." Uncertain of the extent of Suarez's English vocabulary, he expanded on the description. "They concentrate on the efforts of the police to track down and arrest violent criminals."

"And what is your detective called? I know that writers work with one detective who is better than all his colleagues, even though he is usually a drunk."

"Detective Inspector Headingley."

Suarez's eyes lit up. "Ah, But I have read Inspector Headingley. He is a genius. But I think your killers leave too many clues and make life easy for him. This does not happen in real life."

"It might be pleasant to debate the issue with you, Inspector, but may I ask what it has to do with the death of Ms Vardaro?"

"I am making the small talk. Trying to make you feel comfortable, before I present you with the evidence. Giving you a false sense of safety."

"Security."

"*Como?*"

"A false sense of security, not safety."

"Ah. This is so." Suarez accepted the correction with good grace, and reached to a low filing cabinet at his right hand, from which he took a laptop computer which looked suspiciously like Baldock's. "Yesterday, you reported that your laptop was stolen at Alicante airport. Yes?"

"I did. Is that it?"

"It is. Do you know where we found the laptop, Señor Baldock?"

Baldock had a sneaky suspicion that he knew the answer, but he opted for silence and shook his head.

"We found it in the room of Señorita Vadaro. And you know what I am thinking, señor?"

"No. I gave up attempts at mind reading many years ago, so why don't you tell me?"

"I am thinking that you suspected Señorita Vadaro of stealing your laptop, and yesterday afternoon, you challenged her. The argument, it became violent, and you hit her hard enough to make her unconscious, after which you threw her over the balcony. You then left the room in a hurry, because you knew it would not be long before we got there. But you left so fast that you did not have time to search for and find the laptop." Suarez leaned forward, resting on his folded forearms. "What do you have to say to that, Señor Baldock?"

"Balderdash."

Suarez appeared puzzled. "Very well, what do you have to say to that, Señor Balderdash?"

Baldock's frustration began to get the better of him. "My

name is Baldock."

"Then why did you claim it was Balderdash?"

"I didn't. I was expressing an opinion on your theory. Balderdash is another word for tommyrot."

"Señor, I am getting tired of these word games. First you tell me your name is Raymond Ballcock, then it is Baldock, then it is Tommy Balderdash. Would you please make up your mind if only so that I can fill in the charge sheet correctly?"

"My name is Raymond Baldock, and your theory is nonsense. That's what I've been trying to say."

"Ah. So you think I am talking the verbal constipation?"

Baldock hesitated to correct the inspector again. Instead he agreed. "Yes. After lunch yesterday, I went to my room, and I didn't leave again until my agent, Mrs Deerman came to tell me that Xavier had been found dead after falling from her balcony."

"But we have only your word for that," Suarez retaliated.

"The same applies to the rest of the Shortly team."

"This is not so. Aside from yourself, Señorita Vadaro, and Señor Masters, the other members of your party are sharing rooms. The only other exception is Señor Ingels, who is alone because you refuse to share with him. However, we know that he was in the bar all afternoon. You, Señor Baldock, insisted that you wanted a room of your own. You refuse to share. Why was that?" Suarez hastened to answer his own rhetorical question. "Because you knew you had to confront Señorita Vadaro, and you did not want anyone else to know that you would be leaving your room to go to hers."

"Aside from your ridiculous speculation, do you have any solid evidence that puts me in her room?"

"At the moment, no. But it will not take as long to find it. I will need your fingerprints so that we can compare them to those found in the room."

"I have no problem with that. May I ask, have you questioned Gil Masters?"

"Not yet, señor. He has not yet appeared for breakfast and we do not like to disturb the hotel guests. We will get to him.

But I must point out, we did not find his laptop in Señorita Vadaro's possession. I must also tell to you on one other fact. Señorita Vadaro did not fall from her balcony. Our pathologist has confirmed that there are the marks around her ankles were someone gripped hold of her to throw her over. I believe that someone was you."

"And I believe you're talking out of your sombrero."

"*Que?*"

"You're talking nonsense again. Besides, if someone grabbed her by the ankles, there will be latent palm prints. They should be easy enough to compare to mine."

Suarez shook his head. "Not so. Whoever it was covered his hands with gloves."

"Gloves? In this weather?" Baldock's remark at least made Suarez think, but he did not wait for the inspector to pick up the debate again. "I need to think about all this. I tell you, I am innocent, and I will prove that. I just don't know how. Have you finished with me?"

"For the time being. But do not try to leave the Benidorm area, señor."

"Oh, I'm having far too good a time to even consider it."

Chapter Seventeen

Baldock was in high dudgeon when he joined his colleagues for the second attempt at breakfast, and they were not slow to comment upon it.

"If you must know, I am suspected of murdering Xavier," he told them and returned to his eggs and bacon.

"And why did you kill her?" Bernie asked.

"I didn't."

"I know you didn't, but why does Suarez think you did?"

"Because she stole my laptop."

He went back to his meal and allowed the announcement to create a ripple of consternation around the table. As always, when he was in a bad mood, he did not want to speak to anyone. He preferred to be alone, let the irritation work its way through his system. His normal method of dealing with it was to work, but with his laptop held by the Spanish police, and his iPad a poor substitute, he could not.

And of course, the Shortly party would not let the matter rest there.

"Xavier stole your laptop?" Ursula Franklyn asked. "I wonder if Gil knows about this. I'll have to tell him."

Baldock stared sourly at her. "Since when have you been his PA?"

She shrugged. "Since Xavier was killed. He told you yesterday at dinner. I work for the company, remember. I'm not self-employed like you guys, so I didn't have much choice when he told me I was replacing her. Not that it gets me out of the challenges. I still have to go with you and Ian." She became a little more officious. "So, Xavier stole your laptop, did she?"

"It was in her room," Baldock said. "That is as much as I

can tell you. Now do you all mind if I finish breakfast?"

As he tackled his meal again, they dispersed, spreading themselves out amongst nearby tables, and Harry Ingels moved to the adjacent empty seat.

"Hey up, Ray, I'm told you're the man I need to speak to."

Baldock groaned. "You need advice? At your age?"

"I do. The word is that last night you had some chick pull down your pants while another chick took pictures of you in all your glory."

Baldock glared at Bernie on the next table, and she shrugged. "I was trying to get some shorts for you," she said. "I had to tell them what had happened."

"And Masters spread the word, did he?"

"Masters wasn't there," Bernie replied.

Baldock allowed Bernie her explanation and settled his irritation on Ingels. "For your information, Harry, both *chicks* were drunk and acting the goat."

"Masters has set three of us the same challenge," the Lancastrian said. "So all I have to do is find some tart who's drunk and get her to act the fool with me."

"For your further information, those women were not strangers to me. I've known and disowned both of them most of my life." Baldock polished off a fried egg, and washed it down with a large swallow of coffee. "You're not going through with this farce, are you?"

Ingels appeared more resigned than enthusiastic. "What choice do I have? Gil expects results by the time we sit down to dinner tonight."

"He can whistle for his results," Baldock declared. "I won't even be here for dinner."

Listening in, Ursula felt obliged to butt in. "Now, Ray—"

Baldock cut her off. "I didn't know it, but my mother and several of her friends are in town. I'm having lunch with Mother, and I've arranged to have dinner with an old friend; someone I haven't seen for a long time."

"You're making private arrangements on the company time?" The young editor/PA *pro tem*, sounded shocked.

"As you just pointed out, you work for the company. I

don't. And if you recall, I'm here under duress. But if it worries your boss so much, tell him to work out how much the weekend cost and I'll reimburse him for today."

As Ingels wandered away, Ursula and Ian Linkman moved to join him.

"Ray, can we talk?" Linkman asked.

"I give in." Baldock pushed his plate away with a sigh. "About what?"

"This challenge the boss has laid on us," Ursula said. "We're not happy about it."

"First off, Ursula, haven't I just said that he may be your boss, but he isn't mine, and he isn't yours, Ian."

"He's threatened us with sanctions," Linkman protested. "Phillipa is terrified he'll throw out her contract."

"He's threatened me too. Listen, both of you. Just forget about this stupid challenge. He won't go through with it."

"We're not in your position," Ursula pointed out. "We can't afford to take that chance."

Baldock gave the matter some consideration as he finished his coffee and put the cup and saucer with his plate. "I know a woman who might just be persuaded, and after last night, she owes me a favour."

"But Gil wants photographic evidence," Ursula stressed.

"Trust me. I'll arrange it all."

"You're sure?" Linkman still sounded doubtful.

"I told you to trust me, didn't I? Then be good and trust me." Baldock waved a hand at the great outdoors. "There's a beach a hundred yards down that way. Go top up your suntan for the day and I'll handle it." He drummed idle fingers on the table. "While you're here, is there any truth in this rumour that you and Xavier were romantically involved?"

Linkman appeared worried by the question, and looked around as if ensuring that no one else was listening in. "Yes, we were. We've been seeing each other for months. Hell, Ray, there's nothing wrong with it. I'm divorced, she's never been married, but Masters didn't like it. He prefers his PA to be totally under his control. He didn't like the idea that she might settle down with a literary agent and start telling tales out of school."

"So you obviously won't have had anything to do with her death."

Linkman was shocked. "I loved her, for Christ's sake. No way would I ever hurt her, and if I get my hands on the guy who did..." He trailed off, tears sparkling in his eyes.

"I understand how you feel," Baldock admitted, and felt a ripple of pride run through him. Thanks to Lisa he was telling the truth for once.

Linkman left and Baldock glanced at Bernie, who did not look at him, but stared gloomily into a cup of cold coffee.

When the rest of the Shortly party were out of sight, he concentrated on his agent, racking his brain for a line of attack which might weaken her resolve. "Bernie, what's wrong? What has Masters said to prompt you to warn me about him last night, and to make you so glum this morning?"

"I've told you, Raymond, it's nothing you can do anything about."

"In that case, there's no problem telling me, is there? Unless there's something personal between the two of you."

She sighed and looked away, and Baldock fervently wished he had Lisa or better still, his mother with him.

"Bernie, please..."

She sighed again, and brought her gaze back to him. "I said I knew Masters and his reputation at Oxford. What I didn't tell you was that I knew him slightly better than that. He was visiting his old college, and for one night only, he and I were slightly more than friends. You get my drift?" Bernie waited for Baldock to nod. "Well, yesterday evening, before dinner, he reminded me of it. He wants to, er, renew our acquaintanceship."

"Notwithstanding the fact that you're both married?"

"Correct. Naturally I told him where to go."

"But?"

Another long sigh. "Unless I agree, the very same sanctions he's threatened you with will kick in." Her eyes burned into Baldock. "I have to sleep with him, Ray. If I don't, he'll bankrupt the pair of us."

The announcement drove a lance of absolute fury through Baldock. He leapt to his feet. "Right. I'm having this bastard now. What room is he in?"

Bernie stayed him. "He's out. Didn't Ursula just tell you? She's been looking for him since first thing this morning. Besides, taking him on won't do any good. He has the whip hand, Raymond, and he knows it. I don't believe that crap about black belts in karate and no one I know remembers him getting a boxing blue at Oxford, so I'm sure you're big enough to beat seven colours out of him, but you'd be prosecuted, and even if he decided not to press charges, he'd still initiate the sanctions. We'd both be bankrupt within a year."

"But you can't do it, Bernie. You're a happily married woman, for God's sake. You don't play around with other men... or that's the impression I've always had."

"Perfectly true, but what choice do I have? If I don't, he'll kill us both off." Bernie took a tissue to blow her nose and dabbed at her eyes. "I'm not the only one, either."

That particular announcement only drove Baldock into a fresh fit of rage. "What?"

"He's propositioned Phillipa and Tiffany Pittock, Harry Ingels' agent, in exactly the same way, threatening exactly the same sanctions. Phillipa is fuming. She insists that she never signed the contract clauses he's relying on, but when she checked her copy of the contract on her laptop, they were there. Tiffany checked her copy of Harry's contract and they were there, too." She dropped the tissue in the ashtray and drew a fresh one from the pack. "He's screwed us all, and from a woman's point of view, I mean that literally."

Baldock disregarded the sexual connotation. "Have you checked your copy of my contract?"

She shook her head. "It's in the filing cabinet at home. I have a version on my laptop, but I didn't bring the laptop with me. You can check yours, but I've no doubt the clauses are there."

"I can't. The police have my laptop. And anyway, I had

my lawyers look over it and they say it's airtight. It might be on my iPad, though. I'll check when I get back to my room."

"Then we're snookered. All of us."

"I can't understand what his game is. Why take three of your bestselling authors... well, two bestsellers and a reliable midlister, and nail them like this? It's bad for them, bad for the company, bad for everyone."

Bernie shrugged. "I don't know. I'm sure he'll go ahead and clamp down on all three of you in the hope that once you realise he's serious, you'll toe his line. Beyond that, I really don't know what he hopes to gain, unless he's angling after a reduction in royalties in the longer term."

Baldock did not accept it. "According to both you and my lawyers, that would constitute a breach of contract and nullify existing agreements."

"Not," Bernie stressed, "if he had evidence on three women, all of them married, who slept with him." To clarify her point, she went on, "Imagine a year from now, he comes along and insists you take a three to five point reduction in your royalties on pain of telling Oliver that he'd bedded me. Don't you think I wouldn't pressure you into accepting? And even if I could prove that he threatened me into bed, don't you think it would still be the end of my marriage? I'm painted into a corner, Ray, and I have no way out other than the route Masters wants me to take."

"I don't accept that."

"I have to."

"No." Baldock was determined. "There must be something we can do. String him along for the time being, but for God's sake, don't climb into bed with him. Give me time to think about it. I'm a blasted Midthorper whether I like it or not, and most of them are used to playing dirty games like this, even if I'm not. I'm sure I can come up with something."

Chapter Eighteen

Baldock was still furious when he collected his mother from the *Hotel Praia* at a few minutes to one. Masters had not shown his face all morning and there was a general feeling that he had sneaked out and shot off to Valencia or Alicante on business. Meanwhile, on checking his iPad, Baldock could not find a copy of the contract in question.

It was doubly frustrating for him. He was determined to confront the man and give him a good hiding; something Raymond Baldock would never normally consider.

He was still thinking about it, still drawing a blank when he climbed into the taxi with his mother.

"*Carrer el Pont*," she ordered the driver. "Friar's."

While they moved off, turning left onto the broad dual carriageway of *Avenida del Mediterráneo* and its mix of up- and downmarket shops, bars and restaurants, its high rise, mid- to upper-quality hotels, Janet raved about the restaurant.

"You'll like it, Raymond. It's run by an English family, and the food is genuine British, just like you get at home. And it's close to the town centre and the old town if you fancy a bit of quality shopping."

"I don't shop, Mother."

Baldock remained just as taciturn and uncommunicative for most of the ten-minute journey, confining himself to non-committal grunts in response to her enthusiasm.

Friars was a small, discreet place, opposite the end of *Calle Gambo* where the quality shops Janet had talked about, were located. For a Friday lunchtime it was busy, most of the patrons, dressed as Baldock had expected, in holiday wear, their sun hats, thin vests and T-shirts advertising them as British tourists every bit as much as sporting the Union Flag would.

Jimmy, the proprietor, a stocky and powerfully-built man in his mid-forties, was pleased to see one of his favourite customers and showed them to a table in a quiet corner where Janet promptly dispensed with the menu. "I'll have the roast beef, please, Jimmy."

"And what about your toy boy, Janet?"

She laughed. "He's not my toy boy. He's my son."

Jimmy chuckled. "Sorry, gel. What about you then, sonny?"

Baldock glowered. "I'll have the same as my mother... served with a little respect, if you can manage that."

"Ooh." The waiter pouted. "Coming right up, my lord. What you having to drink, Jan?"

"The usual. Easy on the Campari, plenty of soda."

"And for you, boss?"

"I'll have a beer."

Jimmy ambled back to the bar, and Baldock glared again at his mother. "Just how well do the people of Benidorm know you?"

"Oh, not well, but there are a few who have got used to me. I always have lunch at Friar's when I'm here. The food's wonderful and Jimmy gives us a good laugh."

"Us?"

"Tim and me, usually. But Tim's not with me, is he? He'd look a bit out of place on a hen weekend?" Her face became more serious. She reached across the table and took her son's hand. "Never mind Tim. I'm with you, and I worry about you. I worry about Keith, too, but not as much as I do about you."

"Keith? Why do you worry about him? In case he's crashed his lorry or something?"

"No, but he's made a mess of his life because he's feckless. Like your father. He copes. He just coasts through life not giving much of a hoot about anything, and that worries me. But at least he's not living alone. You are. And when I look at you, it's like you have all the problems of the world in your pocket and you don't know what to do with them."

"I'm a success, Mother. And I'm still young enough to enjoy it."

Jimmy returned and placed drinks before them. "There you go, gel, one Campari and soda, and for the gentleman, our finest ale, served at room temperature, allowed to breathe, brewed to perfection, it will tickle the palate—"

"Yes, thank you very much," Baldock interrupted. "Don't call us, we'll call you."

"Careful you don't crack your makeup with a smile." He gestured at the drinks. "Paying for these now are you, or do you wanna add it to the bill?"

"I'll get the drinks." Janet reached for her purse.

Baldock stopped her. "No you will not." He concentrated on the waiter. "Add it to the bill, please."

Jimmy disappeared again and Janet took an approving sip of her Campari, then picked up the conversational thread.

"A success while you're young enough to enjoy it?" she repeated. "But you're not, are you? Enjoying it, I mean."

Baldock struggled for an answer. "My kind of success comes with certain pressures. A novelist, any novelist, is only as good as his last book. I'm earning a fortune, but it can end just like that." He snapped his fingers. "I don't fancy going back to being a hack writer on a tabloid, or even a staff writer on a magazine like *Sleuth Monthly*. That means I have to work exceptionally hard. Run faster just to stand still."

"Raymond, I understand what you're saying, but the truth is you were like this before you went to university. Cambridge only made you worse."

"Well, that's Midthorpe for you. I was bullied, Mother. Gary Lipton and his gang of thugs. And why? Because I was more intelligent than them."

"You never told me."

"Because you know what Dad would have said." He put on a strong, deep voice. "Learn to fight your own battles, lad." He reverted to his normal tones. "Then he'd have gone off to the bookies, the pub or Elland Road."

"I can't answer for your father but I would have tried to do something."

"Telling tales, ratting on someone was against the Midthorpe code," Baldock insisted, switching tack slightly. "It still is, and you know it. Good lord, you refused to identify the culprit to the police when we were chasing those Fiagara pills. If I'd mentioned the bullying to you, if you'd interfered, it would have made matters worse."

"All right." Janet laid her palms flat on the table. "But that was then, and this is now. You're not the only boy who was bullied at school. You're not the only boy who was bullied and became a success. You're thirty-six years old, Raymond, and it's time you got the pole out of your arse."

The colour rushed to his cheek. "Mother!"

"You're the word merchant, Raymond. Isn't language a means of communication? I'm trying to communicate what I feel in the strongest possible way."

He let out an exasperated sigh and made an effort to move the topic sideways. "Did you tell Mandy Cowling that my middle name was Gareth?"

"Yes. Months ago. Before you came to Midthorpe in the summer."

Baldock looked both ways and took a large swallow of beer. "But it isn't. I don't have a middle name. So why tell her that?"

"Well, Mandy has this thing about men whose name begins with G. I thought, if she knew your middle name was Gareth she might, you know, sleep with you. And at the time I thought you were a virgin—"

"What?"

"Well, I know I got mixed up about you and Bernie and —"

"I was not a bloody virgin."

The volume and intensity of their conversation had increased to the point where they were the centre of attention. Memories of The Pantry brought a distinct feeling of déjà vu to Baldock as Jimmy approached from the bar.

The proprietor kept his voice not much above a whisper. "Listen, Jan, you know me. I'm so laid back I'm almost horizontal, but your chitchat is putting the other punters off their dinner. I don't think they wanna hear about your lad's bedtime adventures."

"I'm sorry, Jimmy. Family disagreement."

"Put him over your knee and smack his bottom if you must, but keep it down a bit, eh?"

Raymond glared. "Tell me, does being obnoxious come naturally to you, or have you had training?"

Jimmy leaned in a little closer so Baldock could hear the hiss. "It's a good job your mother is a favourite customer, sunbeam, cos if she wasn't, I'd introduce your head to the pavement. You should keep your sex life to yourself, but if you do need your mum's advice, keep the noise down."

Janet held her breath and Baldock could guess why. Jimmy was a big man. Not tall, but stocky, and despite his slight paunch, a man who appeared as if he could take care of himself. She would not have backed her son against him. But last night, for the first time since he was child, she had seen her youngest son stripped to his underwear, and she knew he had a lean, athletic and muscular physique. Given his genuine surliness, he guessed she was worried that he might take Jimmy on and she was doubtful of the outcome.

Baldock, however, could not recall a single fight he had won in his entire life, and with memories of his ejection from The Pantry at the forefront of his mind, he elected to back down. "Please offer my apologies to your patrons."

As Jimmy departed for the third time, Baldock turned upon his mother and kept his voice to a hiss.

"As that idiot has just hinted, my sex life is my own affair, Mother. I've had my share of girlfriends, and thankfully, none of them have been whores like Mandy Cowling."

"Oh, I don't think she charges for it, luv."

Her observation, a deliberate attempt to lighten the mood and divert her son's attention, did nothing to alleviate his temper. "She is a tart of the cheapest kind. Half the youth of Midthorpe learned biology from her. Mercifully, I was not one of them."

A broody silence fell over the table, broken when Jimmy arrived with their order.

"There you go, children. Roast beef and genuine, homemade yorkie pud."

"Homemade?" Baldock asked.

Jimmy nodded. "The wife defrosted it herself." He smiled at Baldock. "Make sure you eat your greens or there'll be no jelly and ice cream for you."

Baldock smiled back. "Take the words off and clear and rearrange them into a well-known phrase or saying."

"Very funny. You should be on the stage... The next Wells Fargo leaves in ten minutes."

He wandered off again, and they tucked into the food, Janet savouring every mouthful, and she noticed that, despite his constant bickering, her son seemed to be enjoying it too.

"What is it, Raymond? What's wrong?"

He did not answer.

Janet sighed. "They say there's no fool like an old fool. I say you can't fool an old fool, not when she's your mother. There's something wrong, and you're not saying what it is."

He put down his knife and fork and carefully calculated his announcement. "I told you that one of our team was murdered."

"You did."

"Yes, well, the police think I did it."

Chapter Nineteen

Janet almost dropped her cutlery. "They think what?"

Baldock indicated that they should continue with their meal, and as they ate, he gave her an account of the morning's interview with Suarez.

She listened intently, and as he spoke it occurred to him how little credit he had given her over the years. A simple, working-class woman she might be, but under that demure surface was a wealth of experience and an innate intelligence which had remained hidden for many years under the dominance of his father.

He could not recall any time when his father had been physically violent towards his mother. He was sure that Keith, his older brother, would have stepped in had there been any such incidents. But the old man, a truck driver for most of his working life, had a bullying, harrowing approach and a loud voice. It no longer impressed Baldock. It had not impressed him since his early teens, but with hindsight, he could see that his mother, probably concerned for her two sons, had capitulated for many long years.

Now that they were alone, independent of Nick Baldock, that wily astuteness could surface, and it did the moment he had finished his tale.

"The bloody fools. They imagine that you got into a fight with this woman and threw her off the balcony?" She waited for him to deliver a solemn nod. "Didn't you tell them that you can't even punch the air when you score a goal at table football?"

It was not the kind of reputation he preferred to publicise, but it was the truth.

"If you'd been fighting with her, *she* would have thrown

you over the balcony."

"The laptop is the main problem, Mother. What was she doing with it? I don't even recall her standing anywhere near me at the airport, but obviously, she must have taken it, or it wouldn't have been in her room. And I don't know what she was looking for. There was nothing important on it. A copy of my broad contract with Shortly, and one or two ideas for future novels, but nothing else."

"What about this agent boyfriend of hers? This Ian Linkman? Could he have been looking to steal ideas for his clients?"

Baldock chewed through a piece of tough beef and swallowed it, then picked up a serviette and dabbed his lips. "He has only one client. Philippa Killairn. She writes historical romance, so she could hardly use my ideas, could she? No, it has to be more complex than that. Besides, I spoke to Linkman this morning; I don't think he would have hurt Xavier. He was besotted with her."

Janet gave him an elfin grin. "Like you and Lisa?"

He groaned. "Yes, like me and Lisa. The only good thing ever to come out of Midthorpe... Present company excepted. But we're wandering off the point. Linkman—"

"Why do you have such a grudge against Midthorpers?"

The question annoyed him. "You only need look at last night for an answer."

Various memories leapt into her mind, and Janet laughed. "Oh, I haven't had such fun in a long time. Not since the last time I was in Benidorm."

"Yes, you did. And it was at my expense."

She frowned. "I don't think you were there when we played pin the todger on the tom."

"I'm not talking about..." He stopped a forkful of roast beef, carrot and broccoli between the plate and his mouth. "Pin the ... Mother, what on earth has happened to you?"

"The very thing I'd like to see happen to you. I've stepped out of the shadows."

The food made its way to his mouth. Chewing, swallowing and pausing to take a sip of beer, he said, "I don't understand. Stepping out of what shadows?"

Janet, too, washed down a mouthful of food with a sip of Campari. "Life isn't a rehearsal, Raymond. You have to take out of it whatever you can because you're a long time dead. You don't do that. You're haughty and miserable. Everyone can see it. All right, so Sandra Scranton pulling down your underpants and Mandy Cowling taking a photograph was a little over the top, but even allowing for that and your problems with the police and your publisher, you're a proper little ray of gloom and doom."

"Midthorpe," he declared.

"No. Not Midthorpe, or even Benidorm. It's you, Raymond. I said last night, you're unhappy, but you won't admit it. Listen to me. One day you'll wake up and realise what a waste everything has been, and all the money in the world won't put that right. But there's no going back."

"Mother, I am perfectly happy with my life."

"So you keep telling everyone, and yet you carp and whine and snap about everything. Look at the way you treated poor Lisa in the summer."

"I've made it up with her. For your information, she and I spent the night together last night, and we have plans to do so again tonight."

"I know. Lisa told me this morning… well, not that you spent the night together, but that you'd apologised for your behaviour. And it was obvious she still cared from the way she rushed off to buy clean shorts for you."

He ate more food, but his anger was rising again. "While we're at it, I do not carp and whine. I complain when things are wrong. Like this idiot serving us. The man has little or no respect for his patrons."

"You mean he's not some snobby so-and-so dressed in a penguin suit and trying to keep riff-raff like me away." Janet argued. "Jimmy is being sociable. He jollies his customers along with his little jokes. He's not the most original comedian in Benidorm, but he keeps everyone happy while they're eating, and those same people will come back time and time again, because they have good memories of his restaurant. Think, Raymond. What are your happiest memories?"

He took his time thinking, Janet silently reflected as she ate.

Eventually, he said, "I thought they were some of the times I spent with you. But after last night, I'm not so sure. You applauded and laughed along with the rest of them when those stupid bitches did what they did?"

Janet put down her knife and fork. "You're not listening. I love you, Raymond. No one was prouder than me when you got your place at Cambridge. I cried tears of joy when we came to your graduation ceremony. My son, a Cambridge graduate. No one was more pleased when your photograph appeared in all the national newspapers after the success of your first book. I still have all the cuttings at home. And, obviously, I have all your books on the shelf – the ones you sent me - where everyone can see them. Like all mothers, I want what is best for my children, and you are the best. But to become what you've become, something got lost along the way, and one day you'll wake up and ask yourself, 'what have I done with my life'. You make a lot of money. You're much better off than anyone I know. You have an international reputation as a novelist. But deep down you are a sad and lonely young man who doesn't know what it is to enjoy himself." Janet picked up her cutlery again. "Trust me on this, Raymond. You're not the first member of our family to be like that."

Baldock finished his meal, and put down his cutlery. "Keith? Uncle Colin?"

"Me," Janet said and went back to her food.

Working on the last of her meal, Janet allowed a pause which gave Baldock time to consider the announcement. When she had eaten all she wanted, she put down her knife and fork, dabbed at her lips with a napkin and pushed the plate away.

"You?" he demanded.

"That was delicious. Now, jam roly-poly and custard or not?" She tutted. "Life is full of awkward choices, isn't it?"

"Mother—"

"Are you having dessert?"

"No. The hotel leave a bowl of fresh fruit in the room. I'll have something when I get back to the Aranjuez. Mother, what do you mean—"

"What a good idea. I never thought of that." She eyed his drink. "Shall we have another tipple? I'll pay for them this time."

"You will not," Baldock insisted and signalled Jimmy.

He came over and looked down at the plates. "You haven't finished your runner beans."

"I don't like them," Baldock declared. "They give me the runs."

Jimmy pointed into the darkest recess of his restaurant. "Khasi's in the corner." Jimmy concentrated on Janet. "You enjoyed?"

"It was excellent, Jimmy. As always."

"Anything and everything for the fair senorita." He looked to Baldock. "I trust everything was to sir's satisfaction."

"My compliments to the microwave operator," Baldock said.

Jimmy laughed. "He really is a comic, isn't he? You should be up there on the top shelf with the *Beano*, the *Dandy* and the *Daily Mail*." He took up his order pad. "Pudding?"

"Pass."

"Nothing for me, Jimmy." Janet patted her tummy. "I'm looking out for my figure."

He gave a lusty growl. "Plenya blokes in Benidorm who'd be willing to look over your figure, Janet." He placed the bill on the table. "There you go. We take all forms of currency, including cash."

"Plastic?" Baldock asked.

"I've never heard of plastic cash."

Baldock placed his credit card on the table.

"I'll bring you the machine," Jimmy said and crossed back to the bar.

"You didn't order the drinks," Janet pointed out.

"I'll deal with it when he comes back. Mother, what did you mean, when you said it was you?"

Jimmy returned. Baldock sorted out the credit card payment, ordered fresh drinks, and then worked out the cost, plus ten percent of the whole bill before leaving €15 on the table to cover the cost of drinks and a tip. Jimmy delivered the drinks and took away the cash with muted thanks, and Baldock sipped the thin head off his second beer and waited for Janet to answer.

She fussed, pouring the remnants of her first drink into the second, and stirred the mixture. At length she focussed on her youngest son.

"I was twenty-three when I married your father. I was sixty-two when the rotten sod walked out on me to live with the bimbo he'd been shagging. Her from the bookies."

Baldock almost choked on his beer. "Must we resort to the language of the gutter?"

"Why not? It's where your father belongs. And anyway, it expresses my feelings perfectly. I spent almost forty years living in that man's shadow. Everything, and I do mean everything about our marriage was geared to you boys and what he wanted. I admit, he didn't want much. Someone to keep house, cook his meals and make sure he had clean socks in the drawer. When he left, I was shattered. You probably remember. All those years of marriage thrown away for a little cow who couldn't keep her drawers on. I was very ill for a time. I couldn't eat, I couldn't sleep. The doctor had me on antidepressants. Your father and you boys had been my whole life. Even when you two were old enough to leave at home alone, and I went back to work, my priorities were always you and your father. To see it all torn apart like that almost killed me."

"I remember. I went to York to see him, if you recall. Try to talk some sense into the bloody fool, but he wouldn't listen."

"I know you did, luv, and I was grateful at the time. But if you offered now, I'd tell you not to bother. To coin a Midthorpe-ism and to keep the language out of the gutter, I wouldn't pee on him if he were on fire."

This time, Baldock merely chuckled.

"For months I sat in that house brooding," Janet went on. "And suddenly I began to see how bad life had been. I had had no life and at sixty-three, it was all over. I had no past. It was buried under your father's dominance. And I had no future. I was a lonely, old divorcee." She paused to ensure her next words had the right effect. "Then I met a man."

The faint smile of indulgent sympathy faded from Baldock's face, and then the light shone in his eyes. "Ah. You mean Tim?"

"Before Tim." Janet's defiance manifested itself in a glow of pride and pleasure. "A gentleman. A man in a similar position to me. Alone and in his sixties."

"And who was he?"

"That's not important. He's history anyway. What is important is the change he made to my life. I stepped out of the shadows, Raymond. And before your mind goes wandering down the usual Midthorpe dirt track, yes we did sleep together and I'm saying no more than that, so mind your own bloody business."

"It wasn't the first thing that crossed my mind," he replied. "Actually, I was wondering why you've been so secretive. If it hadn't been for that farce with the Fiagara pills during the summer, I'm not sure I would have learned about Tim."

"I never purposely kept anything secret. I simply didn't see what business it is of anyone's but me and my man. I don't inquire after your girlfriends, do I?"

"No. You just make arbitrary assumptions about my sexual orientation."

"For which I apologised." Janet downed a large gulp of Campari. "Listen, Raymond, because this is important. I married your father because I was in love with him. It took me forty years to learn that he never loved me. He just loved the services I had to offer; domestic and other. But I learned that you can move on, that there is another life, and I found it with my gentleman friend. Then, a year or so ago, I got together with Tim and now life is wonderful. When you can see this town, and the bar last night for what they really are – huge fun – then you will be taking the first step to coming out of the shadows and into the light."

"I did see last night it for what it was. A stupid ritual designed to humiliate men like me."

"On the surface, you're probably right. But think about it a bit deeper. You were not humiliated, Raymond, because nobody in this town actually cares. Someone once told me the place should be renamed Beni-who-gives-a-damn-dorm, and that's quite accurate. This place is built for fun, and last night was fun, and most of those in in the pub took it as fun. You were the only one embarrassed by it."

"Because it's not often I strip in public."

"Well you should try it. More than one young woman was looking your way last night."

"And plenty of them were taking pictures. Including Mandy Armitage – I mean Cowling. And that was before she had my underwear down."

"Lisa, too. I saw the sparkle in her eye when she was watching you. She was probably remembering what a good time she'd had with you during the summer, and as I said, she was quick to come to your rescue, and to chase after you when you walked off. And after the way you treated her in June, I wouldn't have blamed her if she'd left you to it." Once again, Janet reached across and held his hand. "Don't end up sad, bitter and lonely like I did, Raymond. I came through it, and I'm now very happy, but when I think about it, my happiness is partly thanks to the death of a woman – Margaret Yeoman – I'd known for many years, which left behind a husband – Tim – who was as lonely as me. You might not be so lucky."

Chapter Twenty

After Janet had a final word with Jimmy, they stepped out into the early afternoon heat, and crossed the road. A line of wooden stalls were open for business. To his delight, Baldock saw that that they were second-hand bookshops, and he spent a few minutes perusing the shelves before he discovered, to his amusement, one of his earlier novels in Spanish, selling at a knockdown price.

After a brief conversation in broken Spanish and English, with the proprietor, he pointed to the picture on the back cover, and then to himself. The stallholder's face split into a beam of delight, and Baldock spent a few more minutes posing for photographs before signing the book, *los mejores deseos, Raymond Baldock*.

"You looked really pleased to find you're famous in Spain, too," Janet observed as they walked on down to the seafront.

"Not as pleased as him. He'll probably double the price now."

As always, the beach was crowded with sun worshippers. Children played in the safe, shallow waters, adults, from the teens upwards slept, read, listened to music on headsets, and slept some more. Adolescents also played in the water. They had to. There was no room on the beach for impromptu games of football or cricket. An inflatable banana, towed by a speedboat and designed to carry several passengers made its way from the shallows towards the deeper waters. A paraglider, again towed by a boat, sat serene on his/her harness in the sky, and further out, almost as an addendum to the background, was the cable ski, pulling a skilled water-skier along at breakneck speed. Closer to them, as they walked along, they paused to admire the handiwork of a sand sculptor, whose creation was a cowboy sleeping alongside his reclining horse. Janet gave a few coins and even her son signalled his approval by taking a photograph before tossing a €5 note in the artist's collection cap.

Janet bought ice cream cones, and they sat on one of the stone benches – spaced at regular intervals – enjoying the vanilla and the view.

"I love it here," Janet said.

"I'd noticed."

"This town is just so full of life. And to be here with my son, it's just... so wonderful." She faced him. "But I still have this puzzle, Raymond. Why did you come in the first place? You're self-employed, so surely you couldn't be forced on this corporate weekend? And Benidorm is not your sort of place, and if you hadn't come, you wouldn't have all this trouble with your stolen laptop and your publisher's secretary. Are you trying to find your roots again? I do wish you would."

"No. I'm quite happy to leave my roots where they belong; in the past. The truth is, I was pressured into it." His features darkened. "And it's been an absolute disaster from the word go. An uncomfortable flight with Mickey Mouse Airways, Xavier's murder, which I'm suspected of committing, I've had half a dozen run-ins with Masters, then there was that farce last night, as if that's not enough, Masters is making ridiculous, disgusting demands on everyone in the party, including me. I tell you—"

Janet cut him off. "Just a minute. Let's take these one by one. Mickey Mouse Airways? What kind of airline did you expect? Virgin Atlantic first-class? This is Benidorm, Raymond, not St Tropez. And this man is making unreasonable demands on you? Tell me more about him."

"Gil Masters. As I said, he's the Chief Executive of Shortly Publishing. He organised this weekend, and he's playing some games as silly as those the women played in the bar last night. As silly, but much more dangerous and dirty, and this morning, I heard of his real agenda."

"Oh, of course. Is he the one you said was an... what was

it? Onanist? One who pulls out before he comes."

Baldock ignored the crude imagery his mother's question raised. "Correct. After what I heard this morning, I mean it even more. You know I'm not a violent man, Mother."

"As a child, if you got into a fight with a spider in the bedroom, you always lost."

"Correct. But if he didn't have us over such a barrel, I would have happily punched him in the face."

Janet finished her ice cream, wiped her mouth and Baldock took both her tissue and his to drop them in a nearby litter bin.

"What has he done, Raymond?" she asked as they walked on.

"He's pulled some dirty stunts, Mother, which have painted Bernie and me into a corner. I'm trying to fathom a way out."

Janet linked her arm through his. "What kind of dirty stunts?"

"Nothing I would tell you about."

"Oh, come on, luv. When it comes to gossip, you're more tight-lipped than your father. How am I supposed to help if I don't know what the problem is?"

"You can't help. This man pulls the strings. He's very wealthy and can do as he likes. If we don't toe his line, he can make life more than difficult for me. He can effectively cut off my income for the next five years." His face darkened again. "All because of one stupid clause in the contract."

"What clause?" Janet began to get irritated with her son. "Come on, Raymond. I'm your mother. Even if I can't help, I can listen."

"Very well. But I'm warning you, it's dirty."

Janet smacked her lips. "Oh, good. I love dirty stories."

He made an obvious but failed attempt to cover his displeasure, and launched into his tale.

They had walked on a further two hundred yards by the time he came to the crunch, by which time Janet was already incensed. Taking a seat by another sand sculptor, this one working on a castle and mosque, complete with streams, waterfalls and a moat, she checked her facts.

"He's demanding that Bernie sleep with him and if she doesn't he'll begin to mess you around?"

Baldock nodded. "To the point of withholding royalties."

"And Bernie has agreed to do it?"

"Bernie is happily married, Mother. No way would she agree, but yes, she will do it. She is willing to compromise her marriage to Oliver in order to safeguard my income… and her commission of course."

Janet's anger began to overflow. "And is he married, this Masters man?"

"Oh yes. I've met his wife a few times. Dominique. Terrible woman. A real dragon."

"So if she found out, there'd be hell to pay?"

"I've thought of that already, Mother, and it wouldn't work. Dominique would probably turn a blind eye. They are, after all, very wealthy, and she knows which side the bread is buttered."

"In that case, you'd probably have to threaten him with public humiliation."

It occurred to Baldock that his mother was thinking out loud.

"What have you done so far?" she asked.

"Nothing, other than ask Bernie to string him along until I think of something. I'm not supposed to know about it, you see."

Janet strummed her lips with her fingers. "This dead woman, Xavier. She was this man's secretary?"

"Yes."

"Has it occurred to you that she might have refused to play along with his filthy ideas? You did say she was romantically involved with another member of your party."

"Ian Linkman. He's Phillipa Killairn's agent."

"So she might have refused, threatened to expose this Masters person. Is it possible then that he killed her and planted your laptop in her room in order to incriminate you?"

It had not and Baldock said so. "Mother, you are a genius. Of course that's what happened."

"I know," she said without any false modesty, "but you're never going to prove it, so it's time we did something." Janet fished into her bag and came out with her phone. "I'm not having him treat my son this way and I'm not having him treat a Midthorper like this."

"Bernie is not your son. And she's not a Midthorper."

Janet brushed her finger up the lock screen to waken the phone, and punched a single icon on the main window, then put the phone to her ear. "You are my son, and Bernie is your friend. I met her last night and I like her, even if I did get confused about your relationship. For the time you're here, she is an honorary Midthorper." She concentrated on the phone. "Tim? It's Janet. Get some of your guys together as quick as you can. I'll bell the girls. Meet me at Winners in, say, half an hour... Yes, yes, I know we said the two parties shouldn't meet, but this is an emergency... Right, I'll see you there."

Baldock frowned. "I thought you said Tim wasn't here."

"No, I said Tim wasn't with me. He's here on Wayne Kenneally's stag do. We're the Midthorpe Maidens and they're the South Leeds Stags."

"Isn't that a little unusual? The stag and hen parties in the same town at the same time?"

"We're Midthorpers, Raymond. A law unto ourselves." Janet concentrated on her phone again. "Now that we have the men organised, let's get some of the girls on board."

Chapter Twenty-One

Early afternoon and Winners was all but empty when they arrived to find Tim with several of the South Leeds Stags, of whom Baldock recognised only Michael Shipston, sitting outside, enjoying the sunshine, drinking beer and mixing with Mandy, Linda Taplin, and Sandra Scranton, all of whom were already on the cocktails and spirits.

"How come Lisa isn't here?" Baldock asked as he and his mother joined the group.

"Because she's like you," Janet replied. "She'd want to fight clean, and this doesn't call for clean fighting. Besides, she has to look after young Chloe, make sure she doesn't get together with her intended. It's bad luck. Now listen to me, Raymond, I don't want you involved in any of these discussions, so just get the drinks in, sit down and shut up like a good boy."

"Mother—"

"Just do it, and don't argue."

Baldock ordered drinks all round, Janet sat alongside Tim and once the refreshments had been delivered, took control of events.

"Raymond has told me in confidence, of certain problems he and his agent are up against. They're dirty and we need to get dirtier to help him."

Mandy guffawed. "Ooh, I love dirty problems and dirtier solutions. What's up, *Gareth*? Can't hack this bint?"

"Mandy, you have been misled. My name is not Gareth, and the problem is not a woman but a man."

"Really?" Mandy's eyes widened with interest. "I didn't know you were that way inclined. What a waste of such a big —"

"You're getting the wrong end of the stick, Mandy," Janet interrupted.

"I haven't had hold of the stick. I just took a picture of it."

Some laughed, Janet sighed, Tim raised his eyes to the heavens, and Baldock tutted. "Mandy, could I have a word? In private?" He looked around. The Square was not busy, but there were still sufficient people nearby to make confidentiality problematic. "Or as near to private as is possible in Benidorm?"

"Sure."

They took their drinks to another table, where Baldock sat facing Mandy, trying to avoid the view beneath her short skirt, and the way her nipples poked through her Midthorpe Maidens T-shirt. Eventually, by fixing his line of sight on the entrance to Beachcombers Bar further down the street, he was able to bring his powers of concentration to bear.

"Last night was unfair. I'm relatively well known, and that photograph is, to say the least, embarrassing for me."

Mandy grinned. "Tough. It's what you get for rising above your proper Midthorpe station."

"Yes, I understand that, but could you manage the lawsuit if it ever goes public?"

The challenge wiped the inane grin from her face.

Baldock pressed his advantage. "You see, if it could be demonstrated that such a photograph was taken without my consent – which it was – and that it could damage my reputation – which it could – you'd be looking at a huge bill in compensation. I'm a famous man. The damages could be so high, that you'd never afford them without selling your house, your car, perhaps even your children and yourself."

"Now hang on a minute, Ray, this was a bit of fun."

"I don't see it in quite the same light."

Baldock fell silent and enjoyed her obvious dismay and discomfort. For the first time since his arrival in this awful town, he felt as if he had some kind of control over events. She looked around, she looked into his eyes, she checked over one shoulder, then the other; she even looked at the mechanical bull, dormant now and covered with a dustsheet, as if it might have some help to offer. Eventually, she took a gulp of her multi-coloured cocktail and honed her concentration.

"So what do you want me to do? Bin the photo?"

"No, not particularly. For one thing, I wouldn't trust that you to get rid of every copy. For all I know, you could have already moved it to cloud storage, or even posted it to your website. No, Mandy, what I want is some kind of compromise. You can keep the photograph on certain conditions."

"Such as?"

Baldock silently congratulated himself. There was some kind of perverse satisfaction to be had from challenging a Midthorper and coming out ahead. He had never managed it as a youngster, but now it was becoming a habit. He had felt the same pleasure during the summer when he bested Ivan Haigh, a shopkeeper with a profitable sideline in stolen car wheels, and he felt it again now that he had Mandy cornered... figuratively speaking.

He leaned forward, lowered his voice, and choosing his words deliberately, he asked, "Are you wearing knickers?"

She guffawed again, drawing attention from the nearby tables where discussions had now begun in earnest. "Course I am. I might like horizontal activities, but I'm not gonna walk through the streets with me skirt up shouting 'come and get it'." She leered at him. "Besides, if you look closely enough, you should be able to see them."

"Pass," Baldock replied. "The man my mother is telling your friends about is causing me any number of problems."

"What? And you want me to drop my trolleys for him so you can blackmail him?"

"No. I think that's what my mother wants you to do. Quite frankly, I'm not sure it will work and if it doesn't, I'm even deeper in the pooh. No, I was thinking more of a favour."

"A favour?" A naughty twinkle had come back to her eye.

"Yes. This man has set me a challenge. I have to persuade a woman to let me take her panties off, and I have to provide photographic evidence of me doing so." He leaned back and relaxed. "It occurs to me that if you would permit me to do that, and allow me to video it, I can take stills from the video, and then we'd be even. And I guarantee that I will do no more than take off your underwear in front of the camera."

"Pity. After what I saw last night—"

"Yes, Mandy. I also guarantee that the video will not see the light of day beyond showing it to him."

Mandy did not waste time thinking about it. "You're damn right it won't because here's how we'll work it. When we're through here, we go back to my room at the Praia and *I'll* video it on my phone. When we're done, I'll either email or bluetooth the video to you."

He remained as doubtful of Mandy as he had been of Masters. "That gives you a hold over me."

"It's a wossname, Brazilian standoff, Ray."

"You mean a Mexican standoff."

"Brazil, Mexico, who gives a toss? I'm married, you know, and Graham turns a blind eye to most of what I get up to, because we make money off my website while I'm doing it. But he doesn't like you. He never did."

"It's mutual," Baldock assured her.

"Yes, well, if he finds a video on YouTube of you taking my clouts off, he'll hit the roof and I'll hit the deck off the end of his fist. After that, he'll come looking for you, and if you remember, he's a big bugger."

Baldock remained nonchalant. "Not impressed. If you recall the stupid picture you took of me last night, and that daft competition, you'll know that I'm a big bugger too."

She chuckled. "In all departments. Listen, Ray, you may be squeezing my booby-doos with the picture I took and filming this kind of stunt—"

"Metaphorically speaking, yes," Baldock agreed.

"What's the weather got to do with it?"

Before Baldock could explain the difference between metaphorical and meteorological, Mandy went on.

"When we're through, I'll have your nuts in a nutcracker."

"Metaphorically speaking."

"There you go again. The sun's shining, Ray. It always

does in Benidorm, and the weather doesn't have nothing to do with what we're on about."

Baldock chuckled generously. "All right, Mandy. It all sounds, er, amicable. A single ground rule, however. Nothing happens other than I take your panties off."

She pouted again. "Shame. You've got one of the biggest —"

"Mandy…"

There was a warning edge to Baldock's voice and she giggled.

"All right. Nothing other than a little knicker-stripping."

Mandy rose and went to join the other Midthorpers. As she did, one of the men got up and crossed over to take her seat opposite Baldock, who struggled for a moment to recognise him.

Wearing a pair of cheap shorts and a South Leeds Stags T-shirt, he appeared to be a few years older than Baldock. Thin and lanky, his dark hair had thinned at the crown, and his skin was pale, other than one or two areas where it had begun to show the pink of an early, Benidorm tan. Baldock concluded that he did not get out often. His brown eyes were sunken and his large ears projected from either side of his head, lending him a simian appearance.

"All right, Ray?" He took out a tobacco tin and began to roll a cigarette, and Baldock's memory clicked into place.

"Ewan Greaves."

Baldock was half-delighted, half-shocked to see a man he had regarded as his only friend in his younger days in Midthorpe. Both loners by nature, neither of them popular with other children and teenagers, Greaves lacked Baldock's intelligence, and on leaving school, while Baldock went to Cambridge, Greaves had never aspired to anything grander than a government training course.

They were the same age, but Greaves had aged terribly. Baldock did not know what Greaves did for a living, but whatever it was, it had not done him any favours appearance-wise.

The two shook hands.

"Well, blow me," Baldock enthused. "I've been with my mother most of the afternoon, and she never told me you were here."

"To be honest, Ray, none of us knew you were here, either, but your ma's just been telling us how you bumped into the hen party last night. Still, it's good to see you. Haven't seen you since you left for Cambridge."

"Well, that's life, Ewan. You lose touch, don't you? So what are you doing with yourself these days?"

"This and that, you know. IT specialist."

Baldock pursed his lips and murmured his approval. "You always were good with technology and that kind of thing. Big company, is it? Your employer?"

Ewan's gaze shifted and he appeared uncomfortable. "No, no. Nowt like that. I'm, self, er, self-employed, you know. Work from home."

"Nothing wrong with that," Baldock approved. "I work at home all the time. When I'm producing a new title, that is. The place can seem like a bit of a prison at times, but you can't have everything. And the big advantage is you can offset a percentage of your household bills against tax. So what is it you do? Security or something?"

"Something like that, yeah. Video and photos. You know."

"We all need to be secure," Baldock said.

He was acutely aware that the conversation was winding down already. How was it possible for two people who had been the closest of friends two decades previously, to have nothing to say now? But then he remembered the main reason others would have nothing to do with them. They were considered boring. If this conversation was anything to go by, the other Midthorpe youngsters had been right.

Greaves puffed on his cigarette. "Your ma was just telling us what this Masters sort has been getting up to. Looks like you're gonna need my help, but I don't have any gear with me, and I'm likely to need some."

"Sorry but the police have my laptop."

"No problem. I've already got one of those. No, Ray, I mean surveillance gear. It's my specialty, you know. Audio and, er, visual surveillance. That kinda stuff. I'll need to buy some tackle, and I'm a bit strapped. I meanersay, we're only here for the weekend and I didn't bring much moolah with me."

"What? Oh. Cash? That won't be a problem. How much are you talking?"

Greaves replied hesitantly. "Coupla hundred euros. Sorry, mate, but this stuff don't come cheap and I will need it."

"No problem." Baldock put on his wealthy front. If it impressed no one else, it would surely impress Greaves. "I'm probably carrying that much. I'll see what my mother has in mind, first."

About to rejoin the Midthorpe crowd, Baldock paused as Tim left his seat and strolled over. As he neared them, Greaves wandered off and Tim's stare followed him.

But just as quickly the stern look descended on Baldock. "Do you know how much you hurt our Lisa last summer?"

Anxious not to get on the wrong side of his mother's closest male friend, yet unwilling to capitulate, Baldock nodded. "Lisa made it quite plain last night, Tim. I apologised and she's forgiven me. Beyond that, I don't think it's any of your concern."

Demonstrating that while he tended to be laid back, easygoing, he was not fazed by confrontation, Tim said, "It's always my concern when someone hurts my girl, just like it's Janet's when someone has a go at you. But if you two are all right, then I'll back off and mind my own." Tim paused. "You are all right?"

"Lisa spent the night with me in the Aranjuez."

Her father grinned. "That's my girl." He glanced again in Greaves' direction. "You and he were big mates when you were kids, weren't you?"

"Yes. A lot of people found him, er, introverted."

"You mean strange."

"I wouldn't say strange, no. And even if he is a bit reserved, he sounds as if he's done well for himself. IT specialist."

Tim laughed. "IT specialist? He's on the dole. He spends

all day pratting about on the internet."

"What? But... Well, how does he afford a weekend in Benidorm?"

"One of his sidelines, I should think. Porn. Takes a lot of porny pics and videos. He reckons he makes more than a sausage sandwich out of it."

"Porn?" Baldock's anger was rising again. His old friend had obviously turned into a true Midthorper, and learned the ability to mask it with convincing waffle.

Tim shushed him. "Keep your voice down, Ray. Yes, porn. Why do you think we need him on this gig? Anyway, come on. Your ma's got it together and she wants to spell it out." Baldock stood, and Tim stayed him. "Word in advance, lad. You're not gonna like this, but we figure it's the only way we can get you and your friend out of the S-H-one-T."

If Baldock was impressed at the firm manner in which his mother held court at the table, he was less than sanguine on her proposed course of action.

"We're all agreed that we need to get this man in a compromising situation, and get it on video," she declared when Baldock joined them. "Mandy, you're happy with that."

"Lead me to him," Mandy said. "I'll give him the time of his life. As long as Ewan can pick up the signal and record it."

Greaves nodded sagely. "Do we know what floor he's on?"

"The eighteenth. Next door to me." Baldock said. "But, listen—"

"In that case, Ray, if we can use your room, we'll be tickety-boo," Greaves declared.

"And how the bloody hell do you suppose I get you through reception and up to my room? Tell them you're my lover?"

"Might work."

"Sod off." Baldock rounded on Janet. "Mother, I'm not happy—"

"We know you're not, luv. That's why we're all here. To help you through this and make you a little happier. Ewan, what kind of range will these receivers have?"

"Hundred yards. If you can get me to the pool at your drum, Ray, I can do it from there."

Baldock's irritation flooded out. "If I can finish a sentence, you don't fight blackmail with blackmail."

"It seems to me that it's exactly the way to fight it," said Michael Shipston, stubbing out a cigarette and rolling another. Shippy, as he was known, appeared as unkempt and unshaven now as he did when Baldock last saw him in the summer. Overweight, looking haggard and bleary-eyed, as if they had just got him out of bed, he went on, "You end up with a Columbian standoff."

Baldock tutted. "For the second time, it is a *Mexican* standoff."

Shippy lit his cigarette. "Columbia, Mexico. Who cares?"

"The people of Columbia and Mexico, I should imagine." Baldock appealed to his mother again. "You can't fight crime by committing worse crimes."

"Exactly what our Lisa would say," Tim volunteered.

"Which is why I didn't ask her along," Janet told them.

"It works for the Mafia," Linda Taplin remarked. "And we're the Midthorpe Mafia. I say get this fella by the nuts and don't let go."

Janet took her son's hand. "Raymond, luv, you're in trouble, and we're trying to help. If you went to the law over it, Masters would carry out his threats against you for landing him in hot water. What we're proposing is not very nice, but it will make him stop and think. Trust us on this."

"Do you know how bad he can make it for me if you go ahead with this?"

"Not as bad as we can make it for him. Isn't that right, Mandy?"

Mandy nodded. "Listen to your mum, Ray. She knows best."

Baldock shook his head, and Janet consoled him again.

"You're to have no direct involvement in this, luv. All you need to do is give Ewan and Mandy the money for the bits and pieces they want."

Beaten, unable to persuade these people to his way of thinking, fervently wishing he had never said anything to his mother, Baldock looked miserably at Greaves and raised his eyebrows.

"I told you. Two ton."

Baldock dipped into his wallet, and came out with €200 which he handed over, then looked at the empty wallet. "Get me a receipt, Ewan. It might be tax deductible."

"And I need about fifty," Mandy told him.

He shrugged. "I'm cleaned out." An idea occurred to him. He needed to be alone with Mandy anyway. Here was the perfect excuse. "Wherever you're going for whatever you want, will they take plastic?"

"I should think so."

"All right. I'll go with Mandy, Mother, but I'm telling you all right now, do whatever you have to, but if anyone asks, I'll deny any knowledge."

Chapter Twenty-Two

With a sinking feeling, Baldock realised that Mandy's destination was a sex shop on the outskirts of the Old Town.

She was thrifty enough to suggest a bus rather than taxi from Winners, and when they got off the bus, not far from Friar's, they wandered up through the main shopping streets, but Mandy was not distracted by the high-priced, branded goods in the classy window displays. Baldock silently applauded her for it. Most women he knew, including his mother, would have taken the better part of an hour to cover the two hundred yards from one end of *Calle Gambo* to the other.

And Mandy was just as focussed and diligent when they walked up the short climb of *Avenida Martinez Alejo*, with its slightly cheaper shops, and turned left into *Plaça de la Creu*, an open, pedestrianised triangle, surrounded by busy eateries, and which led to another, narrower, street of high-class shops, *Passeig de la Carretera*. But no sooner had they stepped into the open area, than she turned sharp right, up a long, narrow street, lined either side by shops, small restaurants, all with residential accommodation on their upper floors, and it was only when Mandy said, "Ah, here it is," that Baldock looked up to find a large, red, vertical sign, declaring 'Sex Shop'.

"Get your wallet out, Ray," She grinned as she made for the door.

Baldock hesitated. He was studying the window display, and uncomfortably aware that of the myriad items on sale, he was uncertain of the purpose of many.

"Er, are you sure about this, Mandy?"

"You want this Masters guy stitched up?"

"Well, I'm not sure—"

"Then this is where we need to be. Come on."

Mandy marched boldly in. Baldock followed more timidly, and he was even more embarrassed to learn that the assistant was not only female, but spoke English about as well as Mandy spoke Spanish and since Mandy's Spanish was limited to *'por favor'* and *'gracias'*, which she pronounced 'grassy arse', he could sense a torrid time ahead.

Utilising a lot of sign language, Mandy managed to make most of her requirements understood, and as she negotiated with the assistant, Baldock looked around the premises with a feeling of dismay bordering on culture shock.

Everyone said sex was a natural phenomenon, but looking around the merchandise on offer, it occurred to him that it was anything but natural.

He was quite accustomed to seeing shop dummies wearing many and varied types of clothing, including frilly underwear, but he had never seen one boasting any kind of proud and erect, strap-on prosthesis, let alone one that was so anatomically accurate.

He had seen magazines before, too, but not like these, and they were published in various languages; Spanish, English, German and French. What did puzzle him was why, like any newsagents, they were ranged on the top shelf. Given the kind of goods the shop traded, and the dedicated clientele who would call, it seemed absurd to put them so high up. The same applied to the DVD videos. While their covers were no worse than many mainstream movies, he had no doubt that the content was much harder, and it seemed pointless putting them out of the reach of children who were not allowed in the shop anyway.

He picked up a metal object, round and bulky at one end, tapered to a rounded point at the other. He was certain the last time he had seen anything remotely like this, it was on the end of a piece of string and used by builders to ensure walls were perpendicular.

"It's a butt plug," Mandy told him while waiting for the attendant to bring out several pairs of lacy knickers. "You jam it up your jacksey for extra pleasure."

Baldock dropped it like it was red hot.

"D'you think your pal would like that kinda thing?"

"I wouldn't know, for the simple reason he is not my pal. I can't stand the man, and I'm sure he feels the same way about me." Baldock's worries began to flood out. "Mandy, I can't say I'm happy with this proposition. I know my mother means well, but I'm shocked that she could come up with such a bizarre idea, and if it doesn't work, I could end up in an even deeper mess."

"Is he gay, this fella?"

"Not as far as I know. He's propositioned several women in our group, and there are rumours that he was having an affair with a woman who died yesterday."

"Then trust your mother. Better yet, trust me. The man hasn't been born who can resist me when I'm hot." Mandy gave him a strange, almost irritated look. "Except you, and I don't know how you—"

"Let's just get on with it, eh?"

Mandy returned to her negotiations with the assistant and, closing his mind to the potential uses and misuses of the equipment for sale, Baldock stood off to one side.

Mandy and the girl were discussing the titillation afforded by a pair of split-crotch panties, when the young woman referred to Mandy as *'señorita'*.

Mandy flashed her wedding ring. "Señora," she declared, pronouncing the word with a hard 'n' and ignoring the more rolling 'nye' afforded by the tilde accent.

"Ah. Sorry." Taking down a pack of novelty condoms, she pointed at Baldock. "*Y, por tu esposo—*"

Baldock interrupted. "I'm not her husband."

He realised instantly that it was not the wisest thing he could have said. The young woman gaped for a moment, then collapsed into a fit of giggles.

"I sorry again. *Por tu amante…*"

"What does that mean, Ray?" Mandy asked as the girl waffled on in broken Spanglish.

"She thinks I'm your lover."

Now Mandy dissolved into giggles.

At length, with an armful of purchases, including the novelty condoms, everything neatly packed into plastic carrier bags declaring *Sex Shop* on the side, Baldock's credit card having been hit with a bill for eighty euros, they stepped out into the shady alley and ambled down the street, back into the bright, afternoon sunshine and soaring temperatures, and soon they were in a taxi on their way back to the *Hotel Praia*.

"You're complaining over the cost," Mandy grumbled, "and here we are taking a taxi. A bus would have saved you a few bob."

"I am not getting on a bus with you or anyone holding three carrier bags telling the world where we've been."

"Oh well. It's your money."

"Yes, and between you, you and Ewan have had a fair slice of it this afternoon."

Back at the Praia, while Mandy marched confidently through the lobby to the lifts, Baldock moved furtively, pulling his sun hat low over his forehead and looking away from the people, staff and guests, milling around the area.

As the lift climbed to the eleventh floor, Mandy berated him for it. "You look like an extra from a James Bond movie. You're attracting more attention that way."

"I have my reputation to think of," Baldock protested as the lift stopped and the doors soughed open.

"Yes, and the way you're behaving, you've just sent it further into the gutter. Now come on."

Slotting her keycard into the lock of room 1102, she pushed open the door and led the way in, and tossed the three carrier bags onto the nearest bed.

"I'm just gonna bell Sandra and tell her not to disturb us for half an hour, then I'll nip into the bathroom and get changed."

"I thought our purpose was to secure this video."

"It is, but you're not gonna take off my normal, everyday trolleys. Oh, no. I need specials on."

"Specials?"

She grinned. "You'll see. Tell you what, though. If I'm gonna help you get the goods on this Masters bloke, I don't understand why you need this video." Her smile turned more lascivious. "Unless it's for your, er, *personal* pleasure."

"Nothing of the kind," Baldock replied injecting as much distaste into his voice as he could muster. "I thought I explained earlier. I need it just in case your plan – correction, my mother's plan – doesn't work."

Mandy disappeared into the bathroom and at a loss for anything to occupy his mind for the moment, his nervousness increasing, Baldock slid open the balcony door and stepped out.

The afternoon sun blazed into the tiny suntrap and broke sweat on his forehead. Screwing up his eyes against the powerful ultraviolet, he put on his Gucci sunglasses and stared down at the pool.

It was, as he expected, busy. Most guests were sunbathing, some preferred the shade. As he looked around the busy area, he could see Sandra Scranton and Linda Taplin. Chloe was there, too, with some of her younger friends. Then he saw his mother, and alongside her was Lisa. Worse than that, when he gazed lustily upon her bikini-clad figure, she looked straight up at him.

Heart pounding, he ducked back in the room.

***

Lisa lowered her shades and stared up at the balcony again. The sun had been in her eyes when she looked up, and she could not be sure, but he was gone.

"That was Raymond."

Janet, on the point of dozing off, stirred. "Hmm? Sorry?"

"Raymond. I just saw him on that balcony up there." Lisa pointed up. "He's gone now."

Janet laughed. "Oh, you have got it bad, haven't you?"

"Got what? Got what bad?"

"Love," Janet replied. "You're so desperate to be with him, you're even seeing him on strange balconies."

"No. Listen to me, Janet. I just saw Raymond on one of the balconies."

Janet patted her hand. "Listen, what would Raymond be doing on a balcony here in the Praia? He's staying next door, and you know how finicky he is. He even paid extra for a room on the top floor of the Aranjuez, so he wouldn't have to mix with the lower classes below, and he probably considers this place a working class dump."

"I swear it was him."

"Someone who looks like him, you mean. I can think of no good reason why he would be here. Can you?"

"No, I can't. But you lot were all meeting at Winners, and Mandy was there."

Janet laughed again. "You don't need to worry on that score. Raymond doesn't like Mandy. He never did."

There was a cautious edge to Lisa's reply. "I know, but it's strange that no one will tell me what went on at Winners."

***

Gripped by complete panic, Baldock was heading for the door when Mandy emerged from the bathroom.

"Hey. Where are you going?"

"I, er, I need to be somewhere else. Urgently."

"Sod that. I haven't gone to all this trouble for nothing."

"We were only making a short video," Baldock pointed out. "It's not like you're going to miss out on an, er, afternoon of passion."

"You never know, Ray."

"I know." He spoke in assured tones which brooked no argument. "Look, Mandy, Lisa is out there. If she learns I'm with you—"

"She won't. Now come on. Let's get this done. I have some sunshine and serious sex waiting for me."

Proving she was not simply the wanton slut he had always considered her, Mandy drew the blinds and switched on the lights. Opening up her smartphone case, she doubled it back upon itself, forming a prop for the phone, and switched it into camera mode. She then positioned it on the dresser, and assessed the lighting, making tiny adjustments to its position until it was as she wanted it.

Starting the recording, she then stood to one side of the bed, and faced the camera.

"Right, Ray, you're gonna need to be slightly to one side of me, or the camera won't catch my drawers coming off."

Eager to be done with the filthy business and out of the room, he strode across, knelt beside her, checked that he was not blocking the camera view, and waited.

"Well go on," she insisted.

"Aren't you going to raise your skirt?"

"Bloody hell. Do you want me to do the job for you?"

Mandy raised her skirt and, looking away, his hands shaking uncontrollably, Baldock whipped her knickers down to ankle level.

"No, no, no." Mandy's temper was on the point of explosion. "For God's sake, Ray, what are you doing?"

"Taking your knickers down."

"You don't just yank 'em down like an old suitcase dragged off the shelf. You have to tease them off. Slowly, gently. Have you never made a porno movie?"

Baldock felt his own temper rising. "Of course not."

"Oh. Right. Okay. No prob. We'll go again." Mandy pulled up her panties and crossed the room to stop the camera. "Before I restart it, let me educate you. You have to lift my skirt, give the camera a good flash of the knickers, then let them down slowly, as if you're trying to turn me – and you – on."

"I didn't think you needed turning on."

"No, but from the look on your face, you do."

"Mandy—"

"Stop worrying about Lisa. She'll never be any the wiser. Now let's go again, and this time, try to do it right."

Mandy restarted the camera, and returned to her spot. Baldock knelt alongside her, still unable to control the shake in his hands. Pushing up her skirt, he found himself confronted with the lacy, split-crotch panties she had bought in the sex shop, and he asked himself why he had not noticed them a few moments ago.

The reason was obvious. Until her outburst, he had not had the courage to look.

Slowly, purposely averting his eyes from the dark thatch at the V of her thighs, he eased them down, past her knees, over her haunches until they were at ankle level, when, leaning on his shoulder for support, she lifted one leg after the other and stepped out of them.

"Smile for the camera, Ray, and show your prize," she told him.

Baldock did as he was told, putting on a forced, sickly smile, and holding up the knickers at chest level. At that point, he also realised that while his face was visible, Mandy's was not. All that could be seen of her were her legs and the dark tangle of pubic hair.

Relieved that the awful job was over, he handed the knickers back, and Mandy stopped the recording before putting them back on.

"I have to get changed and ready for your pal," she said. "Bluetooth is on, on my phone. Switch yours on and pair with mine. Code is factory set, four zeroes. By the time we're paired, I'll be ready and we can transfer the file to you."

"Don't be long," Baldock said, his natural confidence and authority beginning to return. "We have to meet with Ewan before we go to the Aranjuez."

Less than ten minutes later, Mandy attired in high heels, a miniskirt which almost showed her stocking tops and a tight top which exaggerated her already voluminous cleavage, they were back in the lift and on their way down to the pool area, where Baldock ordered Mandy to bring Greaves in.

"I can't go out there. My mother and Lisa are sunbathing. Lisa will see me."

Clucking impatiently, Mandy did as she was told, and returned moments later with Greaves in tow.

He handed Mandy a small, round camera no larger than a cardigan button. "Make sure you place it somewhere where it can catch all the action," he instructed her. "It's magnetic, so you should be able to fasten it to anything metal. Now, Ray, how are you gonna get me into the Aranjuez?"

"With the greatest of difficulty," Baldock admitted. "Do you need to be there?"

Greaves nodded. "The closer the better, as the girl said to her lover's condom."

Chapter Twenty-Three

Passing through the lobby of the Aranjuez, Baldock noticed several police officers about the place, and Suarez talking with Jimenez, the manager.

He assumed they were still making enquiries into Xavier Vardaro's death, but took advantage of their presence to lead Mandy through to the pool exit, where he paused and scanned the crowds taking in the mid-afternoon sun.

After a great deal of debate on the difficulty of getting Greaves into the Aranjuez, they had left him at the Praia, where he took a shaded table by the far perimeter wall, as far from everyone as he could, and where, he had assured them, he would pick up the signal from the fisheye camera he had given Mandy. "As long as Mandy sets it right, Ray, we're in business."

Now, back at the Aranjuez, the police presence made him glad they had left him at the hotel next door.

He scanned the pool area and eventually spotted the Shortly party, on the far side, but they were not on sunbeds. Instead, they sat around a brace of tables close to the bar, deep in debate, like wallflowers ostracised from the general holiday enjoyment.

They were too distant to make out the individual members. Pointing across the pool, towards them, he said to Mandy, "That's our lot. You met Bernie last night, so she'll recognise you. I'm having nothing to do with this idiotic scheme, so I don't even want to see Masters, never mind speak to him. I'll leave you to introduce yourself. Tell them I've gone up to my room to change, or something."

"And how will I know him?"

"He's the oldest man in the group," Baldock replied.

"Leave it with me, Ray. If I don't have this guy in the saddle by half past three, my name's not the Midthorpe Bike."

Wondering how she could be so blasé about such a derogatory nickname, Baldock turned back into the lobby and promptly bumped into Ursula, who smiled diffidently.

"Hello, Ray."

"Hello, Ursula. You can tell Linkman to stop worrying. I've sorted that business."

"Linkman? But—"

"Pulling panties off," Baldock interrupted. "It's done. Did you enjoy your walk on the beach?"

She shrugged. "Ian's a complete numpty."

"I'm sorry?"

"When we left you, we went down to the beach, like you suggested, and he's still wearing these loafers. You should have seen him trying to walk on the sands in them. In the end, I had to tell him to take them off and walk in his socks. Honestly he knows nothing except how to cry over Xavier."

Baldock disregarded most of her tale. "He's wearing socks?"

She looked down at his feet. "Unlike you."

"I passed on the tatty loafers too." Pointing to the expensive, brand name espadrilles on his feet, he gave her a withering smile, and while she carried on to the poolside, he stepped into the lobby.

Once more he noticed Suarez talking with Jimenez. He thought no more of it as he strode to the lift, but at a nod from the manager, the inspector detached himself from the reception desk and hurried over.

"Señor Baldock, please wait."

Baldock stopped by the lift doors, turned and faced the policeman. "What is it, Inspector?"

"I have to speak to you."

"Again? "Baldock displayed no intentions of moving one way or the other even as the lift doors opened. "Why?"

"All will become clear. Please come with me." The inspector gestured towards the counter.

"I'm a British citizen," Baldock announced grandly, "and I think this might constitute harassment."

"I know you are British, señor, but this is España, and you will come with me or I will have you arrested."

Baldock opened his mouth to protest but Suarez carried on speaking.

"Señor, I do not have time to fool around, and I do not want to speak to you here in the lobby where anyone may be listening. I wish to speak to you on a matter of great urgency, but I will do so only in private. Now please come with me before I call for officers to bring you."

Suarez turned away and marched back to reception. Baldock considered ignoring him, but the prospect of being arrested and how it might appear in the British press (he was certain it *would* appear in the British press) swayed him and he followed meekly.

The inspector led him through the pass door to the side of reception, and once inside, to the manager's private office, where once again Suarez took the seat behind the desk and waved Baldock into the chair opposite.

"I was told you can be very determined, señor, but I did not realise it until this morning." Suarez said. "I have no desire to embarrass you in public, so is better that we speak in here."

"I know my rights," Baldock insisted, "and I have already told you that if you think I murdered Xavier Vardaro, then produce some evidence."

"And I will perhaps. But first, I need to establish a few facts." Suarez checked an A4 pad at his right elbow on which was a scrawl of notes. "Shortly Publishing. This is a curious name for a company."

"It's a sort of alliteration," Baldock explained. "An in-joke. Authors, especially the self-publishing ones, are always saying 'I'll be publishing shortly' and that's where the name came from… at least that's my understanding."

"Ah your famous British sense of humour which no one in the world can understand but the British."

"It's quirky," Baldock agreed.

Suarez checked his pad again. "Would it be true to say, Señor Baldock, that you do not like your employer, Mr Gil Masters?"

Baldock gave a ruefully humorous twitch of the head. "I think there's some misunderstanding here. Masters is not my employer. He is my publisher. I'm a well-known author and my work is published by Shortly, but I don't work for them. I'm self-employed."

With Baldock-like haughtiness, Suarez ignored almost everything Baldock said. "I ask again, señor, you do not much like Señor Masters."

"Speaking frankly, I can't stand him. He's arrogant to say the least. Autocratic, dictatorial and completely self-obsessed."

"So you argue with him?"

"I'm sorry?"

"The other members of your party, they say you and Masters you argue a lot since you have been here."

Baldock chewed his lip. "It's complicated, but he's using strongarm methods on many of us. Not just me. I was the only one who had the balls to stand up to him. Look, Inspector, may I ask, is he in any trouble."

"No, señor, but one who argued with him is in trouble. Your dispute with Señor Masters, this led to arguments, si? Some of them very angry?"

"There have been some heated exchanges, yes. That's not illegal, is it? Even in Spain?"

"No, señor, it is not. But to murder Mr Masters because of these arguments is illegal. Even in España."

Baldock chuckled. "I should think so, too. It's still illegal in England to… MURDER?"

Suarez nodded slowly, gravely.

The first thought that crossed Baldock's mind was, *I didn't have to go through that disgusting farce with Mandy.*

"And now you must tell me, señor, when did you last see Señor Masters?"

Baldock was still trying to absorb the news, and had to think about it. "I… I'm not sure exactly. We'd had dinner last night, and we were making our way to the Square. My agent and I, Ms Bernadette Deerman, got separated from the rest of the party somewhere along *Calle Gerona*. Close to the Red Lion. And I think after that we saw them going into *Café Benidorm*. Ms Deerman and I went into Winners. If I saw Masters at all, it was then."

"He was not at breakfast this morning, and he did not arrive for lunch. Your fellow party members have told me this, and of course, I have been waiting to speak to him again on the killing of Señorita Vardaro."

"I can't speak about lunch. I wasn't here. I was with my mother at a restaurant called *Friar's* on *Carrer el Pont*."

"I know *Friar's*. Permit me to tell you, Señor Baldock. Some people in your party suggested he may have gone to Valencia or Alicante on business. But just before one o'clock, the maid went into room 1808 to clean and she found Señor Masters face down in a bathtub full of water. Our medical examiner says he had been dead for many hours, but we do not know precisely when he died."

"So he could have been drunk, slipped and drowned himself," Baldock said.

"He could certainly have drowned, señor, but drunk or sober, it was not by accident. He had a large wound on the back of his head. He had been struck with a bronze bust of Joaquin Rodrigo. I'm told there is one in every room of the top floor."

Baldock had wondered who the bust was in his room, and now he knew and understood. Rodrigo had composed the ever-popular *Concierto de Aranjuez*, a dedication to the Aranjuez Palace, after which the hotel was named.

He brought his mind to bear on the matter at hand. "You're sure he was struck by this bust?"

"It was in the bath."

"Where the water would conveniently dispense with any forensic evidence."

"This is correct. Tell me, Señor Baldock, are you of the weak stomach?"

"I, er, no. I don't think so."

Suarez removed a large photograph from beneath the A4 pad, spun it round and pushed it across the desk for Baldock to study.

Masters was naked, face down in the water, which filled the bath to the brim and had spilled over, as was evident from his white dressing gown cast on the floor beside the bathtub. The wound at the back of his head was clearly visible as a large patch of dried blood. Looking away from the body, into the tub, the bust of Rodrigo could be seen under the water. None of the toiletries and other bathing accoutrements appeared to have been disturbed.

Baldock passed the photograph across the table and Suarez slipped it back beneath the A4 pad.

"At what time were you in the Square last night?"

"Again, I can't be certain but I think it must have been about ten thirty or a little after."

"This is what the others tell me. Yet you did not go into *Café Benidorm*?"

"No. I told you, my agent and I went into Winners instead. My mother and her friends were there."

"Let me tell you what we know, Señor Baldock. We know that almost as soon as he went into *Café Benidorm*, Señor Masters left and he came back here. We know this because the keycards for rooms on the eighteenth floor are very special. They record the times they are used on the hotel computer. He left his key at reception when he went out, and he collected it at ten minutes after eleven. He used it to open his room door at eleven fifteen." Suarez leaned forward and put some steel into his voice in what Baldock imagined was an attempt at intimidation. "We also know that you returned to the hotel and entered your room at eleven twenty."

With typical step-by-step caution, Baldock mentally ran through his options; laugh, shout, scream, swear.

He elected for calm rebuttal. "No, I didn't. I left Winners at just before midnight and I didn't get back here until about half past, and I had a young woman with me."

"The word of a Benidorm good-time girl will not count for much, señor."

This time, Baldock could not avoid irritation. "The woman in question is not a Benidorm tart. She is my girlfriend. Her name is Lisa Yeoman and she's staying at the Praia, next door. I signed her in here as my guest at about half past midnight, and I was with her the whole night."

"Señor Baldock, we know that your key was used at eleven twenty to open your room door. I believe you went to Señor Masters' room and argued with him. I believe he could prove you murdered Señorita Vardaro. I believe this led to an argument and you killed him and then left again to rejoin your friends and your mother and your girlfriend at Winners in time to come back for half past midnight."

"And I believe you're an idiot, but I can't prove it."

"Señor—"

"Listen to me. I can *prove* I was at Winners at eleven twenty last night. I was taking part in some stupid game, and a number of people took photographs. Not only that, but the manager or proprietor or whatever he is, gave me a drink on the house for being a good sport."

"This proves nothing. Those bars are so busy they will not recall the time. And the photographs could have happened at any time."

"Digital photographs have a time and date stamp, Inspector. And if you imagine I could get everyone to alter the time on their phones and cameras, then you really are a fool."

"Your room key was used at eleven twenty last night."

"My room key was with me. What you mean is someone used a key to get into my room."

Chapter Twenty-Four

Baldock's announcement brought Suarez up short. He pondered for a moment, then snatched up the telephone. After delivering gabbled instructions in rapid Spanish, he put down the receiver. "You, señor, will write down the names of some people who took these photographs." He tore off a sheet from his A4 pad, and pushed it across the desk.

"Of course." Baldock fished into his shoulder bag for a pen and began to write out as many names as he could remember. "With the exception of Mrs Deerman, these people are all staying at the Praia."

As he was writing out the names of Mandy Cowling and Linda Taplin, Jimenez entered the office and sat at right angles to Suarez and Baldock.

"I have checked, Inspector, and the door to Señor Baldock's room was opened at eleven twenty. There can be no doubt."

"Using a key for the room or a pass key?" Baldock demanded.

"A room key, señor. A passkey would show a different code."

Baldock passed the handwritten sheet to Suarez. "And does the code for the key that was used match the code for the key you issued?"

"Si, señor. All keys to a particular room are given the same code."

"Well, it wasn't mine."

"It has to be," Jimenez insisted. "There are four keys to your room, señor, and the other three are in reception where they should be."

"I repeat, it was not mine. I was not here at that time."

"Is it possible the time is wrong?" Suarez asked.

"If so, then every time in the log is wrong," Jimenez replied.

"I want you to check the keys," Suarez demanded. "Ensure that there really are three keys to Señor Baldock's room in reception. And I do not mean count them. I mean check that they are what they are supposed to be."

With a slightly grovelling half bow, Jimenez left the room again.

"You're beginning to believe me?" Baldock asked.

"I am giving you the benefit of the doubt, señor. That is all."

Jimenez was gone for some time. Suarez passed part of it by ringing his officers and instructing them to go to the *Hotel Praia* and chase up the photographs, while Baldock ran various scenarios through his mind asking himself who would want access to his room at that hour.

It was only when Jimenez returned carrying a laptop that the penny finally dropped.

"Señor Baldock," the manager said, "I must apologise on behalf of the *Hotel Aranjuez*. I think I know what has happened."

"It would be well for you to explain," Suarez insisted.

"You can see for yourself on the video recording," Jimenez said, and began to run the CCTV video on the laptop.

Without sound, it showed a view of the reception desk, and the timestamp read 2310. Masters, still wearing his bright orange T-shirt and dark shorts, entered through the automatic doors, approached reception and asked for his key. The clerk, Francisco, the same one who signed Lisa in an hour or more later, handed over the key and Masters walked off towards the lift. He had gone only a few yards when he stopped, came back and there was an amused exchange between him and the clerk, during which Masters handed back the key and was issued with another before walking off to the lifts.

"Explain," Suarez insisted.

"Francisco, the night clerk logged the incident but thought nothing of it," Jimenez said. "But Señor Masters asked for the key to room 1807, which is the room of Señor Baldock. He walked off, then returned and explained he had asked for the wrong key. He was laughing about it. Jet lag, he told our assistant."

"Jet lag?" Baldock demanded, eyes wide. "We're only two hours from England."

"This I know," Jimenez replied. "I think he was making the English joke. Si? He then asked for room 1808, and he was issued with it. As you can see, he returned the key to room 1807. But he did not. He gave Francisco the key to room 1422, and Francisco did not check it. He simply put it back in the rack with the other keys to 1807. It is only now, when I have checked it that we know what has happened. The clerk will be told about this when he arrives for work later this afternoon." Jimenez' worried eyes darted from Suarez to Baldock and back. "It was a simple mistake. A moment of lapse by my clerk."

"Perhaps," Baldock said. "But it wasn't a lapse on Masters' part. It was deliberate. He will have observed your clerks at work and guessed he could pull a little substitution stunt on them. And all because he wanted access to my room."

Both men studied him. "How can you know this?" Suarez asked.

"Because I know why he wanted the key to my room. He was planting evidence to incriminate me in Ms Vadaro's murder. If we search my room, we'll find some kind of evidence. I don't know what, but it will be there."

Both men studied him intently, and he felt a glow of pride under their astonished stares.

"I think I know what's been going on. Ms Vadaro took my laptop on Masters' instructions. I guess he was making changes to the contract stored on there. Xavier probably kicked back at him, refused to play ball, they argued and he killed her. Maybe by accident, maybe deliberately. Perhaps she was already dead when he threw her off the balcony. He left the laptop in her room to ensure that you would question me. And late last night he tricked his way into my room to plant more incriminating evidence."

"But who killed Señor Masters?"

Baldock shrugged. "One of our party, for sure. But it wasn't me. You say he had been dead for many hours, but I never left my room last night, and I have someone who can vouch for that."

"Your Señorita..." Suarez checked the list of names Baldock had given him. "...Ye-oh-man. But you say she is your girlfriend, and it may be that you have persuaded her to back up your story."

Baldock sighed. "I did not kill Gil Masters. I never saw him after Bernie Deerman and I lost the Shortly crowd in The Square."

Suarez laid his hand flat on the desk. "I am inclined to believe you, señor, but there is some doubt, and I will again give you the benefit of that."

Baldock's mind slid into overdrive. How would Headingley handle this?

On an impulse, he asked, "Señor Jimenez, do you have security cameras on the upper floors?"

The look of shock on Jimenez' face led Baldock to assume he had just asked whether the hotel provided prostitutes as an additional service for VIP guests. "This would be an invasion of your privacy, señor, and guests like you, on the top floor, are our most influential. We would not do this."

"Very well. You said the key Masters handed back was to room 1422. Who is staying in that room?"

"Señorita Franklyn and Señorita En-der-by."

Baldock's eyes lit. "Then it was definitely *not* a mistake. Since Ms Vardaro's killing, Ms Franklyn has been acting as Masters's secretary, and I think you should question her, Inspector."

"You think she was involved?"

"Almost certainly. Masters returned to his room, then came out again to plant evidence in my room."

The manager shook his head. "Pardon me, Señor Ballcock,

sir—"

"Baldock."

"Yes, sir, Señor Baldock. What you say is not possible. To have done that, Señor Masters could not get back into his room without using the key again, and that would have registered on our system. There is no alert until Juanita, the chambermaid, went in at 12:45 today."

Baldock shook his head. "Not necessarily. Correct me if I'm wrong, but the system only works when someone *enters* the room, doesn't it?"

"That is right," Jimenez said. "It is security. When you leave your room, you do not need the key, and the door locks automatically behind you. We do not need to know when you leave the room. That would invade your privacy. But when you enter, the use of the key registers on the computer. That is one of our security affairs."

"So Masters could have left his room without you knowing it, and gone to my room?"

"Si, señor. But as I have already said, when he returned to his room he would have used the key and we would know it on the computer. He did not use the key a second time."

"I can show you how that's done." Baldock concentrated on Suarez. "Inspector, did you find any Sellotape in Masters' room?"

"Sellotape?"

"Adhesive tape. Such as you might find in any office." Baldock glanced around the manager's office and his eyes lighted on a tape dispenser sitting on a filing cabinet. He pointed to it. "Like that."

"Ah, I understand. I am not sure. Why?"

Baldock picked up Ursula Franklyn's key. "Think about how these keys work. You insert the card in the lock, take it out, the light turns green and then you can operate the handle. But that handle locks again once the door is closed, so if you let yourself out without a keycard you can't get back in."

As Baldock went on, Suarez made hurried notes, and Jimenez listened with increasing horror.

"What you can do is press the lock back into the door and

tape it there so that when it closes, although the handle cannot be operated, the door is not locked. If Masters did that, he could then cut along to my room plant whatever evidence he was planting, a matter of just a few minutes, then return to his room and let himself in without needing his key. To the hotel's computer system it looks as if he let himself in and never came out, and it also looks as if I let myself in and because I came back later, it also looks as if I've been in, left again, and come back again. That makes me the perfect patsy for his murder."

"I see what you are saying, señor," Suarez agreed, "but still it does not make sense. It would seem that Señor Masters knew he was going to be murdered and decided to make you the, er, pasty, as you put it."

"Patsy, not pasty. And I apologise. I meant the patsy for Ms Vadaro's murder. As it happens, it's worked out kindly for Masters's murderer, but I doubt that he was aware of it."

The manager still would not accept it. "I do not believe our rooms are so insecure."

Baldock shrugged more comfortably this time. "Bring me some of that tape and I'll show you. It doesn't have to be tape, either. Blue-tack, plasticine, er silly putty the Americans call it. You can even use chewing gum. A thin wedge of paper in the door might work, but it could be risky. It might dislodge when you close the door."

"Forgive me, Señor Baldock, but you seem to know much about this."

"I write crime fiction, remember."

Suarez smiled. "Then perhaps your super-sluice, Detective Inspector Headingley can tell us who did kill Señor Masters."

"Not necessarily. But I can tell you who didn't. Me."

"I am beginning to believe you, señor, but I cannot permit you to leave the country until I am sure.

"Yes, well, I may be able to help if I can check my laptop. I know a man staying at the *Hotel Dolce*, an old friend from back home, who could examine it and tell us whether or not anything has been changed."

"And you think we do not have such experts here in

Spain?"

"I'm sure you do, but will they have the fluent grasp of English that may be needed?"

Suarez considered this. "I accept what you say. But I insist that this man comes here and he will examine your computer under our surveillance and supervision."

"Very well. I'll get onto him."

"You may go, señor, and thank you for your help."

Relieved that the interview was over, at least for the time being, Baldock stood. "Oh. Am I permitted to visit my friends and my mother at the *Hotel Praia*?"

"Of course, but you must not leave Benidorm without letting me know, and none of your party will be allowed to leave Spain until I am satisfied that there is no involvement."

Chapter Twenty-Five

Baldock made his way back through the lobby and stepped out into the pool area, and was surprised to learn that he had been with Suarez for an hour.

His anger reduced to irritation, it rose again when his eyes fell on the Shortly party, still taking up tables that stood back from the swimming pool. Ursula Franklyn had some explaining to do.

But even as he strode in their direction, a police officer spoke to Ursula and escorted her past him and into the lobby. Chewing spit, Baldock carried on and joined the remaining members of the party.

Bernie greeted him with a weak smile. "You've heard about Gil?"

"I've just spent an hour with the police and all but been accused of murdering both him and Xavier." He signalled a waiter and ordered a coke before sitting down next to Bernie. "I met Ursula at the door an hour ago. How come she didn't tell me Gil was dead?"

Bernie shrugged. "She probably thought you already knew."

Baldock let it go as it occurred to him that Harry Ingels was missing. "Masters was in my room last night," he said, dismissing thoughts of his fellow author. "I think he was planting something on me."

Bernie's eyebrows shot up and the others took a sudden interest in him. "Why?" his agent asked.

"To frame me for Xavier's murder. I think Ursula might know more than she was letting on." He accepted his soft drink from the waiter with a grunt of thanks, and drank gratefully from the glass before explaining to them all what had happened with Masters and the keycards and his theory of the laptop theft.

"It's funny you should say that, Raymond," Phillipa said when he was through. "Gil asked if he could borrow my laptop during the flight yesterday."

"I remember."

"And he borrowed Harry's at Stansted." said Tiffany Pittock. "What has he been up to?"

"I don't know," Baldock admitted and drank more coke. "But I have a man in the hotel next door who may be able to find out. An old friend. He's an IT specialist. The police will let him look at my computer, under their supervision. I'm still betting Ursula knows more than she's been saying."

"She probably wouldn't dare say anything," Ian Linkman said. "Not the way Gil behaved."

"Well he's no longer a part of the equation, is he, and if the cops can't get her to talk, I'll bet I can." He glanced around the tables again and frowned. "Harry. Where is he?"

Bernie smirked, Linkman blushed and so did Katy, while Phillipa laughed and Tiffany struggled to control her mirth.

"I've obviously cracked the joke of the century," Baldock remarked.

"Unwittingly, Ray," Tiffany said. "That friend of yours, Amanda? She joined us and honestly, I've never seen a woman work on a man so fast. Within five minutes, she'd asked to see the view from his bedroom and they were on their way to Harry's room."

Baldock began to shake. He felt his blood run cold as he stared frantically up at the tower block.

"I think Harry must be sleeping it off," Katy commented. "I saw your friend leave about twenty minutes ago."

He transferred his gaze to the Praia next door. "Oh, my God, no. Excuse me, everyone. I, er, I have to see, er… my mother. Yes. That's it. I have to see my mother. Back soon."

He leapt to his feet, and unaware of their astonished eyes following him, hurried through the lobby and out onto the street, where he turned left and scurried down the street to the Praia. After a garbled explanation to the reception clerk, he was allowed through to the pool area, where he found Mandy sitting with Ewan Greaves.

"Mandy, please tell me you didn't—"

"Oh, hiya, Ray," she cut in. "I dealt with your boss. Tell you what, though, you never told me what a porker he is. Talk about a tub of lard."

Baldock covered his face for a moment. "Oh, God, please tell me this isn't happening."

Mandy was momentarily worried. "What is it, Ray? What's wrong?"

"Gil Masters is dead."

Mandy screwed up her face into what she probably imagined was a judicious pout. "Well, I must admit I've been with livelier men. I had to do all the work. But even so, he was still alive when I left him."

"No, you sackless tart. Masters really is dead. You weren't with Masters. You were with a writer called Harry Ingels."

Mandy appeared ready to take umbrage at being called a sackless tart, but she tittered instead. "Oops."

"Oops? Is that all you can say?"

"Well what do you expect me to say? You told me he was the oldest man at the table, so I hit on him. And I must say, he was all for it." She chewed her lip.

"You didn't even have the brains to ask with whom am I having the pleasure?"

"Names, shmames. Men are all the same lying down… well, nearly all the same. Bloaters like him are a bit different." She chewed her lip some more. "I wish I hadn't been quick to upload it now."

More terror struck through Baldock. "Upload it? You weren't supposed to upload anything."

"I know, but he got a bit stroppy when we were through. I said to him, I said, 'if you don't want your wife to know about this, you leave Ray Baldock alone'. He lost it then. Started ranting about you and how he didn't know what I was talking about. Anyway, push comes to shove, he threw me out. He didn't even let me pick my knickers up. I had to knock on the door and ask for them back. So I got a bit mad and uploaded the video to my porn site."

Baldock looked from her to Ewan and back again. "I thought Ewan was dealing with the recording."

"I was," Ewan replied.

"Yeah, well I don't trust you not to bugger it up," Mandy said to Greaves. Concentrating once more on Baldock, she explained, "So I set my phone on video. Quality is a bit naff, but I'm sure his missus will recognise him… or maybe not."

Baldock's head span. "What? What do you mean, his missus will recognise him or maybe not?"

"Well, I titled it, 'Rogering Gil Masters', and if he wasn't Gil Masters…" Mandy trailed off, her meaning clear.

Baldock groaned, buried his head in his hands and shook it from side to side in an effort to make it all go away. "Masters is dead, and aside from his widow having to learn that he's been murdered, she'll be confronted with a hardcore porn video of you doing the business with Harry Ingels in Masters' name. Why do I listen to you people? Why didn't I just tackle him on my own?"

Mandy patted him on the shoulder. "Don't beat yourself up, Ray. We all make mistakes. Even you."

He shrugged her off. "The biggest mistake I made was trusting you to carry out a task which you normally find so easy. You need to remove the video. Now."

She frowned. "Bit difficult. It's already out there and I have four thousand followers on that site. It's probably been viewed a few thousand times already." She chuckled delightedly. "It could even go viral. Especially when everyone learns Gil Masters is dead." She held up her hands, fingers and thumbs forming a rectangle and spread her arms as if spelling out a banner headline. "Gil's last shag." She giggled again. "Or… or… Gil Masters R.I.P. Rest In Pussy."

Baldock groaned. "Give me strength." Forcing control upon himself, he said, "Mandy, you have to take that video down."

"I will. Just as soon as I can."

"And I'd better explain to Harry what's been going on."

"Shunt worry about him," Ewan said. "I think he enjoyed it overall."

Flopping onto a chair alongside Ewan, Baldock made an effort to pull himself together. He would have been in the clear had not Mandy threatened Harry, and when he returned to the Aranjuez, the tubby Lancastrian would undoubtedly have something to say. Right now, however, he had more worries than a rogue pornographic video, and he needed to pull himself together.

"Have either of you seen my mother or Lisa?"

"Funny thing, that," Ewan said, sucking on a beer. "The cops took 'em both into the hotel about half an hour ago. They asked who I was and when I told 'em, they ordered me to stay put." He grinned. "Good job I shut the laptop lid. If they'd seen what I was recording—"

"Yes, yes. I get the picture. Did the police ask for your phone, Mandy?"

"I wasn't here. Remember?"

"Of course not. But they will…, oh my God, and they'll want to see the photos."

Mandy shrugged. "No sweat. I don't care who sees 'em. If I did, I wouldn't put 'em online." She yawned and stretched, thrusting out her impressive breasts. "I'm off for a kip. Nice working with you, Ray."

Baldock shuddered again as she left. He had terrifying visions of his mother, Lisa and the Midthorpe Maidens and himself locked up in an Alicante jail until the Spanish justice system sorted out the confusion.

As if reading his mind, Ewan said, "They wanted to see Lisa's phone and your mam's. And they were asking about Linda Taplin and Sandra Scranton, and Mandy."

Baldock nodded. If nothing else, the timestamps on those phones would go some way to getting him off the hook, leaving him only with the problem of Harry Ingels.

Thoughts of Suarez reminded him of his other problem. "Ewan, someone has been fooling around with my laptop. We're not sure how, but we think it might have been Masters. You promised you'd take a look at it for me."

"No problem, Ray. Got it with you?"

"Not exactly. It's over at the Aranjuez and the police won't let me have it back. I've got their agreement that you can check it over, but you have to do it while one of theirs is watching you."

Greaves stroked his chin thoughtfully. "Not sure about that, Ray. I don't like the cops watching what I'm up to. You never know what they're gonna cook up agin me, what with me being a Midthorper and all."

"You're in Spain, for Christ's sake. They don't know about Midthorpers here."

"Ray—"

"Ewan, I'm in trouble. I told you Masters is dead. Well, the police think I murdered him."

Greaves took out his tobacco tin and began to roll a cigarette. Baldock waited patiently until the smoke was lit, at which point Greaves decided to answer.

"It strikes me that if I look at your computer and it turns out this Masters bloke has been fiddling and faffing it, then you'd have a bigger motive for killing him." He blew a cloud of thin smoke into the clear air, as if placing a full stop to his conclusion.

"That hasn't escaped me, but I didn't kill him." Baldock waved away the cloud of carcinogens. "Listen, Ewan, if I can demonstrate that Masters did do something to my laptop, then it's likely he did the same to other writers and agents, and that gives all of them a motive. He was trying to pull some really dirty stunts."

"Yeah. I know. Mandy told me what you'd told her."

Baldock's heart sank again. "So much for secrecy. If you lot worked for MI6, the country would be under Russian rule."

"Or American."

"No. We're already under American rule. Ewan, will you please help me."

Greaves took another pull on his cigarette. "It'll be difficult. Yeah, okay, Ray. Anything for an old pal. But remember, if the cops ask, I'm an IT specialist."

"Not a porn merchant?"

"Not a porn merchant."

Chapter Twenty-Six

After a gruesome grilling from the Spanish police, during which they learned of Masters' death in the early hours of the morning, both Janet and Lisa were grateful to get back out into the sun, even if the exterior was no cooler.

They emerged from the lobby of the Praia in time to see Baldock and Greaves leaving the hotel for the Aranjuez, and after securing drinks from the pool bar, they sat apart from the rest of the Midthorpe Maidens, where Lisa made no bones about her position.

"I was with Raymond all night, and I know he's innocent, despite what the local police might think."

"Of course he's innocent, dear," Janet replied. "Many things have happened to change my son since he left for Cambridge, but at heart he is the same as he always was; non-violent."

Lisa frowned. "Are you saying he's a coward?"

"Good lord, no. He's not afraid of putting his point of view, and he's more than ready to confront anyone, but he just doesn't believe in violence. From what he told me of this Masters, it would be enough to drive any man to fighting, but not our Raymond."

Lisa took a large swallow of coke and ran the chilled glass across her forehead in an effort to soak up some of the sweat.

"It's more effective if you press it to the back of your neck, luv. There's some kind of temperature controlling doings there."

Lisa did so, and silently applauded Janet for her knowledge... or her ability to get old wives' tales across.

"I'll be blunt, Janet. I feel like I'm left out here. Not by Raymond. I'm sure he'd have brought me bang up to date, but by the rest of you."

"How do you mean, Lisa?"

"Earlier today, you, Linda Taplin, Sandra Scranton and Mandy all met at Winners. Dad rang me and told me he and a few of the men were there, too. Yet no one will tell me what went on. I'm guessing it was to do with Raymond's troubles. It was some kind of problem he had with Masters. Now, I knew about them. He told me first thing this morning."

"And did he tell you how much worse they had got?"

"Worse? You mean Masters' death?"

"No. We didn't know about it at the time. I mean the way Masters was trying to drag that nice agent of Raymond's, that Bernie, into bed."

"No. Raymond never said a word."

"He probably didn't know. Not then. According to what he told me, she only told him at breakfast, and that would have been after you'd left him. Anyway, the thing is, Lisa, Masters was playing some really dirty games and the only way to stop someone like that is to play even dirtier. So we came up with a plan to nail him."

"A dirty plan?"

"A very dirty plan."

"Which is why that creep Greaves was here instead of being at his own hotel with the men."

Janet drifted onto a sidetrack . "Oh, you find him creepy, too, do you?"

"I always did. I never understood why he and Raymond were friends. Talk about chalk and cheese."

"They were both nerds, Lisa, but Raymond was always cleverer. Anyway, to get back to what I was saying, we needed to play really dirty and it's just not your style."

Lisa huffed. "Thank you, Janet."

"Don't take on, so," Janet said. "It's not a criticism. You are a hard-working, honest young woman, and I'm pleased that you and Raymond have made up your quarrel. But you're like him: honest, and if you had been faced with what Raymond told me, you'd have tried to deal with this Masters the *legal* way, and it wouldn't work. The things he was doing were not legal, but they were cleverly set up so that there would never be any way to prove it. The only way you can fight that is to fight even more illegally than he did, so we set Mandy up as a honey trap. She didn't mind... if truth be told, she was looking forward to it."

"But he was dead, Janet."

"Yes, well, we didn't know that at the time. What I'm saying is our way would have worked. Yours wouldn't, so we kept you out of it. If it's any consolation, we kept Raymond out of most of it too, but he had to be with us because he paid for the bits and pieces Ewan and Mandy needed. Now come on, don't be offended, just tell me how you and Raymond are getting on." A naughty twinkle came to Janet's eyes. "Judging from the way you keep seeing him on strange balconies, I think you're falling in love with him."

"Possibly," Lisa replied with a sigh. "He's taking me to dinner tonight... if I ever get to see him. He went out with you earlier today, and I haven't seen him since. I've just noticed him leaving the hotel with Ewan Greaves."

"That'll be something to do with his computer," Janet was obviously pleased to hear Lisa's report on the putative relationship, and she went on to reassure Lisa. "Raymond will get to you. Oh to be young, like you, and so much in love you can't bear to be without him for one minute."

"I don't know about love. It's very early days, and we've only just made up our differences from June." Lisa tried a weak smile. "Don't go ordering any wedding outfits yet."

"Or baby clothes?"

This time Lisa laughed aloud, causing a few heads to turn their way. "Definitely no baby clothes. If Raymond asked me to give up everything, marry him tomorrow and move to Norfolk, you still wouldn't need baby clothes. I'm far too happy in my work to think about a family."

***

Back at the Aranjuez, after informing a police officer of their arrival, Baldock and Greaves sat at a table around the pool, away from the rest of the Shortly party. When Ursula reappeared, Baldock was about to cross the sunlit poolside and confront her, when the same police officer reappeared and informed him Inspector Suarez wished to see him again.

Instructing Greaves to stay where he was, Baldock accompanied the officer into the lobby and through the pass door to Señor Jimenez' office, where Suarez was studying a selection of photographs.

"Ah, Señor Baldock. Please sit." Suarez waved him to the chair opposite. "My officers have spoken to several ladies." The inspector consulted his A4 pad. "Señora Janet Baldock, who I think is your mother, Señora Linda Taplin, Señora Sandra Scranton and Señorita Lisa Yeoman. All of them had photographs of you taken in Winners last night."

Suarez frowned his disapproval and held up a photograph of him with his underpants around his ankles, and for a moment Baldock felt like a naughty schoolboy facing an irate headmaster.

"I have to say, señor, having seen photographs like this, it is people like you who give Benidorm its bad name."

Colour rushed to Baldock's cheeks. Reluctant to express his outrage, he opted for the lesser evil of apologising. "I, er, now look... Oh, er... Yes. Quite. I'm sorry."

"Putting that to one side, the various times on the photographs tell me that you were at Winners between ten thirty-five and eleven thirty yesterday evening. I am satisfied that you could not have returned to the Aranjuez, entered your room, and then gone back to Winners in the time limits I have seen. It confirms that Señor Masters borrowed the key to your room and it was he who went in, not you. I will have something more to say on this in a few minutes. First, I need you to understand, señor, that because we do not yet have a true time of death, I cannot clear you from my list of suspects."

"But Ms Yeoman—"

"It is true that Señorita Yeoman says you were with her all night, but she also agrees that she is your girlfriend. For all I know, you and she may have, er, made up this tale. I do not believe that she is lying and I do not believe you are the killer, but I cannot positively say this, so I cannot remove you as a suspect. You understand?"

Again Baldock was not disposed to argue. "Perfectly."

"Good. Then let us move on to other matters. I have spoken to Señorita Franklyn. Before I tell you what she has said, I must first tell you that these matters are of little interest to me unless they can be, er, linked to the death of Señor Masters. Si?"

"I understand."

"Excellent. When I questioned her, Señorita Franklyn admitted that her employer, Señor Masters, told her to approach reception and tell them she had lost her key, for which she had to pay twenty euros for it to be replaced. She told me this was, er…" Once again, Suarez consulted his notes. "Pork pie. My English, Señor Baldock, is good, but I do not understand why reporting a lost key has anything to do with an English delicacy from the pub, but further testimony from Señorita Franklyn hints that it was untrue. She had not lost her key."

"Pork pie is rhyming slang," Baldock explained. "Pork pie – lie. It means she was lying when she said she had lost her key."

"This is so. I have just said." Suarez chuckled. "What a curious language is yours. We have nothing like this *en Español*. Señorita Franklyn says she does not know why Señor Masters tells her to do this, but with the testimony of Señor Jimenez, the manager, I think we know why."

"He wanted her key so he could trick the clerk into giving him my room key last night."

"Si. This is so. And you suspect that he wanted to get into your room so he could plant the evidence against you in the murder of Señorita Vardaro."

"I do."

"I have yet to speak to other members of your party in detail. I have only initial statements from them." Suarez leaned back, taking his ease. "If we come to the matter of Señorita Vardaro stealing your laptop computer, and we assume she did so on Señor Masters's instructions, do you know why he would want your laptop?"

"I haven't the foggiest."

Suarez frowned again. "Fog? I do not understand what fog has to do with this. I know you English you make small talk about the weather, but—"

"My apologies," Baldock cut in. "It's another English idiom. It means I don't have the vaguest idea what he was doing with my laptop. However, he didn't have my laptop last night, did he? You had it." Baldock considered his position for a moment. "Look, Inspector, my friend, Mr Greaves, is waiting by the pool, and he's quite happy to check the machine over to see if any changes have been made in the last twenty-four hours, and I have an iPad in my room with the same files on it. He could check them both and maybe then we can learn was Masters was playing at."

Suarez beamed his approval. "And I have my man who is expert in these to watch over your friend."

Baldock nodded. "Shall we bring them in?"

"No, señor. We shall take them to your room. I know that you have not returned to your room since our first interview, and while he tests your machine, you can help us point out the evidence you insist Señor Masters placed in you room. If there are changes to the computer , then we know they were made before I first interviewed you and we will take it from there."

Baldock stood. "Very well. Let's get to it."

Chapter Twenty-Seven

Baldock was glad that Suarez insisted on Greaves working in the penthouse room. The afternoon heat was almost unbearable, and he dreaded to think how bad it would have been in the manager's office. It was cramped enough with two of them in there; with the addition of Greaves and a Spanish IT expert, it would have been intolerable.

While his old friend worked, comparing the files on the laptop and iPad, making notes on a sheet of hotel writing paper as he went along, Baldock consulted a mental checklist of the things he still needed to do.

He had to speak to Ursula, he needed to talk to the other members of the Shortly party, and somewhere along the line, he would need to see his mother and calm any worries she may have, and he would also need to shower and change for dinner with Lisa.

Almost as an afterthought, he recalled he would need to see Harry Ingels and offer some kind of explanation for the afternoon's debacle with Mandy.

It did not take the police long to find evidence of Xavier Vardaro in the room. A single earring found under the bed.

"Check it for fingerprints," Baldock invited the inspector. "You won't find mine on it."

"Because you never took it from her. But if it was Señor Masters, we know he used gloves when he threw her over the balcony. And if it is you, we know you used the gloves."

"Then why did Masters break into my room?"

"You tell me. And if you killed him, señor, you should be able to tell me."

Baldock left it at that.

Across the room, Greaves closed the lid of the laptop and shut down the iPad, took up his notes and sat back, while around him, his small audience consisting of Baldock, Inspector Suarez and the Spanish IT expert, waited to hear what he had to say.

It had taken Greaves less than ten minutes to learn what he wanted, and Baldock was surprised and impressed by the speed at which his old friend worked. If, as Tim had suggested, Greaves' *bona fides* were questionable, it did not diminish his skills. Opening and booting up the laptop, his fingers had danced over the keyboard with an impressive accuracy, and menus appeared and disappeared to be replaced by fresh ones so fast that Baldock, who counted his own IT skills as better than average, could not follow them.

And now he was ready to announce his findings. He took his time, carefully rolling a cigarette while he mulled over whatever he had learned.

"You cannot smoke in here, Señor Greaves," Suarez warned him. "You must go out onto the balcony to smoke it, and you cannot go out onto the balcony until you tell me what it is you have learned."

"It's for when I get back downstairs and outside," Greaves said, licking the gummed edge of the paper and finishing the job off before tucking the cigarette in his shirt pocket.

"Well?" Baldock demanded, unable, unwilling to tolerate this limelight-seeking any longer.

Greaves tapped the laptop screen. "First thing that struck me, Ray, was I'm surprised you don't lock these machines up with a password."

"They're reserves, both of them," Baldock explained. "They carry only current files, those which I need while I'm away from home or on a book-signing tour. I back up some essential files on them, too and my contract is on the laptop because I needed to consult my lawyers over it a month ago."

"But you obviously never thought about anyone nicking it?"

"I don't let it out of my sight normally, other than to leave it the hotel safe. I didn't get the option this time considering it was stolen at the airport. And frankly, if I can't trust the crowd at Shortly, who can I trust?"

"Yeah, well, if they're you're friends, you should think about crossing them off your birthday party list."

It seemed to Baldock that Suarez, whose English was quite good, was having difficulty following the debate, but the inflection in Greaves announcement had his attention.

"We are not organising the birthday party, señor, so please do not be distracted. You have found something, señor?"

Greaves nodded. "A document on the laptop which was installed yesterday, and on the iPad, only one doc which was updated this morning about half past seven. It's named journal."

"That was me," Baldock admitted.

"I guessed," Greaves commented. "Lisa must have given you a seriously good seeing to last night."

"That was private," Baldock complained.

Suarez was obviously caught out by the idiomatic English. "Seeing to? This woman, she assaulted you?"

"No." Baldock hastened on to explain. "We had some difficulties and we were making them up."

"Making up? You were inventing a quarrel?"

"No, not making up as in telling stories. I mean making up. Making amends. Putting it right."

"With the manly art?" Suarez held up his fists like a boxer. "Ten rounds. Knockout wins, si?"

"No. Look Inspector, Ms Yeoman and I are, er, lovers. We were having… you know… sex."

"Ah. The nookie. Now I understand. Is an excellent way of making things right."

"According to his diary, it's a dazzling way," Greaves said. "Take the bit where he says the second orgasm—"

"Ewan, can you please leave my sex life out of this and tell us what else you found."

"Yeah. Right. Sure, Ray. The file on the laptop is named Contract Shortly Baldock. It's a PDF, and it was installed at one o'clock yesterday afternoon."

"My overall contract with Shortly," Baldock explained. "Each book has its own contract, but there's an overarching one which covers other, more generalised matters. It's a PDF,

Ewan. How could it be altered?"

Greaves shrugged. "Editing PDFs is not difficult, Ray, if you have the right software or even the right kind of PDF."

"But I don't think I do."

"Maybe not, but I didn't say this had been altered. I said it had been installed."

"Memory stick?"

Greaves nodded at Baldock's suggestion. "More than likely."

Baldock understood. "And if it was replaced at one o'clock yesterday afternoon, it means the machine was not in my possession. It disappeared at Alicante Airport at half past ten yesterday morning. This is Masters' and Vardaro's handiwork, obviously."

"For the moment I will accept what you say, señor," Suarez said. "However, we did not find a memory stick in Señor Masters' room, nor in Señorita Vardaro's."

"Did you look for one?"

The inspector shrugged. "I will check on the matter. For the moment, what difference would there be with the contract after he has done with it?"

"I don't know," Baldock admitted. "The original is in my safe at home, and there's another PDF version on my PC."

Greaves tapped the iPad. "You also have a copy on here, Ray—"

"No I don't I was looking for it earlier."

"Yes you do. It was hidden amongst a few other PDFs and it was called 'consp'."

"Ah. That would explain why I didn't notice it. I thought that was a Headingley plot idea for a conspiracy theory. "

"This entire business sounds like a conspiracy theory if you ask me." Greaves wallowed in his superiority. "If you like, I could compare the two documents. Might take an hour or two, but I should be able to tell you what's what."

Suarez gave the matter some consideration and nodded. "Very well, señor, I will permit you to take away Señor Baldock's machine, but you cannot remove it from the hotel. I will speak with Señor Jimenez, and when you are finished for the day, you will leave the laptop in his safe. Yes?"

Baldock nodded. "As you wish, Inspector."

"I need you to understand, Señor Baldock, that this does not clear your name of the murder of Señor Masters or Señorita Vardaro. In truth, it makes you an even bigger suspect, because this could be the motive for killing him. I know we have the testimony of Señorita Yeoman, but you could have sneaked out of bed while she was asleep and killed Señor Masters."

Greaves collected the machine and prepared to leave. "According to his diary, Lisa screwed him that well, I shouldn't think Ray would have enough strength left to kill anyone."

Chapter Twenty-Eight

Ten minutes later, Baldock joined Lisa and his mother at a poolside table at the Praia where Mandy and Sandra Scranton were larking around in the pool and the rest of the Midthorpe Maidens were idling the remainder of the afternoon away on loungers.

Despite Suarez' instructions, Greaves had taken the laptop and iPad away with him to work at his own hotel. For his part, Baldock felt confident enough of a positive outcome to dismiss the entire puzzle for the time being.

But it was not for long. He had no sooner sat down than Lisa and Janet pressed him for information, and over a soft drink, editing out any reference to his bizarre shopping expedition with Mandy, and her subsequent activity, he gave them a rundown of all that had happened since he returned to his hotel.

Both women were suitably relieved to learn that he was not seriously suspected of the murder, and Lisa sounded glad that the puzzle of the laptop had been cleared up.

"At least it won't distract you this evening."

Misinterpreting her meaning, Baldock blushed and asked, "This evening?"

"You promised me dinner," Lisa reminded him.

"Of course. Mother, you're the Benidorm expert, can you recommend anywhere?"

"Friars," Janet replied.

"I think we could do with somewhere a little less frivolous and more upmarket," he said. "I'll ask Jimenez, the manager at the Aranjuez. He's a local, so I'm sure he'll be able to recommend somewhere."

"The dining room at the Aranjuez, I shouldn't wonder,"

Lisa commented, and before Baldock could take her up on the matter, she changed the subject, bringing it back to his errant laptop. "If Masters took your laptop and made these changes, what was the point? What was he playing at?"

"That is *the* question. As we speak, Ewan is comparing the two versions to see what changes Gil might have made to it. I said all along he had an ulterior motive for getting us all here, and it was to bring pressure to bear on each of us. I can't work out why, though. I accept your idea that he was a control freak, but it still makes no sense. Why go to the trouble of altering contracts, if indeed that's what he's done? Why take the risk of sexual harassment against the women? Why try to tie the authors into what is not only a false contract, but an illegal one, too? From a commercial point of view, it makes little sense."

"And why murder his PA?" Janet asked. "Has this new, flighty little secretary had anything to say about it?" Janet asked.

"I don't know because I haven't spoken to her yet. I know what she said to the police, as I've just told you. She probably knows a lot more which she wasn't saying to Suarez, and as far as he's concerned, none of this contract business is anything to do with him unless and until it can be shown to have a direct bearing on the murders."

"And, of course, it does," Janet declared.

Only half-listening, Baldock asked, "Mother?"

Janet clucked impatiently. "I told you earlier, Raymond, he killed the poor woman. That much is obvious. And it's just as obvious that one of your party murdered him. Nothing was taken from his room, so it wasn't a robbery gone wrong. He was the one fooling about with the computer machines, not just yours, but those of your two friends, too, and according to what you told me earlier, you were not the only one he was trying to, er, stitch up."

Baldock shushed her with a quick glance between his mother and Lisa, but Lisa had already picked up on it.

"It sounds to me like there's a lot more going on than I've been told."

"There is," Janet agreed, "And we don't really want you to know, Lisa, because you would disapprove. For now, let's just say that Raymond and his friends were the innocent parties caught up in this wicked man's schemes, and if you want my opinion, bashing his head in was exactly what he deserved."

"And you agree with that, Raymond?" Lisa demanded.

"Not entirely. He deserved some kind of come-uppance, but you know my feelings on violence."

"Yes, but someone in your party didn't agree with you," Janet said. "It was one of you. Obviously, not you, but what about the others?"

"I repeat, I haven't had time to speak to them yet." Baldock checked the time on his Breitling. "It's getting on for six o'clock, and I'd better get ready for dinner."

"Dressing?" Lisa asked.

"Business suit, I think. I didn't bring a dinner jacket with me."

"I'd better put a proper dress on then."

"Fine. I'll collect you about seven thirty. Enjoy your evening, Mother."

Janet smacked her lips. "I will. Blackbeard's tonight." She cackled. "I may be late out of bed tomorrow morning."

Lisa laughed, too. "Well make sure you kick your toy boy out before breakfast."

The two women tittered. Baldock grimaced.

***

Dressed in his suit, a plain, white shirt and dark tie, Baldock emerged from the lift into the air-conditioned lobby just after 7:20, to find a major argument going on at the reception counter, and he realised at once the identity of the tall, painfully thin woman with a shower of blonde hair covering her slender shoulders.

"You were careless enough to let him be murdered," she yelled, "so the very least you can do is let me have his room."

Less than seven hours had passed since the body of Gil Masters was discovered, and Baldock calculated that in order to be fighting with Señor Jimenez, Dominique Masters must have wasted no time getting from her Surrey home to Gatwick and arranging a flight to Alicante and a limousine to meet her there.

He had met her once or twice in the past and considered her a bitch of the first order. Arrogant, noisy, dismissive of almost everyone and everything except for her own wants or needs, she had been the perfect wife for the equally arrogant and domineering Masters. At least, that was Baldock's opinion, and he often tried to imagine what it would be like to be a fly on the wall of the Masters' mansion on the outskirts of Godalming.

Consistent with his attitude to most people, he considered himself a cut above her, and ignored her as far as was possible, but when compelled to speak to her at formal, Shortly Publishing receptions and parties, it was with a forced civility hovering dangerously close to the rude.

He was certain that she would make her presence felt sooner rather than later, but he had no desire to speak with her now, and headed straight for the exit.

"Baldock. Come here."

Too late. She had seen him.

Halfway across the lobby, he diverted his track and bore down on her.

"Tell these jerk-offs who I am."

"It is *Mister* Baldock, Mrs Masters. Either that or Raymond. And I shouldn't think there's any need for me to tell them anything. You can be heard all over town."

"They won't give me Gil's room," she protested.

To Baldock, it was if she had not heard a word he had said. "It's a crime scene. Their forensic team are likely to be busy there for another few days."

"Gil's personal effects are there. I'm entitled—"

"To nothing," Baldock interrupted. "When they're finished with them, I'm sure they'll be returned to you."

"This is not fair. And I expect you to support a fellow Brit, not take sides with these dago dunces."

He cringed at her derogatory remarks and offered a smile of apology to the manager. "I must apologise for her language, Señor Jimenez. Unfortunately, not all British people are sufficiently well-educated to avoid inbred racism."

"Is all right, Señor Baldock. We are used to English lager louts."

His remark served only to infuriate Dominique further. "I am not a frigging lager lout. I am a wealthy woman, recently widowed, and I expect you to treat me with respect."

"Respect has to be earned, Dominique," Baldock said, "and right now, you're not working hard enough. Now, if you shut your mouth long enough to allow Señor Jimenez to deal with your registration, I'm sure he'll find you suitable accommodation on the upper floor."

Her eyes narrowed to tiny lasers of pure anger. "You wait there, Baldock. I want to speak to you."

"And I want to speak to you, but I have a dinner engagement, so I'll catch up with you later. Probably tomorrow morning." He turned smartly away and with her protests ringing in his ears, marched out of the hotel.

Strolling down the street to the entrance of the Praia, he felt good. Giving Dominique Masters a metaphorical kick between the legs was so satisfying that for a little while it outshone the prospective dinner and forthcoming night with Lisa.

But not for long.

Lisa appeared in a plain, black dress, wearing a little jewellery to offset the dark of her clothing, and like him she was in an excellent mood.

"I've booked us a table at the *Vista del Mar*," Baldock reported as they ambled to the corner of *Avenida del Mediterráneo* to find a taxi. "They don't officially open until eight thirty, but the setting is wonderful and I thought we could enjoy an aperitif on the terrace."

And he was right. Sitting on the headland on the outskirts of the Old Town, the *Vista del Mar* gave spectacular views over both Levante and Poniente beaches, with the stark and sloping *Isla de Benidorm* several kilometres out to sea and roughly central.

As the sun set somewhere behind them, and the first stars began to twinkle in the clear night, they worked their way through *Jamon Iberico*, followed by veal cutlets in red wine, and finished off with an overloaded dish of ice cream in various flavours, the conversation remained fun and neutral, and for the first time in the last few days, Baldock found himself totally at ease.

And beneath it was the rising anticipation of passion to come, which he sensed in Lisa, too.

It was turned ten o'clock before Baldock settled the bill and they strolled from the headland, down through the narrow streets of the Old Town, passing lively bodegas, and cellar bars, pausing now and then to look into the window of late-open souvenir shops.

Stopping at a bar for a small beer while they watched a floor show put on by a pair of flamenco dancers, it was eleven thirty before they were back on *Avenida del Mediterráneo*, and in the taxi to the Aranjuez.

Lisa chattered amiably, commenting on how much she had enjoyed the night, how she preferred it to revelry in Morgan's where her fellow hen-party attendees would be, or even to a flutter in the *Casino Mediterráneo*, where Ian Linkman could be seen strolling in.

Only when they climbed out of the taxi did silence follow, and it was a silence built on the increasing anticipation, the need for each other.

Barely had they got back to the room when they fell to the bed and began that long, slow, tactile climb to the peak of exhilaration and mutual gratification.

And as his eyes closed, sending him into a long and much needed sleep, Baldock concluded that if the day had begun badly, it had ended in the finest style.

Chapter Twenty-Nine

Saturday morning dawned with the familiar, glorious sunshine and cloudless skies.

Despite having finally dropped off to sleep around one a.m. Baldock nevertheless felt refreshed and invigorated when he stepped out onto the balcony just after eight carrying a fresh cup of coffee and his smartphone.

He had reached for his iPad, but when he could not find it, his memory triggered and he realised it was with Ewan Greaves. His dislike of writing by hand bade him take the phone with its word-processing app. The predictive text was irritating, the onscreen keyboard small and fiddly, his fingers too large and bulky for the tiny keys, but it was preferable to his spidery handwriting which, he knew, would be difficult to read when he got around to transcribing it to the computer, especially if, as was likely, that did not happen until after he got home.

After the way Greaves had blurted out extracts from his journal the previous day, he was more careful. He had only included the more intimate details as a reminder of how powerful, almost transcendental, the sex had been on Thursday night. It would be useful for a future Headingley tale. In this update, he remained more circumspect, and encoded the more intimate details. Sex, for example became 'sfx', although the predictive text made strenuous efforts to change it back to the original.

Beyond his adventures with Lisa, he made extensive notes on the killing, the inevitable suspicion that he was involved, and queries on possible motives of his fellow travellers, all of whom he intended to question after breakfast.

If there was a certain autocracy in his assumed right to question them, it was based upon several factors, not least of which was his natural arrogance. He was the only crime writer amongst them, he had spent time with the Norfolk police researching the Headingley novels, and as impressed as he was by Inspector Suarez's thoroughness, he was dismayed by the man's lack of imagination, and that left him reluctant to leave the matter to the Spanish police. They may not want his help, but they were going to get it, like it or not.

"There's an element of selfishness in this," he told Lisa when she joined him on the balcony and she had read his entry. "I don't want to return to the UK with this hanging over me, and yet it's obvious that it must be one of us."

"Not obvious," Lisa argued. "Have you considered that it could be an outsider? Someone not linked to this group. Someone who knew where you would be staying and made sure he – or she – was here waiting."

"No, I hadn't considered it," Baldock admitted. "It's possible, I suppose. Masters must have made more enemies than us. But according to the police, he wasn't robbed, so that's something we'd have to leave to Suarez and his people. In the meantime, I am still going to question the others."

"Is it going to take long?" Lisa asked. "Only I hoped we were going to get some time together today. I missed last night at Blackbeard's, and I'll have to show my face at the Red Lion tonight. I don't want to sound like a wife, Ray, but —"

"I understand completely," he assured her. "I'll be as quick as I can with them."

"And what about her? This dominatrix you were talking about last night."

"Dominatrix... oh, you mean Dominique? What does she have to do with anything? She's simply here to find out what happened to her husband. The police will deal with her." He chuckled. "Or she'll deal with the police."

But he was wrong, as he learned when he joined the Shortly crew, minus Ursula Franklyn, for breakfast at a few minutes to nine.

"Message from Dominique," Bernie told him. "I believe you met in the lobby last night."

Tucking into bacon and eggs, Baldock replied tartly. "We did, and I'm not remotely interested in anything she has to say."

"Well you should be," Phillipa told him, "because she wants to see us all at eleven in the Sports Bar, and judging from her mood it sounds like bad news."

"She can take a flying one," Baldock said and carried on eating breakfast.

His announcement was greeted with shock by his fellows, and muted protests erupted from all. Baldock ignored them and worked his way steadily through his meal, his natural arrogance, once more, driving others to the edge of their tempers.

He was not impressed. He had suffered years of such anger from Midthorpers, who were prepared to back it up with violence if necessary. At the side of them, these people were not even intimidating.

Turning deaf ears on the complaints, he continued eating and when he had finished, he returned to the dining room for fresh coffee, even pausing as he left to ask whether anyone wanted anything while he was in there. Soon, carrying coffee and two slices of toast, which he did not want, but which he had taken great pleasure waiting for, he joined them and buttered the toast.

Finally, he faced them all, his determined eye running round the table to capture everyone individually.

"What is wrong with you people?" he demanded. Pointing to Katy and Dean, he went on, "All right, you work for Shortly. You may have no choice in the matter. But the rest of you work for yourselves. This woman can no more order you around than Gil could. Just tell her where to get off."

There was a brief, uncomfortable since, before Harry Ingels spoke up. "I'm not speaking out of turn here, but remember Gil had something on us. Yes, and that cow you sent after me was determined to square him for it, wasn't she? Only she picked on the wrong man."

"I can only apologise for that, Harry. I didn't know Gil was dead at the time, and she was too stupid to ask your name."

"That don't explain the game you were trying to play," Ingels retorted.

"The same dirty game Gil was already playing."

Baldock's reply caused Ingels' ears to colour. "Yes, well, right now, what's to say Dame Domino isn't gonna play the same game? Especially if she has the same hold over us."

"She doesn't and she won't," Baldock replied.

Once again his announcement was greeted by silence. Surprised silence this time.

"How do you know?" Linkman asked.

"Because unlike you people, instead of fannying around worrying, I took action, and I don't mean randy Mandy Cowling. Xavier stole my laptop on Thursday so Gil could install a copy of the contract on it. Now why would he do that? Because he's made some changes to that contract. I don't know what, but I will before the day is out. Unfortunately for him, I'm a pain in the bottom. I carry an iPad with me, and the original contract is stored on that."

Baldock took more satisfaction from the stunned faces that greeted his announcement. If only he could get that kind of reaction from a Midthorper, his life would be…

He ceased the internal search for triumph. "I'm convinced he killed Xavier. He left the laptop with her to implicate me, and then, after leaving you lot in The Square on Thursday night, he wormed his way into my room to plant further evidence on me. The police will want to check your laptop, Harry, and yours, Phillipa. I think the reason Gil borrowed them at Stansted and on the flight was to install the altered contract on them."

"What kind of alterations has he made?" Tiffany Pittock asked.

"I said, I don't know yet, but I have a suspicion Ursula does. Anyone know where she is?"

"With Dominique as far as we can work out," Bernie replied.

"Then I'll want to speak to her before I speak to Dominique. As matters stand, I have a man looking at my laptop to ascertain exactly what Masters did. Whatever it is, I'm guessing he did the same to you two." Abandoning the rest of his coffee and toast, he stood up. "Unfortunately, as Inspector Suarez has pointed out, it means we are all prime suspects in his murder. I'll bid you all a cheerful good morning, and enjoy your meeting with Dominique."

With a superior glow, he marched back through the dining room, and into the lobby. He was making for the exit, when Ursula stepped out of the lift.

"Raymond," she called after him, and he paused.

She hurried over to join him. "Raymond, where are you going?"

"Out."

"You will be back, won't you? There is a meeting with Mrs Masters at eleven."

"Not with me, there isn't." He glanced around and spotted a vacant sofa by the windows. "Come over here."

"I'm—"

"You're coming with me for a minute, Ursula, or I'll have a word with Inspector Suarez and tell him what I believe you really know."

Meekly, she followed him to the settee. Baldock installed himself at one end, and allowed Ursula to settle into the other. She sat with her back straight, knees projecting from her plain, white shorts, and clamped together, sending out an aura of prim virginity, which Baldock guessed was wholly at odds with her demeanour on the few occasions he had met her at Shortly's London headquarters. She did not look at him, but focussed on the fronds of a potted plant several yards behind him over his right shoulder.

"The inspector and Señor Jimenez told me that Masters insisted you pay for a replacement key at reception, even though yours was not missing. What was Masters up to?"

"I don't know."

"Try again."

"I will not try anything again. Xavier was Gil's PA for the last five years, and I only filled in when she was on holiday, or like now. I like my job so I do as I'm told and—"

"And the fringe benefits are all horizontal."

"None of your business," she retorted. "I'm good at my job, and one of the things it entails is confidentiality. Gil only ever told me what he wanted me to know, and only then when I acted as his PA, and it's not my place to bring anyone else up to speed on his activities."

"It is when those activities are criminal. Listen, Ursula, I'm not going to run to Suarez with this. Aside from anything else, it's nothing to do with him, but whatever he was doing is the probable motive for his murder, and you could be hampering a criminal investigation."

She sighed. "I'm saying nothing, Raymond. Suarez told me you had someone looking at your computer. The results should tell you all you want to know, but to put it together, you need one other piece of information." She stood, ready to leave. "He and Dominique were divorcing. Now what do I tell Dominique when you don't show up?"

"Tell her I said she can get stuffed."

Ursula marched away, and Baldock stepped out of the hotel into the soaring heat of the morning, ambled down to the beach, where he picked up a copy of *The Telegraph*, before climbing into a taxi.

"*Hotel Dolce*, please," he instructed the driver, and turned to the crossword.

The taxi pulled out and up the road, turning left at the second lights onto *Calle Gerona*. The indoor market was open on the right, attracting its share of British tourists. Also on the right, outside the twin, ungainly towers of a brace of Sol hotels, a film crew was at work. It was the location for a well-known TV comedy, but Baldock could see no sign of any of the stars and he guessed the crew were taking establishing shots. It called to mind the proposed TV production of his Headingley novels, an idea which had excited him when it was first mooted, but which had paled somewhat thanks to the length of time negotiations and the commissioning process had taken. It was nothing to do with him. He was not even writing the scripts, merely collecting his share of the rights income, but he had asked, and been granted permission to visit the locations once production got under way.

Once past these hotels, where *Calle Gerona* forked left towards the Brit Quarter, the taxi carried on, drifting right with the road along *Calle Derramador*, moving in a west-ish direction, towards the outskirts of Benidorm. At a patch of open ground, where the renowned Sunday and Wednesday markets were held, the driver turned left into a grid of narrower streets and after a couple more left and right turns, pulled up outside the *Hotel Dolce*.

A tall, and narrow high-rise block, built of redbrick, it fitted in well with its surroundings of similar hotels, each with their own niggardly plot of concrete where the pools were located. Although the lobby was smart, there was an element of the three-star about it which disappointed Baldock. He noticed that he was the only person carrying a British broadsheet. Everyone else seemed to be carrying or reading *The Sun* or *The Mirror*, or in some cases, *Bild*.

Introducing himself at reception, he asked for Greaves, and was directed towards the pool area. Stepping out into the bright sunlight once again, he was greeted by the familiar sight of people lounging around the pool, sleeping off the previous night's excesses or cavorting in the water. Loud music emanated from the pool bar where a queue waited for service. Baldock noticed, quite inconsequentially, that most of those at the bar were wearing wrist straps which identified them as all-inclusive guests, and despite the hour, they were ordering copious amounts of local lager.

As he wandered round the crowded area, seeking his old friend, he bumped into Tim Yeoman and Michael Shipston.

Tim greeted him cheerfully. "Hey up, Ray. Slumming are you, lad?"

"Oh, hello, Tim. Actually, I'm looking for Ewan."

"Dracula, you mean." Tim waved in the direction of the rear wall and a shaded table where Greaves sat smoking and hunched over Baldock's laptop. "He's over there."

"Dracula?"

"He doesn't like the sun," Shippy explained. "Freckles and

he was a marmalade when he had hair."

While the two men went on their way, Baldock wove his way through loungers and tables, to join Greaves. "Morning, Ewan."

"Oh. Hiya, Ray." Greaves hastily shut down whatever he had been doing with the computer.

"Did you find anything in those documents?"

"Hmm. Oh. Yeah. Hey. Did I ever?"

Rolling a fresh cigarette, he worked on the mousepad to call up a set of documents, and when he was ready, he put a light to his smoke, and half turned the computer so both he and Baldock could see.

The screen was divided vertically into three sections. The two versions of the contract took up the centre and right, while on the left was a column dedicated to highlighting the differences.

"I copied the iPad version onto a memory stick, converted it for Windows, and installed it on your laptop." Greaves chuckled. "Do I know what I'm doing, or do I know what I'm doing? Two operating systems which don't like each other but I—"

"Yes, you can save the self-congratulation for later, Ewan. What did you find?"

"I copied both into your word processing package, and ran a comparison. They're the same for most of the doc, but look at this.

It was a single paragraph. In the centre was the original, which read:

The author grants to the publisher the first option on all future works in the series. In the event that the publisher shall reject such future works, the author retains full rights and on notifying the publisher of his intention to do so, may at his discretion take them to another publisher without forfeit.

"Now look at the other one," Greaves invited.

The author grants to the publisher the first option on all future works in the series. In the event that the publisher shall reject such future works, the author has the option to bring the work up to the standards demanded by the publisher. The publisher shall retain the right to publish for a period of not more than five years.

The publisher shall have first option on all future works published and unpublished from the author, and shall retain those rights for a period of not more than five years from the date of first submission. The author may not, without the express permission of the publisher offer any works to any other publisher.

Baldock's blood began to boil. "The bastard."

Greaves shrugged. "What was he playing at?"

"He was trying to stitch me into his company whether I like it or not. No wonder my lawyers couldn't find anything wrong with the damn thing. They saw the original version."

"Trouble is, Ray, what are you gonna do about it now he's brown bread?"

"Nail his wife to the cross," Baldock fumed as he collected his laptop. "Thanks, Ewan. Do I owe you anything?"

"Well, a few bob would come in handy, but if I can keep that tackle we bought for yesterday's exercise, I'm cool."

"It's yours with my compliments. I'm going back to the Aranjuez. I need to speak to some people before I set up Dominique Masters as a dartboard. Thanks again."

He was still, bitterly angry as a second taxi took him back to his hotel, but through his anger he began to run various scenarios for Masters's outrageous actions. Everything, he finally decided, was down to whether he had made the same adjustments to the contracts belonging to Phillipa and Ingels, and before he arrived at the Aranjuez, Baldock knew that he had.

It was coming up to eleven when he got there and met with the others. At his insistence, both Ingels and Phillipa returned to their rooms and brought their laptops. When he checked them against the comparison document Greaves had left on his machine, he found the same, restrictive clauses on theirs.

"You may need to dig into your files at home and recover the original as I've done," Baldock explained. "As I said to my IT friend, this explains why my lawyers couldn't find anything wrong with the contract. They didn't see these changes. They saw the original."

"So what's the legal position with this?" Ingels wanted to know.

"Tricky," Linkman ventured, but Bernie pooh-poohed him immediately.

"It's not tricky at all, Ian," she declared. "It's illegal and as such Masters is in breach of contract. If you were so minded you could rip it up, withdraw the rights and go somewhere else."

"That might be all right for Ray and Phillipa," Ingels complained, "but I don't sell anything like the numbers they do. I don't think I'd get anyone to take me on."

"Why don't we talk to Dominique and see what she has to say?" Linkman suggested. "Surely if we point all this out, she'll backtrack on it. I'm sure we can come to some agreement."

Baldock sneered. "This planet you live on, can you still get Sky TV?"

Tiffany Pittock checked her watch. "We're late for the meeting anyway. Dominique will be spitting blood."

Baldock picked up his laptop. "By the time we're through with her, she'll be spitting teeth… her own."

Chapter Thirty

As Tiffany had predicted, Dominique was furious at their tardiness. Sat at the head of the same table her late husband had used on their first day, with Ursula at her side, she began with a rant aimed at all of them.

"When I call a meeting for eleven o'clock, I expect you to be here at eleven. Not a quarter past."

"We got held up," Linkman said. "And before we go any further, can I offer, on behalf of all of us, our sincere condolences on Gil's untimely death."

"I didn't call you here to listen to you grovelling. As far as I'm concerned, he got what he deserved and I'm glad to see the back of him, but it changes things… a lot… a great lot."

Preferring to keep his mouth shut for the moment, Baldock allowed Phillipa to respond.

"In what way?"

"I've heard the story from Ursula, and you three, you, Ingels and especially you, Baldock, have been giving Gil serious hell ever since you got here, and I'm damned if I know why. Jesus, who was paying for this gig? Shortly, that's who. And you've done nothing but hassle him. Well, I won't stand for the same crap. I'll cut your contracts before I'll let you walk over me."

"You've been officially appointed the new Chief Executive, have you?" Baldock asked.

"Appointed, hell," she snapped. "Gil launched the company on the back of my money, not his own. I've always been the majority shareholder. I've appointed myself the new Chief Exec."

"And the fact that you were in the process of divorcing Gil has no bearing on anything?" Baldock demanded.

Her colour rose. "Who told you about that?" She cast a sour glance at Ursula. "It doesn't matter. To answer you, smartarse, yes it has a lot of bearing."

"I'm glad you speak English rather than writing it," Phillipa commented and Baldock silently applauded her for speaking up.

"And what is that supposed to mean?"

"You speak it poorly," Phillipa replied.

"It also means that Gil probably ran rings round you," Baldock added. "Tell me something, did Gil ever tell you the purpose of this alleged team-building weekend for which Shortly so generously paid?"

"Team building, wasn't it? The clue is in the name, Baldock. It's one of these crazy ideas he brought back from Harveys."

"Harvard," Phillipa corrected.

"Wherever."

"Yes well, it might be advantageous if you shut your mouth for a moment and allow us to enlighten you," Baldock suggested.

"I—"

"I told you to shut up, didn't I?" Baldock paused a moment to ensure Dominique would not interrupt. "While we were waiting at Stansted, Gil borrowed Harry's laptop, ostensibly to check something online. During the flight, he borrowed Phillipa's, claiming he had to rough out a memo and save it to a memory stick. When we arrived, he had Xavier steal my laptop, made changes to it, then murdered Xavier. And while we were all out team building on the first night, he planted evidence on me." He purposely narrowed his eye on the new CEO.

"You can prove all that, can you?" Dominique guffawed, "And you three were stupid enough to let him fiddle with your laptops? You get all you deserve. Don't come whining to me that he's changed your manuscripts. Put them right. It's what you get paid for."

"It's not that simple, Dominique," Bernie announced. "Gil made changes to contracts, not manuscripts, and Raymond has proof of those changes. He did the same to Harry and Phillipa, and they, too will have proof of those changes when they get home and check the originals. He was an officer of the company, and even though he is no longer with us, Shortly Publishing can be held responsible for his actions."

A murmur of agreement rippled round the table and Baldock took up the reins.

"Unless you stop screaming about what you will and will not do, and start listening, Dominique, our lawyers will be queuing up to crucify Shortly for breach of contract, restrictive trade practices, invasion of privacy, falsification of legally binding documents, blackmail, coercion, attempting to pervert the course of Spanish justice, and any other little charges they can dream up, amongst which I'm sure Phillipa, Tiff and Bernie, will insist upon sexual harassment, while I will demand an explanation and damages for his attempts to compromise my reputation."

As he spoke, he had watched her mouth fall further and further open until she was gaping.

"I… er… Right, Ray. Say no more—"

"It seems to me," Baldock interrupted to fill any chasm her waffle might create, "that this was Gil endeavouring to sidestep any efforts from you to oust him as CEO in the aftermath of your divorce. He wanted to show the board how smart he was, and how he had bound we three to Shortly for the next five years. To do so, he changed our contracts, which means, technically and legally, the original contracts are now null and void, and open for renegotiation. And before you begin to fight, I have both documents secured on my laptop, my iPad, and on a memory stick and in cloud storage. And I have witnesses in the shape of an independent IT consultant, and two police officers from the Benidorm division of the *Policia Nacional,* and a further witness in the shape of Señor Emilio Jimenez, the manager of the *Hotel Aranjuez*, the same man you subjected to vicious, racist harassment last night, and who is ready to testify that by sleight of hand, Gil secured a key for my room late on Thursday night, and used it to gain access to said room so he could incriminate me in

Xavier Vardaro's murder."

"I see where you're coming from, Ray—"

Rubbing as much salt into the wound as he could muster, Baldock cut in on her again. "With all due respect to Harry, he doesn't set the world on fire with his books, but they are excellent, midlist titles. Phillipa and I are in a slightly higher league, and I estimate the damages to us three will run into millions. That's not to mention the amount Bernie, Tiff and Ian may demand, or the Shortly employees, who were also given outrageous tasks to fulfil. Furthermore, his attempt to point the finger at me when Xavier was killed will result in even higher, personal damages." He glared at Dominique. "Now who's in the S-H-one-T?"

Dominique smiled thinly. "I'm sure we can sort this out."

Having allowed her to complete a sentence, albeit a brief one, Baldock went on the attack again. "I hope so. Because we also have to look at the goodwill aspect. In the event that we were to bring down your house of cards, none of us would be likely to have anything to do with Shortly again. You would instantly lose two bestselling authors and a reliable midlister, and how many others will run for it when they learn what has been going on?"

Dominique reverted to type. "If he was here, I'd cut off his tackle and feed it to him for Sunday lunch."

"Something I would dearly love to see, but which, alas, will not be possible considering his sad demise." Baldock paused to let the full implications sink in, then carried on again. "Inspector Suarez is, naturally, more interested in the murders of Xavier and Gil death than any contractual and other arguments we may have with you, and there is a strong possibility that one of us delivered the fatal blow. That, too, is not going to look good on Shortly's CV, is it? I can see the headlines now. Outraged author, or agent, smashes crooked murdering publisher's head in then drowns him just to make sure he's dead."

More silence followed, during which Dominique metaphorically squirmed.

Phillipa took up the attack. "So, Dominique, now that

you're through shouting the odds, and you know where we're coming from, what are you willing to do to put matters right?"

When she finally spoke, she was meek and compliant, more hopeful than confident. "Go back to the way things were?"

Baldock smiled and slowly shook his head. "You'll have to do better than that."

She became decisive. "All right, all right. I need to pass this to our legal eagles. I'm not trying to duck it, but I need to know where we are and what we can do. The lawyers will need formal depositions from all of you including you members of Shortly staff, as to what's been going on here this weekend. From there, I'll have our lawyers assess the potential damage, and if we can, we'll reach some kind of agreement. How does that sound?"

"A lot better than insisting we get down on our knees and beg," Ingels said.

Dominique was obviously relieved to hear it. Patting her brow with a tissue, she took a long drink to help calm her nerves, and then scanned those present again.

"Gil is dead. Someone wasted him. Ray's just hinted that it had to be one of you. Do we know that for sure? I mean, could he have been attacked by thieves or something?"

"If he was, they didn't take anything," Bernie replied. "Let's get sensible, Dominique. The only people with any real motive are we nine."

"And if I may point out," Baldock said, "Gil opened the door to whoever killed him. Because of the security set up around rooms on the top floor, we know that the key was not used after Gil let himself in at eleven-fifteen. He opened the door to his killer."

Even as he said it, Baldock could see the hole in his argument. If Masters had left the room with the door unlocked to plant the evidence, then an opportunist thief could have slipped in then. But even as he thought of it, he knew it had not happened like that. Nothing had been stolen.

He elected to say nothing, but laid his eye on Masters' PA.

"I suspect Ursula knows a sight more than she's letting on," Baldock said.

Ursula stiffened at the mention of her name. "I know nothing more than I told you in the lobby."

Baldock took up her challenge. "You know why Gil wanted the key to my room."

"No, I do not."

"As a liar, I'd stick to working as an editor-cum-PA if I were you," Baldock declared. "Ursula, no one is accusing you of anything—"

"I am," Dominique interrupted. "I'm accusing her of screwing my husband."

Baldock blanched. "That's a personal matter, and I'm sure you'll sort it out in an, er, adult manner. What I'm trying to say is that no one is accusing her of any involvement in Gil's scheming or his death. But if you feel, Ursula, that you cannot tell us, then tell Mrs Masters. She is, after all, your new boss."

The level of expectancy around the table increased in direct proportion to Ursula's discomfort.

Dominique regarded the woman with dagger eyes. "If you know, spit it out."

Ursula sighed. "He wanted to get into Ray's room. But he did not want anyone to know it."

"The earring?" Baldock asked.

"He said he was returning your laptop which Xavier had taken at the airport."

Baldock was satisfied. "A lie. By that time, the police had the laptop."

"Well, that's what he told me," Ursula insisted.

"All right. Let me ask you this, Ursula. He installed fake contracts on all our laptops. He must have used a memory stick. Where is it?"

"I think the police have it."

"I'll talk to them and get it back," Dominique said.

"No you bloody well won't," Baldock retorted. "That's evidence against your company in our favour. No way will I let it fall into your hands so it can be conveniently wiped. At least, not until we all have copies of it."

"You think I'd be bothered to cover up for that jerk?"

"No, but you would be willing to cover up for Shortly Publishing."

"You sound as if you don't trust me," Dominique objected.

"That's because I don't trust you," Baldock replied. "I'll speak to Inspector Suarez and see if I can get copies of the memory stick for each of us. To drag this debate back to where it was a few minutes ago, prime suspects in Gil's murder are we nine. Can we all account for our movements during Thursday night to the early hours of Friday morning?"

"Can you?" Ingels demanded.

"As it happens, Harry, I can. I signed my girlfriend in as a guest late on Thursday night, and I was with her all night."

Ingels was not persuaded. "It seems to me very opportune. First you won't share a room with me, then, all of a sudden, your girlfriend turns up. That sounds like meticulous planning and for my money—"

"She was in Benidorm before us," Baldock cut in. "I didn't even know she was here until Gil dragged us down to The Square on Thursday night, which is where I met her. If I planned it, I did so off the cuff, but even if I did, she can still vouch for me."

"Yes, well, having met her—"

"Not Amanda Cowling, you idiot," Baldock interrupted again, more irritably this time. "Amanda was a honey trap, not my girlfriend. And it didn't take you long to get caught in the honey, did it?"

"Bog off."

"Like watching two schoolboys," Phillipa commented. "As Raymond has asked, can we all account for our whereabouts during Thursday night and Friday morning?"

Dominique made an effort to exert some control. "Gil was with you all in a bar in the town, was he?"

"No," Tiff replied. "We all made our way to The Square, as Raymond said, but he and Bernie went their own way, while we all went into the bar, but Gil didn't stay long. He ordered a round of drinks for everyone, then he got a text message and said he had to get back to the hotel to attend to some urgent business."

"That urgent business being the planting of evidence in my room," Baldock said. "Ursula, was the text from you?"

Masters' new PA nodded. "Before we went out, he told me I was to ensure I knew where you were, and then send him the message."

"And what did it say?" Dominique asked.

"Clear." Ursula addressed the whole table. "That was all. It was meant to indicate that Raymond was somewhere nearby, and not in his room. As we went into *Café Benidorm*, I saw Raymond and Bernie hanging back. When they went into Winners, I sent the text. A minute or two later, Gil left the bar and made his way back here." Ursula looked more uncomfortable as the minutes passed. "I'm sorry, Ray, but I had orders from Gil. I had to keep an eye on you. He knew how, er, temperamental you can be, and he needed to know if you decided to come back here, but when I last saw you, you were sat outside Winners having a drink with a middle-aged woman."

"My mother."

Ingels guffawed. "I thought you said she was your girlfriend."

Baldock's eyes narrowed on him. "If you talk about my mother like that again, I will not be responsible for what happens to you."

"And trust me, Harry, Janet Baldock would make bigger mincemeat of you than Mandy did." After Bernie delivered her opinion, she addressed the rest of the table. "I can vouch for Raymond up until about half past eleven because I was with him. That was when I came back to *Café Benidorm* trying to rescue a pair of shorts for him."

"You needed fresh shorts?" Dominique grinned broadly. "What the hell kind of party were you people involved in?"

"You're upset because we didn't invite you?" Baldock was beginning to tire of the concentration on his appalling night. "Some woman vomited over my shorts."

He realised instantly that it was not the wisest admission

he could have made, when the table dissolved into tittering laughter.

"What was her head doing anywhere near your shorts?" Ingels asked.

"I wasn't wearing them at the time." Realising the risqué interpretation they would put on his words, Baldock closed his mouth quickly.

"Ray, you're digging yourself deeper in," Bernie noted with a sad smile.

"Then forget about me," he replied testily. "What about the rest of you? Did you all stay together for the rest of the evening?"

There was a general murmur of agreement that they had, indeed, stayed together until around one in the morning, but there was less agreement on what happened after. One or two took taxis back to the Aranjuez, Tiff and Bernie walked back together, Linkman and Ursula did likewise but separately. All insisted they were back in their rooms by one thirty and stayed there for the rest of the night.

"One of us is lying," Baldock declared. "But whoever he – or she – is, I'm confident they'll have left traces for Suarez's forensic team."

"But if not, will they let us go home tomorrow?" Linkman asked.

"I should think so. A European arrest warrant will soon drag the miscreant back." Baldock got to his feet. "For now, I'll see if I can get a word with Suarez and get copies of Gil's memory stick."

There was a further murmur of general agreement, and he left the room.

He found Suarez in the manager's office, where the inspector greeted him cordially, and listened while Baldock outlined the issue.

"Si, Señor Baldock, we found memory stick, but we cannot open any of the files on it. They are all locked with a code. You think this may point to his killer?"

"I'm not sure," Baldock confessed, "but there is a chance that it might. And Masters was obviously being ultra-careful with the material he had. If you'd like to copy the files onto another memory stick, Inspector, I'll have my friend look at it. See if he can break them." He offered a blank memory stick to Suarez.

"Of course, of course." The inspector jammed the stick into the manager's desktop tower, and took the blank from Baldock. After a moment or two, the files were busy copying and Baldock asked about being allowed to fly home.

"I see no reason to detain any of you," Suarez replied amiably, "But the case is not closed, and when we have the evidence, we shall call upon your famous Scotland Yard to make the arrest and fly the guilty back to Alicante."

Baldock refrained from pointing out that Scotland Yard would hardly be likely to carry out such a menial arrest, but instead accepted the copied memory stick from Suarez, and bid him 'good morning'.

It was only as he got back to the lobby that he realised it was no longer morning, and he still had not made good his promise to Lisa to spend time with her.

Chapter Thirty-One

"There you go, Ray. I've removed the passwords so anyone can open and read the files."

Greaves, still hidden in the shade around the pool at the *Hotel Dolce*, swivelled the laptop round so Baldock could study the file list.

There were only four such files, the first three of which were named, *Contract HI, Contract PK, Contract RB*. Harry Ingels, Phillipa Killairn, Raymond Baldock.

Greaves was still waffling proudly on his IT skills. "Trouble with nurks like this Masters sort is they think they're smart when they lock a file up with a password." He took out his cigarette rolling material. "But they don't reckon with guys like me. Y'know. Blokes as knows what they're doing."

"Obviously not. I don't suppose there's any point my asking how you do it?"

Greaves tapped the side of his nose. "Secrets and lies, Ray. Ask no secrets and I'll tell you no lies. Besides, if I told everyone how it's done, do you know how much money I'd lose in an average year? A good hundred quid. Maybe more."

Baldock buried most of his natural scorn. "As much as that? Well, we can't have that, can we?"

He opened up, Contract RB, and ran quickly through the pages, seeking the specific clause, and it was, as he suspected, a copy of his contract with Shortly Publishing containing precisely the changes Greaves had found earlier, and which had been installed on his laptop. Checking the other two contract files, he found that those of Harry and Phillipa were the same.

He closed them down, and concentrated on the fourth file, named Background. It had been prepared in a word processing package, and when he opened it, he found, much to his surprise, that his name comprised the first two words in the document.

Ray Baldock is a woman-hater. Not sure if he isn't gay. Solution: give him a task that involves getting close up and intimate with a total female stranger.

Baldock could feel his gorge rising, but he suppressed it. Alongside him, Greaves looked at the screen with interest.

"I never figured you were that way, Ray? Especially after the way you reckoned you'd shafted Lisa so many times."

"Bugger off, Ewan. You're as ill-informed and prejudiced as this damned idiot was." He waved wildly at the screen indicating Masters as the idiot he was talking about. "I am not gay, I am not a woman-hater, I have never been either. I am a bachelor. So are you. Does that make you gay?"

"No."

"There you are then."

Baldock returned to his reading.

Harry Ingels is a fat bastard, completely unattractive to women. Solution: give him a task which involves a total female stranger getting up close and intimate with him.

Ian Linkman is easy. No point exposing his gambling addiction. Everyone knows about it already. But the threat of a call to Sammy the Shark should be enough to make him pressure the Killairn bitch. And I don't care if he does fancy Xavier. I can shut her up too

The employees will do as they're told or end up back on the unemployment line, and I'll deal with the other three women personally. By the time the weekend is over, I should have enough ammunition to keep the vamp at arm's length.

The document ended there but for a single paragraph which had probably been added later.

That jerk, Baldock never even suspected. He blamed the airport people. The machine is left with the Vardaro bitch. That should be enough to cook his goose but I'll be in his room later just to make sure. I win. Period.

By now, Baldock was gripped with a rage that was barely under control, and the target could not be hit; he was already dead. From a slightly more positive point of view, this final paragraph made it clear that he had been alive sometime after visiting Baldock's room on Thursday night. But for how long?

"Can you tell me when this document was last accessed and changed, Ewan?"

Greaves nodded. "About ten minutes ago."

Baldock's face fell.

"When I hacked the password from the registry, and then changed the document properties to eliminate the password, it automatically overwrote the last time it was modified." Greaves shrugged. "Sorry, Ray, if I'd known you needed to know that, I'd have made a note."

Irritating, thought Baldock. Although it was clear that Masters was alive after delivering the laptop, the time of death could not be narrowed down any further.

"I didn't know either," he admitted, "and it's not your fault." He removed the memory stick and shut down the laptop. "All right, Ewan. Thanks for this. I'm sure the other members of the party will thank you for it, too."

"Good. Tell them I prefer their thanks in cash."

Baldock dismissed his friend's hints and for the fourth time, and took a taxi back to the Aranjuez.

By now, he had made the journey across Benidorm so often, he felt he knew the place as well as he knew Leeds. Probably better, given that he had not lived in Leeds for the last two decades.

It did, however, mean that he was not distracted by the sights and sounds of the town as they passed through it, and he could disregard the driver's invective hurled at other road users. At least, he assumed it was invective, judging from the bad-tempered manner in which it was delivered.

While a busy Saturday in one of Spain's most popular resorts passed him by, he considered the death of Gil Masters.

It was, he concluded, entirely apposite. He had been the architect of his own demise. His egotistical attempts at complete domination over those around him, including those, such as Baldock himself, who did not work for him but were only contractors, had sparked and orchestrated the chain of events which led to his murder.

And it was obvious who had done it. As the cab weaved its way alone *Avenida del Mediterráneo*, the driver juggling for position, hassling buses and private cars alike, cursing pedestrians, most of them dressed in holiday clothing, who tried to cross against the lights, Baldock sifted the information he had gleaned from the memory stick, and narrowed the suspects down to just three people. He dismissed two of those immediately, for the simple reason that they were sharing a room and if one of them had been missing, the other would have pointed it out by now.

Arriving back at the Aranjuez, he paid the taxi driver off and was about to enter the hotel, when an irritated Lisa hurried up to him.

"Raymond, I thought we were going to spend some time together today."

"What? Oh, er, yes. I, er… I'm sorry, Lisa, but I got bogged down on this Shortly business."

"Right. And your phone's broke? It's forgotten my number, has it?"

"No. I, er, look, I'm sorry. Yes, I should have rung." He looked anxiously up at the Aranjuez, and then down the street to the Praia. "Come on. What say I buy you a drink right now? Your hotel. Not mine. They'll be waiting for me and they'll only start asking questions again."

Mollified, Lisa fell in step alongside him and they strolled down the hill, into the Praia, where they joined his mother around the pool, and he ordered drinks for them.

Other members of the Midthorpe Maidens were sleeping on loungers, two were larking around in the water, and his mother had been on the point of nodding off when they joined her. She woke up and as their drinks arrived, a vodka and tonic for Janet, a beer for Lisa and soft drink for Baldock, Janet asked why her son looked so gloomy.

"It's Masters' murder. I'm sure I know who did it, but I'd never be able to prove it, and if I made an accusation and I'm wrong, it could cost me a fortune in damages."

His words brought both Lisa's and Janet's attention into full focus. "You know who did it?" Lisa asked. "Who?"

"We want every detail, Raymond," Janet insisted. "Just to make sure we can all agree that you have it right."

With a wry smile, and fond memories of the scenarios he had so often written for Detective Inspector Headingley, Baldock told them the whole tale.

"But you have no proof," Janet echoed when he had finished. "In that case, luv, you have to force him to confess."

"Mother, there is nothing to say he was there, nothing to say he did it. Everything is circumstantial. I simply know it's him and I know why."

"There are times, Raymond, when I despair of you. You live alone and yet you have not the slightest bit of the domestic about you." Janet smiled. "Why not get everyone together at your hotel, and I'll show you how to prove it."

Mystified, bemused by the changes he saw in his mother, he did as she asked. Thirty minutes later, the whole of the Shortly party were gathered around a table near the pool at the Aranjuez, with Baldock, Lisa, Janet, and Inspector Suarez holding court.

Baldock had spoken in advance with Suarez, who had listened and dismissed the idea as impossible to prove. He changed his mind when Baldock explained what they were going to attempt.

"If it goes wrong, Señor, we will not support you."

"Are you happy that Masters murdered Ms Vardaro?" Baldock had demanded.

"Of course."

"And do you want Masters' killer?"

Suarez agreed that he did.

"Then there's no other way."

Suarez acquiesced and after ordering two of his men to station themselves discreetly in the background, joined Baldock and the group in a shaded corner of the pool area.

Baldock opened proceedings. "Thank you for coming, everyone. I've spoken with Inspector Suarez, and he has graciously conceded that we can all go home tomorrow, and I think we should thank him for that."

"Why?" Ingels asked. "We didn't kill Masters, or Xavier so it's only right that—"

"That's not quite true, Harry," Baldock cut in. "If you recall, we decided earlier that we are the only people who had a motive to kill him. We're the ones he was trying to railroad, so it's obvious that it had to be one of us."

"And you know which one?" Dominique asked.

"I do." Baldock laid extra copies of the memory stick on the table. "These are for each of you, but I will tell you in advance, there is an extra file on the original, which I have not copied to the remainder. When we're through here, you can have it if you wish, but I warn you in advance, it contains some highly disparaging remarks about you, Harry, you, Linkman, and me. It's none too flattering about you, either, Dominique."

"You should have put it on the copies," she protested. "For all we know, you could have tampered with it."

"Inspector Suarez has the originals, and he has the password for them, so you can guarantee it has not been altered."

"Then why leave it off, Ray?" Bernie asked.

"Because it contained information about the killer, which if he had seen it, might have tempted him to kill again in order to cover his tracks. Or at the very least make a run for it."

"Him?" Phillipa asked, ignoring most of his declaration. "It was a man?"

"Yes. It was a man…" Baldock scanned the table, his eye melodramatically taking in Ingels, Linkman and Dean Quarmby. "Wasn't it, Ian?"

Linkman stared up open-mouthed, and for a moment Baldock thought he was going to confess. He did not. The gape turned to a broad grin. "This is a joke. Right?"

"Wrong. It's no joke. You killed him because he was threatening to expose your near-bankruptcy and gambling problems to people you'd rather did not know about them. I don't know who Sammy the Shark is, but I'm guessing it's someone you owe large amounts of money to, but who doesn't know where to find you. Either that, or he's not aware that his chances of getting his money back are lower than my chances of getting into the England rugby team, and I would never get into the England rugby team because I hate the game."

Sweat broke on Linkman's face. "This is so much bull."

While everyone stared in stunned silence, Janet took up the reins. "You were very clever. You covered your tracks really well. Dropping him into the bathtub and throwing the murder weapon in there, too. It all helped to remove forensic evidence. And if the police did find any latent traces of you in the room, well you were not alone, were you. A lot of people had been in that room before and after Mr Masters's arrival. Other guests, cleaners, and for all you knew, other members of your party. With no one to argue differently, if the police could prove you had been there, you could have claimed to have visited anytime since you got here. So there was nothing to place you there at the time of the murder, even if the police could narrow that time down."

Linkman's face turned to a mask of hatred. "Listen to me, you old bat—"

"That, Linkman, is my friend's mother you're speaking to, and you should show some respect," Lisa protested.

"Please, Lisa," Janet insisted softly, before going on to the sweating literary agent. "An old bat, I might be, Mr Linkman, but like most old bats, I've spent a lifetime picking up trivia which people like you, particularly men, ignore. For instance, when did you last polish those shoes?" She pointed at his ever-present loafers.

"How the hell should I know? Who bothers to polish shoes?"

"My son. Because I brought him up to do so. You're a very untidy man. If Raymond dressed like you, I'd hound him to smarten himself up a little."

"Yes, well, I'm not a mummy's boy."

"One more veiled insult, Linkman, and you'll be a non-mummy's boy with a broken nose," Baldock warned.

"Don't threaten, dear," Janet ordered her son. "You were never any use in a fight, and you know it." She turned her attention to Linkman once more. "I might also ask you, who comes to Benidorm with nothing but a pair of leather slip-ons?"

"I do," Linkman insisted. "I like 'em. They're comfortable."

"Either that or you can't afford better because your gambling problems have taken all your money."

"Now, look here—"

"Do you know what that stain is on them?" Janet interrupted, pointing to the visible white marks on the shoes' uppers. "It's water damage. And it happened when you filled the bathtub and dropped Mr Masters in it. The water overflowed… all over your shoes and caused those white marks."

Alarm spread rapidly across Linkman's features. He had lost his anger, and began to sound a retreat. "No, no. You've got it wrong. I was on the beach on Friday. With Ursula. That's where my shoes got wet."

"Wrong," Baldock said. "Ursula told me you couldn't walk on the sand in those shoes. You had to take them off. Is that right, Ursula?"

She nodded. "Bang on, Ray."

"It's rain," Linkman squealed. "It rained and they got wet."

"My party has been here since Thursday morning, just like yours," Janet said, "and the only rain we've seen was a brief thunderstorm in the early hours of Friday morning, but you claimed you were back here and in bed by then. No, no, your shoes got wet in the bathroom when you dropped Mr Masters into the tub and it overflowed."

It seemed to Baldock that the whole table held its collective breath. For a moment he thought Linkman would try to brazen it out further. But to his relief, the front collapsed and tears sparkled in the man's eyes.

"I didn't go there to kill him. He was on his balcony and I

saw him. I knew he'd killed Xavier, and I was gonna have it out with him. He admitted it. She'd threatened to blow the whole contract scam wide open. I told him I'd tell the cops, he told me to go ahead, but if I opened my mouth, the loan sharks would get to know where to find me."

"This would be about two in the morning?" Baldock asked. He knew the answer already.

Linkman nodded. "I left *Café Benidorm* early and went to the casino. I was on my way back when I saw him."

"And that's when the confrontation happened?"

Linkman nodded. "He said if I didn't shut up and get Phillipa to toe the line, he'd make sure the shark found out where I lived."

"And what did Phillipa have to do?" Baldock demanded.

"Sleep with him."

Baldock fumed. "So he could get a hold over her and coerce her into his nasty little plans, giving him more power when it came to the crunch with the board of directors and Dominique."

"I told him there was no way I could do that. I may be some kind of low-life, but not that low. I said I was going to the cops. Then he lost it. Started calling me all sorts of names; and Phillipa, and you, and Harry, and Bernie. I lost my temper, too. He took a swing at me. I hit back, he fell on the floor and I was blazing mad. I just grabbed the first thing I could lay my hands on, that bronze bust thing, and I hit him with it." Linkman calmed a little. "Then I realised what I'd done, so I tried to cover my tracks. I took his phone, broke up the SIM card and flushed it down the toilet. Then I smashed the phone up and threw the bits in the sea when I was on the beach with Ursula, on Friday." His eyes scanned the tables, begging them. "I'm sorry. I swear I didn't mean to kill him. But he killed Xavier and I did save your skins."

"We shall have to see what the judge has to say about that, Señor Linkman." Suarez snapped his fingers and his men marched to the table. "And I already know what the judge will say about another English lager lout polluting our coastal waters with an unwanted mobile phone." He drew a finger across his neck. "You will go with my people and make the statement. Si?"

Linkman nodded and left with the officers.

Suarez beamed on them. "I would not like to meet you down the English dark alley."

Baldock blushed modestly. "Kind of you to say so."

"I was talking to your mother, señor. The rest of you, please enjoy what time you have left in Benidorm." With a half bow, he left them.

As he left, the table around them broke into various muttered conversations.

"There is just one thing, Mother," Baldock said as Suarez disappeared into the building.

"What, luv?"

"It's *salt* water that affects leather, not tap water… even Spanish tap water. And as you pointed out there was a thunderstorm the other night. He probably got caught in it."

"I know. I was sat on the balcony watching it. His shoes might have got wet walking back to the hotel from the casino and there would be enough salt in the rain and on the ground to stain them. But he did lie about the time he got back, didn't he?"

"Yes, but—"

"I was sure he wouldn't know the difference. Any man who dressed so shabbily wouldn't know what kind of water affects shoe leather."

Listening in, Phillipa managed a weak smile. "As Suarez said, Mrs Baldock, I wouldn't like to meet you without a bulletproof vest."

Chapter Thirty-Two

There was a huge party that night, spread across several of Benidorm's better-known bars, involving the Midthorpe Maidens, the South Leeds Stags and the Shortly Publishing group, which included Dominique who was celebrating having got rid of a liability – her husband – and acquiring complete control of a medium sized company.

Baldock joined in, loosening his usual strict discipline sufficiently to let him perform a duet with his mother on the karaoke while others took pictures and videos.

It was almost two in the morning before he and Lisa returned to the Aranjuez, and by the time her libidinous thirst had been quenched, it was getting on for three.

He woke a little after ten, to find a note from Lisa saying she had returned to the Praia to pack for the journey home.

He rang the lobby. Ordered a late breakfast to be delivered to his room, and at the same time, organised a late checkout for himself. Their flight was not until ten thirty in the evening and the airport shuttle would not arrive until seven thirty.

After breakfast, he sat on the balcony with the returned laptop open, making extensive notes on all that had happened.

My opinion of Benidorm has altered slightly, but not much. I still think it's a working class cesspit, but the presence of Lisa and, to a lesser extent, Bernie, has made me feel a little more benign towards the place. But it will be a cold day in hell before I come back.

Inspector Suarez paid a courtesy call at twelve to thank him for his efforts.

"If it had not been for you, Señor Baldock, I do not know that we would have caught this man. And yet, you know, I feel some pity for him. It is a terrible thing to be caught up in gambling fever and to lose the love of your life."

"I wouldn't feel too sorry for him, Inspector. He could have gone for counselling at any time for his addiction. It was his choice not to, and no matter how deeply in debt he may be, it's no excuse for murder."

"We do not think murder, Señor. We think manslaughter. Based on his testimony, it's the best we can hope for. For now, I bid you *adios*. For you, there will always be a warm welcome from the Benidorm police."

They shook hands, Suarez left, and Baldock returned to his journal.

At one forty-five, the phone rang.

"Raymond, it's Lisa. We're at Winners and the balloon has gone up. We need your help."

"Lisa, we're too old for these games. I don't want any silly ceremonies congratulating me."

"This is no game, Ray, and it's not about you. It's Chloe and Wayne. Just get over here."

It was just after two when he finally reached The Square to find that, as Lisa had said, all was far from well. She and his mother were sat off to one side, consoling a tearful Chloe, while across the street Tim and Michael Shipston were trying to calm an angry Wayne. Mandy stood anxiously by looking uncomfortably guilty.

Baldock hesitated, wondering where to go first. In the end, he opted for his mother and girlfriend. "What's happened?"

"Mandy left her phone lying around," his mother explained, "and Wayne picked it up. There was a photo on it from Thursday night. Chloe snogging and groping some stranger."

Baldock recalled seeing a couple trying to eat each other as he and Bernie made their way to Winners. "Well, I said it was odd having the hen and stag parties in the same place at the same time, but surely it's all part of the absurd Benidorm ritual."

"If the truth be told, Chloe was blathered out of her head on Thursday night, but you're right, Raymond, it is Benidorm, and in the grand scheme of things, it doesn't mean much." Lisa agreed. "But Wayne doesn't see it quite the same way."

"So why call me?"

"We thought you might be able to do something, before these two people ended up separated forever?"

"Me?" He was not so much surprised as shocked that Lisa imagined he would be able to do anything. "What can I do?"

"Talk to Wayne. You're a man aren't you?"

He sneered. "There's always been some debate about that. Especially on Midthorpe."

Lisa's temper was on the point of boiling over. "Then make an effort to prove them wrong. Lay the law down. You're good at challenging everyone, so challenge Wayne. Give him some kind of cover story to get Chloe out of this."

"Surely she can think of her own cover story? She's a Midthorper. Lying should come naturally to her. It's a Midthorpe speciality."

"He won't speak to her. You tell him some lie."

He shook his head. "I'm no good at lying. Never have been."

"Oh, sweet bloody Jesus, I can't believe this is the same man who riveted me to the mattress these last three nights."

Lisa's remark, angry though it was, caused Janet to smile discreetly, and then blush when she caught her son's disapproving eye.

Lisa unclenched her tight fists. "Raymond, you are a successful novelist. You spend your entire life sat in front of a computer screen making up stories. Well make one up for Chloe and Wayne. And do it quickly before it's too late."

She hurried back to the tearful Chloe.

Janet shook her head sadly. "You always say people from Midthorpe won't listen to you, Raymond. Perhaps now is the time to make them listen. And Lisa is right. You do spend your life making up stories."

Her words stung. She did not understand. The Headingley novels were stories, yes, but they had a core of reality which was far removed from thinking up something to cover the actions of a young woman who had had too much to drink.

As far as he was concerned, her actions were inexcusable, anyway. Over the top. Just like that farce when Sandra Scranton pulled down... his...

His thoughts came to a stuttering halt. Tim and Shippy were still trying to encourage Wayne. Janet and Lisa were back with Chloe, offering platitudes, no doubt, in an effort to bring her some comfort. Mid-way between them sat Mandy, looking more uncomfortable by the minute. Baldock crossed to her.

She went straight on the defensive. "It wasn't my fault. He was nosying, looking through the pictures on my phone. He shouldn't have even picked it up."

"I'm not blaming you, Mandy, but perhaps you shouldn't have left it lying around." Baldock told her. "Your phone. Does it still have that stupid picture of me on it? The one you took on Thursday night?"

Her smile was not remotely seductive for once. "I have a lot of pictures of you on it, Ray."

"You know the one I'm talking about."

"Yes. It's still there. And I won't get rid of it. Not after what I did for you the other day."

"You mean, er, doing the deed with the wrong man?"

"I didn't know he was the wrong man."

"You never stopped to ask, did you? Lend me your phone."

"Want me to Bluetooth the picture to you?"

"Just lend me your phone."

Doubt crossed her features. "I dunno. I mean, I don't want you getting rid of it, either, and if you're thinking of making calls on my phone... well, you're the rich fella. I can't afford calls to—"

"I'm not making calls and I'm not getting rid of the picture. I want to try to make a point. Just lend me your bloody phone for a few minutes, and be prepared to back up everything I say if necessary."

With some reluctance, she passed him the Samsung and as he crossed the pavement, she followed.

Snatching a chair from an adjacent table, he sat facing the

depressed and angry Wayne.

Tim, inherently aware of what was going on, stood up and backed off.

Shippy did not. "He don't need your help, Ray."

"I'm told different, so just bugger off, Shippy, and let me speak to him."

"Hey, careful who you're telling to bugger off."

Baldock glowered. "I'm telling you, you stupid sod. Now clear off."

Shipston looked as if he was going to stand his ground.

Baldock glared. "Go… away."

Shippy glanced around and at a signal from Tim, who had moved to a separate table, drifted into the background.

Baldock called up Mandy's photo album and began to scroll through the thumbnails as he spoke. "Ever read any of my books, Wayne?"

"Why would I wanna read books?" The response was bitter, surly, aggravating.

Baldock kept his cool. "Because they're fiction. Tales. Tall stories."

"I don't read bleeding books."

Baldock found the image he was looking for and opened it. "You watch movies don't you?"

"What if I do?"

"It's the same principle. The writers and actors make you believe that what's happening on screen is real. But it isn't." He turned the phone so that Wayne could see the photograph. "Here, take a look at that."

Wayne looked at it, and his lip curled. "Right, right. You've shown the world what a big knob you've got to go with your big head and your big bank account."

"One more comment like that and I'll give you a big nose. It'll be twice its normal size until the swelling goes down."

Wayne moved as if to get up. "Try it—"

"Sit down, you idiot, and listen to me." Baldock paused until Wayne was seated again. "Contrary to your mouthy opinion, I was not showing the world how big my, er, member is. That picture was one of the most humiliating moments of my life. I had little to do with it other than being the fall guy for Mrs Cowling and Mrs Scranton. And why did they take it? Because it was part of a game they were playing in this bar. A puerile, juvenile game where they had to get a photograph of a man with his underwear removed."

He took back the phone, and thumbed through the images again until he came to the one of Chloe and her mystery man. He once more showed it to Wayne.

"That picture is part of the same thing. Another idiotic, delinquent dare. For God's sake, even my mother took part in it. Chloe was just inebriated enough to accept the challenge. She was no more unfaithful to you than my mother was ready to spend the night with the fool she was groping."

It took moment to sink in. "A game?"

"You're on your stag weekend. Were you not playing games last night?"

"Yeah, but they weren't like this. I just had to have me picture taken holding some tart's bubs."

"And Chloe had hers taken holding some man's... well, you know. What's the difference?"

"I wasn't snogging the tart."

"Only because no one thought to include it in the rules." Baldock waved across The Square. "Look at the state of her, man. You've broken her heart. And why? Because you can't see further than your own jealousy. Now do yourself a favour while you still have the chance. Get over there, tell her you're sorry, kiss and make up, then get your stags away for their last afternoon so the hens can enjoy theirs too."

Despite Baldock's schoolmaster tones, Wayne looked across at his fiancée, leapt from his chair and ambled across to her. He stood alongside her at first, then crouched beside her, and although they could not hear what he was saying, Chloe gradually began to listen. Then Janet gave up her chair so Wayne could sit.

Tim pursed his lips and nodded. "Nice one, Ray."

It was as close to a compliment as he could expect from a Midthorper.

"Raymond, you are a genius," Janet said.

"I've been telling you that for years, Mother." He handed the phone back to Mandy. "You should lock those images with a password. That way, they can't cause any further problems."

"I will, Ray."

"Hey, Mandy," someone shouted from the bar.

She glanced at the waiter. "Right with you, Guillermo." With a grin she dropped the phone on the table. "Here. Look after that. I'm off for a last quickie. It won't take long."

Janet frowned. "I hope she means a quick drink."

Tim shook his head. "She doesn't waste time, that girl, and that fella's name begins with a G." He took Janet's hand. "We'll catch you later, Ray."

Tim and Janet wandered off, and Lisa arrived to take their place.

She took his hand. "That was brilliant."

Baldock shook his head. "I don't know why I always end up lying for Midthorpers."

"Always?"

"Didn't I end up lying for Peter Lipton in June?"

"So you did." Lisa picked up Mandy's phone and began to thumb through the images. "She's a dirty cow, this one. Look at all the filth on here. It's a good job the police didn't see this yesterday, or…" she trailed off. Her brow furrowed, her cheeks coloured. She pressed a button on the phone and watched as a video unfolded. As she watched, her eyes riveted to the screen, her colour up came further, and Baldock realised it was not embarrassment but anger.

She turned the phone to face him. "What is this?"

He faced an image of himself sliding Mandy's panties down to her ankles.

"Oh, that? I thought she'd have got rid of it by now. We didn't need it anyway."

"Didn't need it? Didn't bloody need it? Why? Because you had me in your bed?"

The volume of her complaint rose with every word until most of The Square could hear. Twenty yards down, her father and his mother turned to listen.

"Lisa? What are you talking about? That's—"

"I can see what it is." She slammed the phone on the table, stood and stormed off, hurrying past her father and Janet. Baldock's mother looked anxiously after Lisa and then to her son who was already on his feet hurrying after her.

He caught her at the bottom of The Square, grabbed her by the arm and spun her round to face him.

"Take your hands off me or I'll make sure you can never sleep with Mandy Cowling or any other woman again."

"Lisa, you're not giving me a chance to explain."

"What's to explain? You were taking her pants off."

"Yes, but—"

"Just get away from me, Raymond. I don't want anything to do with you."

"Fine, but at least allow me to explain first."

She struggled against his powerful grip but he would not let go. Lisa clenched her free fist and lashed out, catching him on the nose. As blood dripped down his Hilfiger T-shirt, he sat down on the ground and she leaned threateningly over him, to the delight and applause of onlookers from the Beachcombers Bar.

"Next time, I'll break your bloody teeth," she yelled, and got a cheer from the onlookers. "If I ever see you again, it will be too soon."

Baldock sat up and watched her march away, stiff-backed and furious. And deep inside, he decided he could not blame her.

THE END

The Midthorpe Murder Mystery series:
A Case of Missing on Midthorpe
A Case of Bloodshed in Benidorm

The STAC Mystery series:
The Filey Connection
The I-Spy Murders
A Halloween Homicide
A Murder for Christmas
Murder at the Murder Mystery Weekend
My Deadly Valentine
The Chocolate Egg Murders
The Summer Wedding Murder
Costa del Murder
Christmas Crackers
Death in Distribution
A Killing in the Family
A Theatrical Murder
Trial by Fire
Peril in Palmanova
The Squire's Lodge Murders
Murder at the Treasure Hunt
A Cornish Killing

Fantastic Books
Great Authors

darkstroke is
an imprint of
Crooked Cat Books

- Gripping Thrillers
- Cosy Mysteries
- Romantic Chick-Lit
- Fascinating Historicals
- Exciting Fantasy
- Young Adult and Children's Adventures
- Non-Fiction

Discover us online
www.darkstroke.com

Find us on instagram:
www.instagram.com/darkstrokebooks

Printed in Great Britain
by Amazon